THE POLAR BEAR
AND THE DRAGON

PERILOUS PASSAGE

THE POLAR BEAR AND THE DRAGON

PERILOUS PASSAGE

DEBBIE WATSON

Debbie Watson

MISSION POINT PRESS

Readers are encouraged to go to www.MissionPointPress.com to contact the author or to find information on how to buy this book in bulk at a discounted rate.

MISSION POINT PRESS

Published by Mission Point Press
2554 Chandler Rd.
Traverse City, MI 49696
(231) 421-9513

www.MissionPointPress.com

Cover and interior illustrations by Mark Pate, except for the illustration on page 48, which is by Mindy Indy.

LOC no.: 2022923670

Softcover: ISBN: 978-1-958363-54-6
Hardcover: ISBN: 978-1-958363-53-9

Printed in the United States of America

Many thanks to my amazing support team! To editor Neil Walker for his patience and dedication to excellence, Chelsea Flagg for her skilled coaching, and my husband Dave for his love and willingness to listen to countless revisions.

Chapter One

SWEET REVENGE

Edna hadn't always been cruel, but a string of catastrophic events struck during a crucial time in her life and triggered the young woman's transformation. The decades that followed brought unbearable hardships and much suffering to those she loved. Edna tried to stay brave, but she mourned the loss of joy and laughter and missed her friends terribly. Each night she fell asleep hoping the sun would return to brighten her world, but every morning was just as gray and dismal as the one before.

Wishing for miracles and longing to find heroes, she was drawn to brilliant but evil schemers, naively mistaking their ruthless pursuit of power for bravery and intelligence. She felt terribly deceived as her so-called champions gave up and disappeared into oblivion like so many other tiresome cowards. Sneering in disgust at their weak spirits, Edna chastised herself for being so naive and vowed she'd never be deceived again. In that defining moment, her heart turned to ice and any lingering signs of humanity vanished. The transformation into a cruel, pitiless monster was complete.

While the turbulent times defeated most of her peers, Edna became a clever opportunist, thriving on the misfortunes of others. Driven by her insatiable appetite for power and prestige the young wizard perfected her vast skills and won many challenges.

Although Edna had gained respect as a dangerous opponent and clawed her way to the top, she had one more goal to achieve.

It was unthinkable for a woman to become a clan leader, but Edna had ceased following the rules a long time ago and arrogantly assumed she could seize one of the coveted positions. With her eye on Yagdi's most highly esteemed wizard clan, she goaded their leader into battle, and won so masterfully no one dared question the transition of power. Edna never looked back and through gritty determination remained at the helm for over a century, batting away any who dared challenge her position as if they were nothing more than insignificant insects!

The formidable woman was frighteningly unpredictable and her extremely short fuse was easily ignited. Many things displeased the ancient leader but acts of cowardice or betrayal guaranteed swift and certain justice! Her clan members wisely refrained from risky behaviors because they'd witnessed their leader's grim pleasure in exacting severe punishment for any form of treachery. When her eyes sparked in irritation, they hastily retreated to avoid her angry eruption.

The woman's devious mind and quick wit were supreme, and arguably her best assets. Many, including the renowned Mergan, grudgingly confessed the clan leader had outmatched them at one time or another, and wizards rarely admit their own failings. Edna held the same respect for Mergan's vast abilities even though they didn't see eye to eye on most things of importance. Her admiration for the old wizard was a rare honor bestowed on a mere handful of her peers.

The two powerful wizards often found themselves adversaries because each used their powers for very different reasons. While Edna didn't hesitate to use her wizardry for personal gain, Mergan considered such behavior an abominable misuse of their gifts and wielded his immense powers only to defend Yagdi's peaceful citizens. Their incompatible philosophies became clear to all when Edna waged a brutal war to seize power, a war that didn't end well for her clan and their allies.

After losing the battle, Edna and her clan were shackled and dragged before the tribunal to face the consequences for their traitorous deeds. Fully expecting her clan to be set free, the haughty leader soon tired of the tedious proceedings. She considered their trial a mockery of justice and a complete waste of time. It was difficult to play nice, but she remained cleverly deceptive. Edna was able to keep her anger and resentment hidden until she discovered how terribly she'd misjudged the outcome.

When the judge shouted "guilty!" Edna jumped out of her seat and shook her fist, vowing she'd revenge all those who'd participated. Their punishment was severe. They had to choose between banishment and leaving Yagdi forever. Neither were good options, but Edna and her clan chose to leave their world rather than spend the next century in the horrid lifeless desert in the far southern region of Yagdi. Edna solemnly promised to keep her clan away, but never intended to do any such thing. The judge seemed to fall for it, but the dolt still felt it was his duty to warn the clan they would suffer severe consequences if any dared return.

Their loss and cruel exile were so devastating that Edna's disheartened clan members threatened to leave her, hoping life would improve with a fresh start in a different group. Of course, Edna never blamed herself but placed all responsibility squarely on Mergan and his allies. His lofty ideals had gotten in her way yet again, and the irate woman would make sure her arch enemy paid dearly.

When she felt enough time had passed, Edna led a select few of her best minions on a covert operation back to Yagdi. Their return was well planned, and no one witnessed their arrival. Stumbling upon the tunnels twisting through the heart of the Great Yagdian range was a stroke of luck. The caves near her clan's new home were the perfect hiding spot for their weapon of mass destruction, a powerful ancient creature named Sylern!

. . .

"Some weapon that dimwit turned out to be!" she huffed, anger stirring once again. "Sylern should have been our ticket to power, but he failed miserably," she growled. She'd provided her overgrown guard dog with the absolute best information so he could keep track of activities throughout Yagdi, but he'd still gotten it wrong. By the time Edna discovered Sylern was impossibly challenged when it came to thinking for himself, it was too late to alter her plans. Mergan, Traveller, and their annoying alliance defeated Sylern far too easily and foiled her operation.

"I must give credit where it's due," she admitted to herself. "In a way, I'm partly responsible for my own defeat! I never dreamed Randolph would discover he was a wizard; his mother worked so hard to keep our family history a secret. Although he had yet to uncover all of his powers, the newbie had still impressively neutralized Sylern's army." Her distant relative was now in the alliance, and an enemy she would battle, but Edna couldn't help feeling a bit proud.

Any idiot can spy and report, so Sylern might still be of use. Sending her well-trained thug on a scouting mission to earth, with the purpose of spying on the chosen ones' families would be a good test. If he completed this simple mission successfully, and without asking for help every second, she might keep him around.

Debating with herself was far more enlightening than tiresome discussions with others, and this evening's conversation was proving productive. She'd checked her plans for their return to Yagdi many times but wisely studied them once more, giving herself last-minute advice as her clan made final preparations for tonight's sneak attack.

Satisfied her plan had no hidden flaws, Edna located the most significant phrase in her entire plan. With a dramatic flourish, she underlined, "First order of business will be to appoint the new queen of Yagdi!" Throwing her pen down for the last time, Edna shouted, "That will be me, of course!"

Sitting back in her chair, Edna proudly crossed her arms. "Yes, it's time to put this difficult century behind us! However, I look forward to spending the next as Queen of Yagdi." Smiling wickedly, she hissed, "That which I covet above all else is within reach, and retribution will soon be mine!" At long last, Edna would return and punish all Yagdians who'd banished her clan so heartlessly.

To pull this off, Edna's minions must follow every detail perfectly. "They all fear my wrath, and that's a strong motivator, so I don't think anyone will bungle their job on purpose," she mused. Because some had too few brain cells to follow simple orders, she'd demanded their mandatory participation in daily practice sessions. She was now fairly confident everyone could perform their job, but to seal the deal, she'd threatened to leave behind any who didn't step up and do their part.

"That was the ticket!" she grinned slyly. Rolling her shoulders to get out the kinks, she stood up and stretched, then began walking around her small quarters. She'd been at it for hours and needed a little exercise. "So, what else is new? Planning for our return has ruled my life for decades, and the piles of blueprints filling all those trash bins outside my door proves I've been busy. But it's all been worth the wait. I'm confident there is not a single flaw in my plan for our return."

Looking in the mirror, Edna smiled and straightened her hat, then winked at herself. "You'll be a fine queen indeed, Edna, and how sweet it will feel to crush your accusers!" Frowning as bitter memories returned, Edna clenched her hands angrily. The outrageous sequence of events that led to her clan's exile were as vivid today as they'd been a long century ago. "How dare they!" she muttered angrily.

The labyrinth of tunnels was buried far too deep for direct access to Traveller's precious portal, but there was an advantage hidden within that. The clever Yagdian bear would never discover her clan's location and wouldn't even suspect they'd returned. "She's another who holds my respect, and a good one to keep in the dark," she murmured, fully aware of Traveller's far-reaching abilities and contacts. Uncovering the location of the entrance to the bear's portal had been challenging, but she'd done it. Spies were positioned along the path leading to the mighty Yagdian's gateway and her seer would alert her when the alliance entered the portal.

Squatting down, Edna unlocked her safe, and smiled to find her seer right where she'd left it. "There you are my friend, safe and sound," she cooed, "Your role is critical in our successful takeover. I'm relying on you to alert me when the alliance enters the portal, so you must remain under lock and key a few more hours!" she apologized. Placing it back in the safe with great care she locked it once again and stood up.

Leaving her plans open on the desk, Edna left her suite and headed to the control room for one final inspection. The tall woman's high heels made her appear larger than life, and she enjoyed their authoritative clatter as she marched along the granite floor. Savoring the excitement in the air, Edna smiled happily, and gave everyone she passed a thumbs up to show her appreciation for their hustle. "How sweet it is!" she thought.

"Tonight, we reveal our presence to all Yagdians!" she shouted to a surprised group of her followers. Waving excitedly, they yelled, "We're ready for your marching orders!"

Chapter Two

SENSING DANGER

Traveller and her alliance were feeling more lighthearted and happier than they had in many months. They'd just crushed Sylern's devious plan to rule Yagdi, which saved the peaceful citizens from a long, brutal war. "Hopefully that beast's gone for good, and peace will last!" Traveller thought as she plodded up the steep mountain path leading to their portal. They hadn't captured the horrid ancient being, and that was a nagging concern for the Yagdian general. "You were amazing, Randolph!" she said suddenly, turning to the newest member of their alliance.

They'd walked so long in silence, Randolph looked at his friend in surprise. Recovering quickly, the earth wizard grinned and teased, "Well of course! But which of my amazing feats are you referring to?"

"Good one, Randolph! Whichever title you prefer, Earth Wizard or Dream Jumper, they're both you, and your arrogance grows more like Mergan's every day!" Traveller said, her eyes twinkling with mischief.

As she'd expected, Mergan took the bait and growled, "Personally, I don't see the resemblance! Our dream jumper has a long way to go to match wits with me!"

Traveller grinned. "You never fail to amuse me, dear friend. I've treasured your friendship and your alliance in battles for many decades and look forward to many more."

Mergan opened his mouth, but words failed him. "I have never seen you tongue-tied, dear wizard," Randolph said mockingly, "and I will forever cherish this rare moment!"

"Seriously, gentlemen," Traveller broke in. "I've been thinking a lot about Sylern. I fear that creature's disappearance may be temporary. I suspect after licking his wounds, our enemy may return to finish what he started! I won't rest easy until that creature's found and put somewhere he'll never escape!"

Feeling personally responsible for the disastrous turn of events, Randolph sighed and shook his head. "I never expected he'd react so quickly! What good am I as a Dream Jumper if I can't use my ability to enter dreams when most needed? If I'd used my skills more effectively, I might have learned Sylern had a trick up his sleeve to use if things went sour!"

"You were key to his defeat, Randolph!" Traveller reminded her friend. "You just recently discovered you're not only a wizard, but one with very unique powers as a dream jumper. That ability allowed you to find his stronghold and soundly defeat that beast! All Yagdians will forever be in your debt!"

"Not if he returns!" Randolph grumbled.

While each continued their musing over the dilemma Sylern presented, the three powerful companions followed the rest of their group up the path. Traveller grinned as she watched the two teens laughing and teasing each other. Their chosen ones had learned many new skills and used them effectively to protect Aiden until the young dragon could return to follow his father's mighty footsteps as King of Yagdi.

"Whitney and Edward are amazing in every way possible!" she said proudly, breaking the silence once again.

"They are remarkable!" Randolph and Mergan agreed in unison.

Laughing and shaking her head, Traveller quipped, "What's it going to take for you two to admit you're becoming so alike?"

before turning serious once again. "I'm glad we could celebrate defeating the enemy, and I realize the party was very much needed after all that we've been through, but I fear we may have stayed a bit too long. The light's fading quickly, and if darkness descends on us before we reach the portal, it could present unforeseen problems."

"You have a point," Randolph agreed. "The dread I felt earlier is gone, but I worry it may have been a warning. Of what, I have no idea!"

"What dread, Earth Wizard?" Mergan demanded. "This is news to me, so please explain yourself!"

"A sense of dread struck during the celebration. I still don't know what caused it and have no idea what to make of it," Randolph admitted. "Maybe it's a good sign that it disappeared and hasn't returned," he added hopefully.

"Your worry may come from uncertainty," Mergan suggested. "Who knows what could be lurking out there, hiding somewhere in the wilderness?" he muttered, scanning the hillside. "The battle just ended, and we don't know whether all of Sylern's recruits have been rounded up."

Winking at their dream jumper, he offered a rare compliment. "The only ones we've captured are the creatures locked in the beast's expansive paddocks, and we owe that good fortune to our earth wizard."

"Mergan's right about that, Randolph!" Traveller agreed. "That was a remarkable accomplishment! I agree it's wise to stay vigilant, and following the others is a good plan. We can defend our friends from prowling enemies sneaking up from behind while encouraging their speedy ascent up the mountain."

"Any one of us could handle a few strays, including Whitney and Edward! And that goes for Aiden and Ellie as well! Our new king and fierce Yagdian panther would stand up to any and all who are foolhardy enough to threaten our alliance," Randolph said with uncharacteristic bravado. "Now how about we follow Traveller's advice and hustle up this path!" he added, leading the other two up their narrow, winding route to the portal.

Following a particularly wide, sweeping turn, an unsettling sense of foreboding struck Traveller, and she stopped short to stare worriedly in every direction. "What just triggered my warning system?"

The Yagdian bear's sense of danger was never wrong. Although it remained cleverly hidden, she had no doubt a threat of some kind awaited them. Closing her eyes, she let her mind explore. Scouring the area thoroughly, and finding nothing suspicious the frustrated bear muttered, "Something is very wrong!"

"When will it end?" she sighed, plodding forward once again. "Escorting our young chosen ones back to Earth should feel like a wonderful adventure, so why do I get the sudden sense we're racing for our lives once again?"

Sensing Traveller's concern, Whitney stopped in the middle of the path and turned around. "Is everything okay?"

"I'm not surprised you picked up on that, Whitney. Your skills have become truly amazing, and sensing approaching danger and others' unspoken worries are among the most impressive." Traveller said proudly. "But to answer your question, yes, everything is probably okay. Something seems off though, so we must all remain alert and attentive to details. Look for anything that might seem out of place," she cautioned. Raising her voice so everyone could hear, she added "Let's move a little quicker. I'd like to get to the portal well before we run out of daylight!"

"Something's bugging Traveller," Whitney said, leaning toward Edward. "What do you think's going on?"

"No clue, Whit," Edward admitted. "Sylern fled in defeat, so I can't imagine what it could be. But I heard her warning to move fast, so how about we make it interesting?" Pointing up the trail, he continued, "Let's race from here to that last bend up ahead!"

"You're on, Biker Boy!" Whitney screamed, racing away.

"Not fair! But I'll catch you!" he yelled.

Whitney was fast, but any contest brought out the beast in Edward. Putting on a herculean burst of speed, he soon caught up to his friend then slowed down to match her pace. "Told ya!" he yelled with a triumphant grin.

"I let you catch up, Biker Boy! So, get over yourself!" she laughed.

"I'm going to miss them!" Traveller admitted to the sleek panther who'd run up to walk beside her. "In a way, I think you're the lucky one, Ms. Ellie. I envy your decision to stay with Whitney and Susan. If my duties didn't define my life, I might be sorely tempted to spend a nice, extended vacation on Earth."

"That would be amazing!" Ellie purred. "Try to make that a goal for the near future. It would be good to gather often, with nothing to worry about, no gathering intel, no war plans. Just a group of friends spending time together!"

"I'll make that my number one priority," the bear promised. "Right now, I have to get us safely back to Earth."

Hearing her friend's worried tone, Ellie put her long nose into the air, her whiskers moving rapidly back and forth as she sniffed the breeze. "I don't smell anything out of the ordinary," she began to say when Traveller stopped and hissed, "Did you see that?"

"See what?" Ellie asked, looking around nervously.

"Those eyes, over there, near that scrubby pine," the bear said urgently, pointing toward a tree, very small and grotesquely deformed from living in the harsh elements so far up the mountain. "Whatever it was used those twisted branches hovering low to the ground as a convenient hiding place."

"I don't see anything," Ellie admitted.

"Neither do I, not anymore," Traveller sighed. "Ellie, I feel like I'm losing my mind with worry. You know my sense of danger is always accurate, and it's been on full alert since we passed that huge bend back there."

"Oh dear!" Ellie said. "How about I scout ahead and report back?"

"Just like old times!" Traveller said with a strained smile. "None of this makes any sense, and there's no evidence to support my growing concern. However, once again, you soothe my worries by offering a wise solution. Yes, become our eyes and ears for what lies ahead, but don't stray too far. I don't want to worry about you too, dear friend!"

Watching the sleek panther until she rounded a bend and disappeared, the bear frowned worriedly, then continued walking. "How could Randolph have been so worried at the celebration, but not feel any threat now?" she wondered. Her small world should feel safe, especially now that Sylern was gone, but Traveller couldn't deny she sensed an ominous presence.

The mountains were high in this remote Yagdian territory, and with the path so often shrouded in clouds and fog, their gateway remained hidden to all but the alliance. She'd traveled this path many times and never sensed the presence of anyone or anything unexpected. This time, however, it felt different, and the troubling sensation grew more threatening as they climbed higher.

Spotting a pair of ravens flying high overhead, Traveller let her keen eyes carefully examine their behavior. Although she concluded the birds seemed innocent enough, the bear continued to watch them. The mountain's wicked wind currents carried the ravens right over the path they were walking. They soared out of sight, then battled their way back against the wind. Making wide, sweeping turns, their path brought them right back over the alliance.

This odd behavior was repeated several times. As the pair looped to fly over them a fourth time, they suddenly dove head-first right toward Whitney and Edward. Traveller moved to block what she thought might be an attack, but the ravens veered off at the last minute. "They're behaving like spies, but if that's true, for whom?" she muttered.

"What's that?" Whitney yelled, pointing to something in the dense vegetation just off the trail. "Traveller, come look!"

"Too many unexplained occurrences!" the bear muttered. Turning away from the ravens, she raced toward the teen. "Show me!" she demanded, throwing up a cloud of dust as she skidded to a stop.

"I don't see it now," Whitney admitted. Gathering up her courage, she ran toward a spot just off the path and pointed. "It was right here, not three yards away from Edward and me!"

"Describe what you saw!" Traveller said sharply.

"I don't know!" the poor teen cried. "It looked like one of those horrid mist creatures from my nightmares. I even saw its red eyes! But that's impossible! We captured all of them, right?"

"That was our assumption!" the bear growled angrily and stalked off the trail. Stopping abruptly, she yelled, "Something was here! The vegetation is trampled and there are food crumbs all over!"

Turning to Aiden, she yelled, "Fly high, young king! Look everywhere with those sharp, dragon eyes, and report anything you see!"

Aiden leaped into the air, and with a few strokes of his massive wings, the young dragon was soaring high above the alliance. While exploring their route to the portal he noticed the ravens, but they flew out of sight and didn't return. Not aware they were suspects the young dragon disregarded the pair as inconsequential. The winds were vicious, and Aiden was above the portal in no time. "Nothing suspicious anywhere," he muttered and turned back.

Landing effortlessly in front of the giant bear, the young

dragon said, "I didn't see any—" just as Ellie came flying down the path and interrupted him.

"I found nothing worrisome, Traveller!" she reported. Noticing her news hadn't eased her friend's worries, Ellie asked, "Should I be apologizing? I thought I was sharing good news!"

"I started to say the same thing, before I was rudely interrupted that is," Aiden said, grinning at the panther. "I saw nothing other than a pair of ravens who understandably spread their wings and flew away quickly. There were also two rather large rabbits not too far up the path, and that was all." Aiden added.

"Both reports are strange!" Traveller said nervously. "Rabbits don't live here! I've never seen any rodents this far up the mountain! And I'm surprised neither of you detected anything that drew your suspicions. Truthfully, your reports make me worry all the more because they defy my sense of danger! But I appreciate your efforts!" the frustrated bear said with a heavy sigh.

After pondering for a moment, Traveller snapped to a decision. "Everyone, follow me! We must move twice as fast!" she urged. As if she needed any further hints of danger, the bear sensed an unnatural presence and looked toward the peaks just in time to see a brilliant flash of light. It went out almost immediately, but she continued to stare and caught another brief flicker of light. "Just as I suspected! I'm now certain that was some kind of signal," she thought grimly, moving forward with even greater urgency.

Chapter Three

DISASTER STRIKES

"At last!" Traveller sighed with relief. They'd made it to the portal without further incident. However, while the bear was eager to get this journey behind them, Whitney and Edward ran up to her with an alternative plan.

"We know you're feeling uneasy, but this could be our last chance to watch a Yagdian sunset! Think we could spare a few minutes?" Whitney asked hopefully.

"Come on, Traveller! Even if something's lurking out there, we're all more than capable of beating our enemies," Edward reasoned.

"Think about it! What could possibly go wrong in a few short minutes, Traveller?" Whitney chimed in.

The teens considered their points well-chosen and possible game changers, but their hope evaporated when Traveller said, "I don't feel good about this. You know my sense of danger is pretty accurate, and I'm not liking what I'm feeling right now."

Putting her hands on her hips, Whitney stared fearlessly into Traveller's big brown eyes and said defiantly, "I don't feel any warnings, Traveller. We all know the tingling in my neck would be going crazy right now if something was near, right?"

This could be the last Yagdian light show they'd ever see and watching two stars set over the mountain peaks was truly a memorable experience. Traveller understood why they were pushing to stay, and she had to admit the girl's argument held merit. The fact that Whitney didn't sense imminent danger was something to consider, and the sunset and their journey home would be lightning fast.

Watching her young chosen one carefully, Traveller reached out and touched the stones hanging from a leather cord around the girl's neck. "They're a bit warm, but that could be due to the late afternoon light reaching them. Do they feel any different to you?" she asked softly.

"You know I always heed their warning, Traveller. But I'm not getting a hint of danger from any of my stones," Whitney answered honestly, hoping to reassure her friend.

"Hmmm," Traveller mumbled. Even without any sign of danger from Whitney or her stones, there were so many reasons not to linger. "I still think it best if we head home, and we must do so right away!" Traveller cautioned.

The disappointment on their faces tipped the scale, so she growled, "This is against my better judgement! We can stay, but as soon as the sunset's over, we must all race to the portal! Do I make myself clear?" and gave them both her best no-nonsense scowl.

"Crystal!" Whitney yelped excitedly and ran to a boulder. "Come on, Edward. Best seat in the house!" she squealed, looking into the sky as she patted the spot next to her. Yagdi's sunsets were spectacular, and this time was no different. "It's even better than I remembered!" Whitney sighed, putting her head on Edward's shoulder.

The others crowded around the teenagers and waited patiently for the sunset to end. The small purple and giant yellow stars dropped closer to the horizon, but hovered just above the snow-capped peaks, as if hesitant to leave. When the two stars finally fell behind the mountains, bright bursts of light shot over the peaks, flooding the valley with dazzling color. The evening sky turned a deep purple as bright green and yellow rays exploded into a million colors overhead. Whitney and Edward gasped and reached up, as if trying to touch the magic surrounding them.

The show was over as suddenly as it began, but the group remained silent. "I believe that was worth the wait," Traveller said quietly, then gently shoved Whitney and Edward with her broad shoulder. "However, it's time we left!" and led everyone to the portal.

One-by-one, the alliance entered and disappeared. When it was their turn, Whitney reached for Edward's hand and smiled. "Ready to go home, Biker Boy?"

"I'll follow you anywhere!" Edward grinned back, linking their fingers.

They were almost to the entrance when Whitney cried, "Oh, no! Not now!" and looked over her shoulder nervously.

"Whit, what's happening?" Edward asked, spinning her around and cupping her elbow with his free hand.

"My neck's tingling!" she groaned. "Something's going to happen...Oh man, that stings!" she gasped, falling to the ground. "I've never felt such a powerful warning, Edward!"

Edward leaned over and looked so worried, she grimaced and stood up. "See, it's better," Whitney lied. As suddenly as it struck, her pain disappeared, and she blew out a relieved breath. Seeing Traveller poised to race back to them, she waved and yelled, "I'm okay. Honest! We can talk about it back on Earth! We're right behind you!"

Sensing her decision could have critical consequences, Traveller was terribly torn and lingered, anxiously watching her young chosen ones. Finally, the worried bear decided she could best protect Whitney and Edward if she went ahead of them because that would position her to confront any enemies lying in ambush. "I'll clear the way for your safe return!" she yelled, hoping she'd made the right choice as she prowled back into the portal.

"Traveller will take care of any danger in the portal!" Whitney said confidently as she and Edward watched their friend disappear.

As the portal whisked them away from Yagdi, Whitney felt the familiar butterflies and grinned up at Edward excitedly. Suddenly, she couldn't wait to see her mom. "We'll be back on Earth in no time! What's the first thing you're gonna do?"

BOOM! A thunderous explosion interrupted Edward before he could answer. "What was that?" Whitney screamed, holding his hand in a vice grip. "I don't know, Whit!" he shouted as another equally powerful eruption rocked the portal. Whitney's eyes widened in terror, and she moved closer to her friend as loud, high-pitched squeals and groans erupted from everywhere at once. Staring at each other in shock, they felt the portal shudder as smaller eruptions rumbled far below. Then it screeched to an abrupt stop, tossing the teens into sharp rocks they hadn't even seen in the inky darkness.

They clung to each other as the portal undulated up and down, pitching them wildly back and forth, with Whitney struggling to stay upright. "I can't stand any longer, Edward! I need to kneel!"

Suddenly, the crazy movement stopped, and an ominous stillness settled in. "It's way too quiet!" Whitney murmured, fearing the silence more than the chaotic eruptions. It was so still they could hear her voice echo through empty spaces far below.

"Edward, are we going to make it home?" she cried, looking wide-eyed at her best friend.

• • •

Unaware of the chaos behind them, the weary travelers were greeted by the invigorating, fresh scent of pine as they stepped out of the ancient keeper of their portal. Taking a deep breath, they looked around with pleased expressions. The majestic Michigan white pine had guarded this spot for centuries, and stood so close to Lake Superior her long branches swooped over the rocky shoreline, providing shade on hot summer days.

Traveller heard the welcome sound of waves lapping over rocks along the shore and grinned. "We made it! We're on Ellie's Point, and only a mile to your house, Whitney!" she said with relief, turning around to greet the teenagers. But they weren't there!

"Whitney and Edward should have been right behind me! Where are they?" she cried and began pacing back and forth impatiently. The minutes passed by agonizingly slow. Finally, she stopped pacing and turned to her friends.

The alliance had circled around her, and all were frowning worriedly. "The kids should be here by now! Why didn't I let them go ahead of me?" she cried frantically. "You all know my warning system is never wrong. It followed me the entire way up the mountain path! Then, just before I entered the portal, Whitney was struck by a warning powerful enough to bring the poor girl to her knees. I was torn, and uncertain how best to protect our kids, but finally decided to go on the offensive and run interference," the distraught bear explained, looking apologetically at each of her friends. Shaking her head sadly, she moaned, "It appears my decision to go first was horribly misguided!"

"We can't both have been feeling unsettled without good cause!" Randolph agreed. "There must be something we missed, and I fear if neither of us could detect the enemy, it must be deviously clever!"

"Exactly right!" Traveller groaned. "And I'll be nervous until the kids join us, but we've waited too long!"

Trying to comfort them both, Randolph put his arm around her broad shoulders and said softly, "I hope their delay is nothing serious and we won't have much longer to wait!"

"I don't intend to wait another second!" Traveller announced determinedly. But when she turned toward the portal, Aiden and Ellie moved in to block her path, staring at her in dismay and confusion. Both frowned and shook their heads, as if warning their friend to go no further, then turned and stalked toward the portal and stopped in front of the entrance. Both the dragon and panther seemed baffled, as if they'd just discovered a confusing puzzle they didn't understand.

Traveller was mystified when they growled menacingly and grew increasingly impatient watching them slowly and thoroughly sniff around the entire entrance, top to bottom. But, when they suddenly attacked the massive tree trunk, sending bark flying in every direction, she yelled, "Aiden, Ellie, explain! I'm already frightened for the kids, and you're not easing those fears! What's going on?" Completely ignoring her pleas, both continued to shred the bark surrounding the entrance to their portal.

Chapter Four

EXPLOSION!

"It's gone! Who stole my seer?" Edna shrieked.

"I really did it this time!" Patrick muttered. It had been an idiotic idea to grab Edna's toy and hadn't been worth the risk because her seer hadn't cooperated! Now, if they discovered he'd taken her precious object, things would go very badly for the young wizard. "I'm a goner if I don't think of something quick!"

He'd really thought Edna and her clan would conquer Yagdi because he'd peeked at little bits and pieces of her plan, and it looked brilliant. If they'd been successful, he would've had a sweet position with lots of wealth and power!

"How could I have been so naive to think I could ride that woman's coattails to fame and fortune?" the trickster groaned, hoping it wasn't too late to scheme his way out of this mess. Patrick was now convinced Edna and her clan's days were numbered, and desperately wanted to leave before things went south. The trickster never held allegiances for long anyway because there were always greener pastures. "If I stick around now, I'm going to end up imprisoned with the rest of 'em!"

But Edna's spies were everywhere, and the thought of getting caught made him shiver. The consequences of deceiving her were enormous! The ancient wizard was powerful, and if any of her minions learned you were planning to escape, they hunted you down like a common criminal and locked you up until their leader took over. Patrick had witnessed Edna toy with a few unfortunate victims before she sentenced them and if he didn't play his cards just right, he'd end up with the same fate, and that was terrifying!

Once you were in the clan, you remained a member for life! Sure, he'd signed an oath to that effect, and pledged his allegiance to the clan. But his fingers had been crossed behind his back and that negated his promise, didn't it? However, this was a particularly tricky situation because Edna was such a formidable opponent!

"I just wanted her seer to get me out of here!" Patrick moaned. His new scheme was still in the developmental stages, but it could bring him millions! The young wizard was done following that tyrant and ratting on her plans to conquer Yagdi could be the most lucrative scheme he'd ever come up with! He'd have to leave the clan without getting caught and that had never been done, but the trickster was determined to reach the supreme commander, and always found a way to get what he wanted.

Patrick had earned his reputation as a scheming trickster because he was an expert performer. He could fool anyone into helping him out of difficult situations, and the motivation to find the commander of Yagdi and report Edna's activities was powerful! "That's my ticket to fame and fortune and truly could be worth a ton!"

Wanting to open the door, but afraid of what might be on the other side, Patrick gripped the handle uncertainly. He knew they'd begun searching for the thief because loud alarms were blaring urgently. He needed to get out of here, and fast, because if they were onto him, his room would be the first place they'd look. "I'll run into the tunnels where they can't find me and finalize my plan once I get far away from here."

Desperately hoping to get Edna's seer back where it belonged before they caught him, Patrick tucked her precious item inside his long shirtsleeve and cautiously opened the door. The alarms were so loud the young wizard covered his ears as he gaped at the chaos in the halls. Intent on reaching their outraged, very unpredictable leader, no one even noticed when Patrick slipped in among them.

Moving stealthily, the young wizard followed the flow of frenzied clan members. Although he remained vigilant, he needed more information and so he grabbed a youngster racing by. "What happened?"

"The enemy alliance just got away!" the kid answered, shaking loose, and racing away before Patrick could ask any further questions.

Still needing details, Patrick caught up to a nervous wide-eyed wizard who was also hurrying by. "Can you tell me what's going on?"

Slowing down for a moment to catch his breath, the wizard looked grimly into Patrick's eyes, saying "Whatever you do, avoid Edna! She's looking for the thief who stole her seer, and I pity that poor soul when she catches him! It was supposed to alert her when the alliance entered the portal, but it wasn't where it was supposed to be. They all got away except the two teenagers called the 'chosen ones.' They're trapped in the portal now, and that's the only good news!" And with that, he raced away.

"This is really bad!" Patrick muttered anxiously, sorely tempted to turn around and head away from Edna's room. Deciding it was safest to remain hidden within the crowd, he moved into the flow of traffic, but stayed close to the wall in case he needed to disappear quickly.

As he approached Edna's room, the leader and a dozen of her minions marched into the hall. Turning away quickly, Patrick hid behind a group of young clan members. Peeking between two rather burly characters, he watched the frightening woman move purposefully through the crowd, surrounded by a mob of guards.

Patrick needed to return Edna's seer, and the coast seemed clear, at least for the moment. Staying safely in the shadows, the trickster moved slowly and deliberately toward her room. Just as he reached the door, someone grabbed him from behind. The sudden jolt caused Edna's seer to fall out of his shirt, and he gasped, "I can explain!" as it dropped to the floor. Before he could finish, two guards grabbed his elbows, and dragged him down the hall, shouting, "We got him! We caught this scoundrel red-handed!"

The minions marched him right up to Edna, and proudly shoved him into the angry woman's outstretched arms. Patrick looked up nervously as her long fingers wrapped around his arms. The wizard's black eyes sparked with such fury the trickster grimaced, realizing there was no chance of escape.

• • •

Aiden and Ellie suddenly stopped their vicious attack on the huge white pine and cocked their heads to listen.

"What do you two hear?" Traveller asked, out of her mind with fear.

"Alarms!" Aiden growled in confusion. "The blasts are very far away but it sounds like some kind of warning."

"We never should have left the young ones behind!" Traveller growled. The danger she'd sensed was upon them, and Whitney and Edward were still missing!

"The kids are in trouble!" she yelled, racing toward the portal, but excruciating pain struck, forcing her to the ground. "I'm feeling their fear!" she cried. Breathing heavily, the bear stood up slowly and limped toward the tree.

"STOP!" Aiden bellowed, seconds before a thunderous boom rocked the entire area. They listened as multiple eruptions rose to the surface from far below the very deep roots of the ancient tree. Then, to their shock and horror, a dark cloud billowed out of the portal, filling the air with thick, black smoke.

Covering their mouths and noses, they watched the opening to their portal disappear. When the smoke finally cleared, the ancient pine showed no signs of the portal. It was as if it had never existed!

Looking every bit as menacing as his father, Aiden roared, "What just happened?" and raced to where the portal had been, just moments before. Touching the trunk with his long nose, the young dragon murmured the same magical words he'd used to open the portal just days earlier. This time it simply shuddered then stood completely still.

"It's here!" Traveller moaned, looking meaningfully at Randolph. Falling to the ground, she began rocking back and forth, wailing, "The threat I sensed has found our young chosen ones!"

Her allies had never seen Traveller lose control like this, and they rushed forward to surround her. Hoping it helped a little, they stroked her beautiful white head and murmured, "it'll be okay, dear friend," over and over, but she continued to moan and rock back and forth.

Crouching in front of the huge bear, Mergan saw tears threatening to fall from her anguished brown eyes, and said softly, "Come now, dear friend. We're all in a state of shock, but we must think clearly!" Taking her face between his hands, the wizard waited until he had Traveller's attention then gently cautioned, "To do that, we must control our emotions and keep our minds clear! Do you understand? We can figure this out together."

"I'll get to the bottom of this!" Aiden growled and stalked off, but returned minutes later, visibly upset and confused. "I just contacted my father. Neither Whitney nor Edward remains on Yagdi and no one in my family has heard from them!" he reported. Shaking his head, he muttered in confusion, "How could that be? They both had our gifts when they left the celebration and should have used them to contact us. So, why haven't they?"

"We must keep trying, even if it means a slow process of elim-ination!" Mergan bellowed determinedly, standing up and plant-ing his wizard staff in the sand near the tree. Bowing his head, he began whispering all the magical phrases he could think of. Finally, his shoulders slumped, and he turned to the rest. "My staff is no help. I can't see anything inside the portal!" he admit-ted glumly.

"Let me try!" Traveller offered, rising slowly. Pulling out Ryuu, her tiny dragon seer, the bear placed it in a giant paw, and sup-pressed her guilt so she could focus on contacting their missing teenagers.

After several unsuccessful attempts, Traveller turned away from the tree and sighed, "Our devices appear to be blocked by something. We need to come up with another plan, and quick!"

"It's true we don't yet know what became of our two chosen ones," Mergan agreed. "However, our actions from this moment forward must be driven by the assumption they still live."

Saddened both by the disappearance of the two teens and the extreme distress on the faces of his dearest friends, especially Traveller, the wizard watched the bear carefully as he continued, "We all know how creative those two are when it comes to solving problems. Therefore, we must believe they will do so again."

Chapter Five

INTO THE DARKNESS

"Something's happening to our portal! What if we don't make it back to Earth?" Whitney cried, furious at herself for delaying their return. "We could be home by now, but I had to see one more sunset!"

Edward nodded grimly, but reasoned, "We can't be certain of anything right now, can we, Whit? Anyway, what's done is done!"

"Oh, man!" Whitney groaned as a low tortured sound reached them from deep inside the portal.

"Look out, Whit!" Edward yelled, reaching out to grab her hand just as the portal suddenly shifted. Thrown off balance, he flew into another sharp rock. "That stung!" he hissed, rubbing his arm.

"Are you okay?" Whitney asked, touching his sore arm gently. Searching for the truth, she frowned up at her friend. "We're in big trouble, aren't we!" and leaned against her steadfast rock of support. "I'm really scared, Edward. None of this feels right!" she whispered.

"Let's hope the portal fixes itself soon," Edward said, peering nervously into the darkness surrounding them. Leaning in close, he said softly, "Truth is, I agree. I think we're in trouble, but I promise to do everything I can to keep you safe!"

All hope completely vanished when another loud explosion rocked the portal, much more powerful than the ones before.

"Edward!" Whitney screamed as eruptions rumbled toward them from deep, empty spaces below. "It's getting closer! Do you think our friends made it out of here?"

"I hope so, Whit! But hang on tight! I think things are about to get worse!" Edward shouted as a gust of wind blew in, attacking the stunned teenagers with sand and debris. Dragging them into its ever-tightening vortex, the strange phenomenon lifted the shocked teens and spun them through the air in wild spins.

Spitting sand out of her mouth, Whitney shrieked, "Hang onto me! Don't let go, whatever you do!" gripping her friend's hand so tightly her nails bit into his palm. Clinching her jaw determinedly, she shouted, "We're a team!" She wouldn't allow this freak of nature to separate them because the thought of losing her best friend forever was too horrifying to consider!

Drawing her wizard staff in close, Whitney was trying to figure out how to battle this strange force when they were flung even higher, then suddenly released to fall into the depths of the portal. "Edward, hang on!" she screamed.

Their arms and legs flailed helplessly, but the teens miraculously held onto each other as they tumbled through the narrow canyon at dizzying speeds. One wrong move in any direction would send them crashing against nasty, jagged rocks inches away.

Clenching Whitney's hand tightly, Edward remained focused on the rock wall, wishing there was something he could do to keep them from hitting, but they were falling too fast, completely out of control. The best he could do was stay close to Whitney, and if it became necessary, he'd use his body as a shield to protect her.

As if she'd read his mind, Whitney squeezed Edward's hand and shook her head. They'd been in so many dangerous situations in the last few days, she had to believe they'd survive this one too. The trick would be staying together *after* they survived this crazy freefall! They were 'chosen ones' with many skills, but she and Edward had just begun to discover what they were truly capable of. Now they were alone and would have to uncover their talents without the guidance of Traveller or Mergan. "We can do this!" she murmured grimly.

"Look out!" Edward yelled, pulling her away from a nasty-looking rock shelf jutting out of the wall, just inches from their heads. "That was way too close!" he cried as they flew by.

Shaken by that near miss, Whitney joined Edward to focus on the path ahead and spied the deadly obstacle first. "We're gonna hit!" she cried, pointing to the massive boulder. Edward's hand tightened around hers, a feeling that was surprisingly reassuring given their dire situation.

It had taken a herculean effort, driven by desperation and determination, for Whitney and Edward to stay together. But suddenly an invisible force came out of nowhere and yanked them apart! It all happened so fast Whitney couldn't react quickly enough, and she watched in horror as Edward drifted away. "Edward, come back!" she screamed, frantically reaching toward him. It felt like she was moving in slow motion, and every time she got close, he drifted away.

They were still falling toward the boulder, but now their descent seemed much slower. Whitney felt the smack when her head hit and heard the sickening crunch when Edward landed nearby. She laid on the hard surface with agonizing pain pulsing through her brain, and for a short time, all she could see were tiny bursts of light.

"I must've hit pretty hard!" she said, feeling the bump on her head. Unable to hold her arm up any longer, she let it drop and stayed still because everything hurt when she moved.

Suddenly she realized Edward hadn't said a word. "Edward, are you okay?" No response. Not a groan, nothing! Starting to panic, but also feeling like her head was going to split apart, she had to find out if her friend was okay. Fighting the overpowering urge to close her eyes, Whitney spread her arms wide and felt around in the darkness.

"Where could he be?" she muttered. Ignoring her screaming head Whitney tried to stand up, and as she braced herself, she felt the tips of Edward's fingers! "Thank goodness!" she cried, laying back with a sigh of relief.

But he wasn't moving! Concerned all over again, she cried, "Edward, can you hear me? Are you okay? Say something!" but he still didn't answer.

Thinking the worst, Whitney beat the ground and sobbed, "I'm so sorry, Edward! You're in this mess because of me! Who knows where we are, and what happened to the rest of our friends!" Feeling lonely and frightened, Whitney desperately needed their connection. Choking back tears, she reached out and wrapped her hand around Edward's arm. "This is no way to repay you, especially after all you've done for me since we left Earth!"

The steady pulse in his wrist told her Edward was still alive, so what was wrong? "Please wake up and talk to me!" she pleaded. Suddenly, she remembered reading an article about people in comas. Doctors were still baffled by the strange disorder, so a great deal of research had been done trying to figure them out.

A person in a coma looked like they were sound asleep. Although they didn't react to things around them, there was plenty of evidence pointing to the strong possibility they could hear people talking to them. In many cases, that was enough to wake them up.

"Maybe that's exactly what's wrong with Edward," she thought, feeling a twinge of hope. "You know I'm an expert at talking, Edward, so let's get started!" she said. Although she was anxious to begin, Whitney couldn't help the yawn that escaped. "I'm not that tired, so what's that about?" she wondered, but shrugged it off and started talking.

"I owe you so much, Edward! I can't believe all that's happened in such a short time! We left Earth to help our alliance fight an enemy threatening to take over Yagdi. Before war even started, Sylern captured me. I was so frightened and felt so alone, but you risked your life to rescue me!" she said softly, squeezing his arm as she blinked rapidly, trying to keep from crying all over again.

Rolling onto her back, Whitney put an arm over her eyes as she yawned once again and whispered, "I hope you can hear me! I'm not going anywhere without you, I promise!"

Losing her battle to stay awake, Whitney cried out "Mom, I'm so sorry! I feel so alone!" As soon as she closed her eyes, darkness swooped in and wrapped itself tightly around her, pulling her into a deep, dreamless sleep.

. . .

"Whitney!" Susan cried, bolting upright and sucking in long, ragged breaths of air. Still haunted by her daughter's frightened voice crying out for help, her wide, terrified eyes peered into the darkness. "The nightmare felt so real!" she moaned, wiping her damp forehead with trembling hands. "She sounded so lost and alone!"

Leaping out of bed, Susan almost tripped over the little snow goose jumping up and down, trying so hard to get her attention. "Not now, Looa," she scolded, throwing on her robe, and shoving her feet in the slippers she'd kicked off by the bed. "Maybe Whitney had another nightmare and called out to me in her sleep!" she thought, yanking her door open, and racing down the hall to her daughter's room.

Shoving the door wide open, Susan flicked on the light. Squinting in the sudden brightness, she noticed two things immediately. Her daughter wasn't there, and her bed was made. Collapsing onto Whitney's bedspread with its bright yellow sun, surrounded by blue water, Susan remembered their shopping trip downstate. Whitney had begged for this bedspread until she'd given in. Putting her head in her hands, trying not to cry, Susan struggled with what to do next.

Following Susan into Whitney's room, Looa jumped up and down once again until the distraught mother gave in and drew their little rescue bird into her lap. Stroking the tiny bird's silky feathers, she sighed, "We can only sit here for a second!"

Wide awake now and thinking more clearly, Whitney's mother began wondering if there was a message hiding in the silence of their house. Pulling Looa in closer, she closed her eyes to listen and shivered as a hint of something important crept into her mind. It felt ominous and grew louder and more insistent as she continued to focus her attention on the agonizingly elusive nugget of information.

"There's something there but I can't see it. Whitney, where are you?" Susan cried. Suddenly she understood and her eyes opened wide. Her daughter had not been in their house, or anywhere near, when she'd cried out for help. Susan's heart had heard the distress in Whitney's voice and woke her from a deep sleep.

The deafening silence was proof their house was empty, and Whitney was gone! Her daughter was in trouble, and she'd go to the ends of the earth to help her. But first, she needed to find out where her daughter was. That was a problem! How could she find Whitney when her heart no longer heard her voice?

She couldn't just sit there doing nothing, so Susan leaped up and ran to the stairway. Grabbing the banister, she slid more than ran down the stairs and into the kitchen. Whitney wasn't there, so she pulled open the door to the deck. Still no Whitney!

Speeding down the hall to her vet office at the back of the house, Susan flung the door open so forcefully it slammed against the wall. She'd desperately hoped to find her daughter sitting in her leather desk chair reading about animals, but the room was empty!

Sagging against the doorframe, Susan dropped to the floor and screamed as the truth sank in. Her daughter was gone! Deep down, she'd known that from the moment she woke up.

But her search had just begun, and she wouldn't stop until Whitney was safely back home! Standing up, Susan squared her shoulders, and marched back into the kitchen. Grabbing her phone off the counter, she dialed 911 and paced back and forth impatiently as she waited for someone to pick up.

"911! What's your emergency?"

"Finally!" she thought. "This is Susan Wagner, and my daughter is missing!" she cried.

"I'm here to help," the operator said soothingly, trying to calm the poor woman. "Can you give me more details, such as your daughter's name, age and the last time you saw her?"

"Her name is Whitney, Whitney Wagner and she's thirteen. She went to bed here in our house last night and she's not there now!" Susan reported, trying to keep her terror in check long enough to relay the information coherently. "The more I can share, the more they'll be able to help," she thought.

"So, your daughter has been gone for three or four hours, ma'am?" the operator confirmed.

"Yes! Yes, that's about right," Susan answered, drumming her finger on the counter.

"We'll send an officer out, but if nothing seems out of order, we'll most likely wait twenty-four hours before taking further action. We'll leave that up to the officer in charge. Often, especially with independent-minded teenagers, the missing person returns on their own," she explained.

"Missing person?" Susan shouted. "Her name is Whitney, W-H-I-T-N-E-Y! Please call her by her name!"

"I understand," the operator said soothingly. "Look for Officer Rick O'Neil within twenty minutes. I'm here too if you need me."

"I know the O'Neils," Susan said. "Their dog Jessie has been a patient of mine for several years. I'll be waiting for Officer O'Neil," she promised, dropping the phone on the counter.

"What have I missed? Where are you, Whitney?" she cried out. Finding Looa at her feet once again, she picked up the little bird. "Thanks for being here, little girl! Officer O'Neil better get here quick!" she muttered, then put her face into the bird's feathers and sobbed.

"Get a grip! Whitney needs you!" she muttered and raced upstairs to throw on a pair of jeans and sweatshirt.

Chapter Six

HELP ARRIVES

Hearing the loud, authoritative knock, Susan raced to the door and flung it open. "I don't think you'll find anything, officer O'Neill. But Jessie might," she added hopefully, looking for his skilled tracker dog.

Directing Susan toward the brightly lit kitchen, Rick pulled out a chair and encouraged her to sit down. Sitting down next to her, he tried to comfort their amazing veterinarian, covering her hand with his. "No Jessie tonight, but that's a good idea. She's an excellent tracker, and if need be, I'll bring her into the case."

"I never thought my daughter would become a 'case' in a missing person investigation," she cried, near tears once again. Clearing his throat, Officer Rick said softly, "I can imagine! We'll get to the bottom of this, Susan," and pulled a notepad and pen out of his pocket.

He gently questioned Susan for several minutes, taking extensive notes the entire time. "It's apparent your daughter was here and asleep when you went to bed. Now we must find out what happened between then and when you woke up and discovered she was missing," he said gently. "Can I have a look around?"

"By all means!" Susan encouraged. "I'll go with you!" and started up the stairs, motioning for Rick to follow. "This might be the best place to start," she suggested, leading the officer into Whitney's room. He looked around for a minute, then walked over to her closet and opened the door. Pushing clothes, games, and a large beach bag out of his way, he scoured every inch, wrote something in his notebook, then closed the door and looked under her bed.

"Does he think I wouldn't have already looked everywhere she could be hiding?" Susan wondered, growing increasingly frustrated. But she held her tongue, curious about what he'd written.

"Did you find something of interest in the closet?" she asked.

"Honestly, I was more interested in what appears to be missing," he explained.

"What did you find?" she asked impatiently.

"Plenty of dust," he said, then hurried to explain the significance. "That's not a problem, but I found no dust in one of the corners and wondered what might have been sitting there recently."

"Oh, I see!" Susan answered, mystified. "Whitney and I don't keep secrets, but I can't tell you what she keeps in her closet," she said, suddenly feeling like an irresponsible mother.

Rick noticed her discomfort immediately. "I didn't mean to imply anything. It's just something that stood out. It might be nothing."

"It might be important, though!" she frowned. "I wish I could help! There is something odd, though," Susan added. "Our cat Ellie always sleeps with Whitney, but she's missing too. I don't know if that helps, but it's something," Susan said hopefully.

He jotted the information down then suggested, "Let's continue our search." Susan picked up Looa and followed Officer O'Neil through the house, onto the deck and even down to the beach.

After shining his flashlight, and walking ten yards in every direction, he sighed and turned his light off. "I'm sorry, Susan. Whitney's not in the house, and it's too dark to look for clues outside."

Coaxed by her disappointed sigh, he said, "I'll tell you what. If your daughter hasn't returned by midday, call me and I promise to come back right away, and I'll bring my very capable assistant with me. Jessie has the most amazing sense of smell and has proven to be invaluable many times. She can lead us down a trail, even days later."

With a sympathetic smile, Rick touched Susan's shoulder and promised, "If Whitney doesn't come home, we'll do everything in our power to find her, Susan." Touching the brim of his hat, he turned and walked up the hill to his patrol car and drove away.

Dragging herself back up the long flight of stairs and into the house, Susan acknowledged there would be no more sleep tonight, and sat down at the kitchen table. "No matter what, I'll never stop looking for you, Whitney!" she vowed.

Putting her head in her hands, Susan replayed everything she and Officer Rick had done, wondering if either of them had missed anything. She couldn't think of anything else to do or anywhere else to look and groaned, "Come on, Whitney, show yourself!"

Walking back on the deck made her feel somehow closer to her daughter, and the sun would rise soon, so she dropped into one of their Adirondack chairs to wait. It wasn't long before Looa the little snow goose climbed into her lap. Wiggling its way up to her face, its tiny beak tickled as it swept back and forth across her damp cheek. "If anything happens to Whitney, I'll never forgive myself, Looa," she murmured.

Refusing to believe her daughter was so far away that she'd never find her, Susan desperately tried to convince herself that her heart was wrong. Looking up, she discovered the sky was brightening and felt hope for the first time.

"Whitney, please find a way to tell me where you are!" she whispered to the rising sun. Rushing to the rail, she scanned the beach once again, but still didn't see her daughter. Turning back into the kitchen she started a pot of coffee, hoping the caffeine would help her think. She needed to come up with a concrete plan of action, and quickly!

The coffee was taking forever! Full of nervous energy and needing something to do while she waited, Susan picked up the phone. It was way too early to bother Edward's grandparents, but she called her friends anyway.

Cathy surprised her by answering on the first ring. "Susan? What's wrong?" she asked, sounding very concerned.

"I hope nothing!" Susan answered. "Cathy, are Whitney and Edward with you?"

"You know, Edward often gets up early to get in a long bike ride," she mused. "Hang on. Let me check."

Impatiently thrumming her fingers on the table, Susan heard Cathy yell, "Jerome, check the garage for Edward's bike!"

Holding her phone in a vice grip, Susan nervously chewed on a nail and waited.

"Susan?" Cathy said with a catch in her voice.

"Yes? I'm here!" Susan answered quickly.

"First, there's no sign that Whitney's been here!" Cathy reported. Not knowing if that was good or bad news for her friend, she continued quickly, "Edward's bike's not here either, but that's nothing new. The strange thing is that his bed's been made, and he NEVER does that before his early bike rides."

Susan was ready to jump in with more questions when Cathy said cautiously, "It's like he never slept here last night!"

"Thanks for checking," Susan said quickly "I hope Edward's just out for a bike ride! But I'm really getting worried about Whitney!" she admitted. "I've looked everywhere except Ellie's Point. She could have gotten up early and gone out there rockhounding. I'm headed there right now."

After a slight hesitation, Susan shared everything. "Cathy, you should know when I couldn't find Whitney anywhere, I called

911." Hearing her friend's gasp, she continued, "I know. That's a big step! Officer O'Neil showed up within the half hour and we searched everywhere. We even walked the beach. There were no prints to follow, just some strange large indents in the sand by the water's edge. He wasn't sure what to make of it, but we both agreed it wasn't Whitney, and there was only one set of prints. He took extensive notes but said he'd wait a few hours to see if Whitney came home on her own before returning with Jessie, his tracker dog. That's as far as we got!" she moaned.

"That is a big step, but I completely understand. If Edward doesn't come home by late morning, I intend to do the same thing! In fact, while Jerome and I are waiting for Edward, we'll drive out to the camper. It's a longshot, but it's possible the kids are there. After that, we'll swing by your place. This is no time for you to be alone, Susan!"

"Good idea to check the trailer! And thanks! I could use your company," Susan said gratefully, then hung up and walked over to the kitchen window. Their house was perched high on a sandy bluff and provided a commanding view of the "Big Lake" and the mile-long peninsula in front of their house.

Susan rubbed her sleepy eyes then gazed toward Ellie's Point and pondered her next move. She was certain that Whitney was in trouble, and the peninsula was the best place to look for her. So why was she dragging her feet? "Because it feels like I'm going in the wrong direction!" she moaned.

Whitney's frightened voice had terrified her, and that fear for her daughter hadn't gone away. If anything, she was growing more worried by the minute. But for some strange reason, she no longer felt a sense of urgency to race out to Ellie's Point. Susan felt lost and lonely, like the bond between them had been severed. Not completely, she quickly corrected herself, but it was frayed and weakening. Even more, she feared her daughter was feel-ing their connection fade too. Her heart knew that Whitney was somewhere she couldn't go, but it was too frightening to consider the possibility she'd never find her!

"I can't just sit here doing nothing!" Squaring her shoulders, Susan vowed, "I'll never stop looking for you, Whitney!" With renewed determination, she marched down the long flight of stairs to the beach and headed to Ellie's Point.

Chapter Seven

THE TRICKSTER

Glaring down at the young wizard, Edna snarled in disgust. "You try my patience to no end, young trickster! Your grubby little hands stole my seer so I couldn't track the movements of the alliance! We didn't discover they were in the portal until our secondary alarms went off, and by then it was too late!"

"You're right!" Patrick cried. Edna's minions had caught him red-handed, so it seemed pointless to say anything more, but he took this one last opportunity to defend his actions, foolish as they'd been. "Yes, I stole your treasure, but I just wanted to borrow it to see into my future!"

"You don't need a seer to uncover what your future holds because I can tell you it's been shortened considerably!" Edna announced angrily.

"I was at your door, trying to return it to you when your minions caught me! What more proof do you need that I didn't intend to keep it?" Patrick cried defiantly.

Eyeing the powerful woman warily, he continued, "I know it was wrong. But I didn't know you needed your seer at that very moment to complete your victorious return to Yagdi! I would have never intentionally ruined almost a century of planning. Please believe me!"

Throwing her arms up in frustration, Edna ran a hand through her hair and began to pace. The room turned deathly quiet as the clan members watched their leader, anticipating the speedy pronouncement of a severe sentence.

Edna had found the young wizard's youthful spunk and energy exhilarating and admired his devious schemes. In fact, she considered his ability to deceive others a wonderful asset and had been considering Patrick for a position of power once they returned to Yagdi.

Unfortunately, too many had seen his bold act. The young wizard must be punished to maintain her position of power. The powerful leader ran a tight ship and could not tolerate deceit from her followers. Anyone foolish enough to betray her never lived long enough to see the dawn of a new day, and Patrick couldn't be the exception to that rule.

Edna was fully aware he'd bamboozled his way out of many tight situations, but she was a master at ensnaring her enemies and doubted the young wizard was good enough to outwit her. Just to have a little fun, she would enjoy probing the trickster's beguiling mind for any hint of lies, and her method of coercing the truth never failed!

Whirling on Patrick, Edna pointed a long, twisted finger toward him and screamed, "You're a foolish wizard and must learn there are consequences for bad behavior!"

"Believe me, I know that!" Patrick whimpered, sorely tempted to get down on his knees and beg for mercy. That usually worked in his favor! But he'd already apologized profusely, and nothing had penetrated the wall she'd erected.

Edna would punish him because he'd deceived her, and the clan expected justice. So, the trickster sucked in a painful breath and looked away, bracing for the inevitable. *No one* disrespected the powerful leader without paying dearly!

Leaning in threateningly close, the ancient hissed, "Almost every member of the alliance made it back to Earth safely because of you!" Backing away, she threw out some bait to gauge his reaction. "Lucky for you, young Whitney and Edward remain trapped in the portal. That means we have a chance to kidnap their precious 'chosen ones' and may need your services. For that reason alone, I might let you live for the time being, young trickster!"

"I can't take back what's already been done, but I can fix my mistake!" Patrick blurted, eager to promise this woman anything to get out of trouble.

"I'll find the young chosen ones and bring them back to the clan. You can do as you will with Whitney and Edward, just leave me in peace!" he begged, hoping that would satisfy her.

"Please believe me!" Patrick pleaded silently, squirming uncomfortably under Edna's suspicious glare. If she suspected he wasn't being completely truthful, the young wizard feared he wouldn't survive much longer — unless he thought of something fast. The powerful woman remained silent and continued to glare at him, increasing Patrick's doubt that his plan would succeed.

He'd gone into this knowing it would be almost impossible to fool Edna because she was so well equipped to detect all forms of deceit. But the trickster was out of options! He'd become a master at crafting cunning lies and deceits. It was a loathsome hobby, but those very skills had gotten him out of trouble many times in the past. However, this was a very challenging situation that called for unusually creative thinking. Today's performance must be flawless, or Edna would see through it immediately.

"Let me catch the kids and bring them back!" he declared. "If I fail, I pledge my allegiance to you. I will be your servant, waiting on you hand-and-foot every second of every day! You will want for nothing, my queen!"

Crossing her arms, Edna growled menacingly, "You stole from me, and there were witnesses. How can you expect me to believe your so-called vow?"

Trying to mask their excitement, the wizards moved in closer and held their breath in eager anticipation.

Grateful he was wearing long sleeves, the trickster made sure his hand was concealed under the shirt's wide cuff. Crossing his fingers, Patrick cast his eyes down in a show of respect and knelt before Edna. In a valiant effort to mask any sign of trickery, the young wizard looked up at her and raised his free hand, vowing "I solemnly swear, before you and the entire clan, if you pardon my misguided decision to steal from you, I will find Whitney and Edward and bring them to you."

Patrick stole a quick glance as he stood up and caught the doubt in Edna's stern glare. "She didn't buy it," he thought and braced for the worst possible outcome.

"I shall uncover the truth in your vow," Edna sneered as she sauntered slowly and purposefully toward him. Raising her arm, the powerful woman sent a bolt of electricity into Patrick. It struck with such force his entire body began to shake uncontrollably.

"What more do you want from me?" he moaned, slumping to the ground, and covering his ears in a frantic attempt to stop the pain in his head.

Callously ignoring the young wizard's agony, Edna continued her assault on his mind, smiling with grim satisfaction as she watched the trickster writhe on the ground.

"Do you even have a heart?" Patrick screamed, struggling to concentrate through the fog of pain. Somehow, he found the strength to keep the truth hidden from Edna, despite her painful mind probes.

Finally, Edna stood back and crossed her arms. "Groveling never works, simpleton! Get up at once!" she snapped.

Unsteady and fearing he might fall, Patrick rose slowly. Struck by a wave of dizziness, he instinctively reached out for support and grabbed Edna's shoulder because she happened to be right there. Catching the evil grins on the faces of the other wizards, he realized they were standing far closer than he'd remembered. Captivated by the show, they'd indeed moved in and were now surrounding both the wizard and their leader. Patrick swayed and almost fell when Edna yanked her arm away. Everyone thought that was hilarious and began to laugh. It sounded more like annoying high-pitched shrieking, but Patrick was embarrassed and frowned. That only made them laugh harder and the young wizard gaped as their faces turned terrifyingly ghoulish.

The bizarre scene was so distracting, Patrick wasn't aware Edna had snuck up behind him. When one of her long fingernails raked down his back, he instinctively leaped and twisted in midair, then kicked one leg straight out.

Deftly avoiding his fancy footwork, the ancient leader grabbed Patrick's hands and held them tightly behind his back. He could feel her hot angry breath on his neck. "I'm going to let go but leave your flying feet on the floor!" she hissed.

Turning slowly and cautiously, he found Edna glaring down at him menacingly. Tapping a long fingernail into his chest, she warned, "We'll be watching your every move from this point forward. If you stray from your promise the consequences will be more severe than you can possibly imagine. Do you understand, scheming trickster?"

Patrick winced when she used the despised nickname and vowed for the millionth time to repay the arrogant wizard who'd given it to him. Many of his peers remembered Mergan fondly and even admired his skills, but Patrick chose to believe his own slanted version. The trickster convinced himself that Mergan had treated him very poorly and those warped memories turned rock-solid over time. When others attempted to point out the flaws in his perspective, Patrick refused to listen.

It had happened so long ago, but the wounds from wizard school went deep, and the bad memories stung now as much as they had decades ago. Patrick had always suffered from low self-esteem and took offense when anyone looked at him sideways! When his errors in judgment hurt others, he never claimed responsibility but deflected the blame onto some other poor, unsuspecting soul.

In fact, Patrick made Mergan his primary scapegoat for all the trouble he had in school. He even pinned his poor social skills on his teacher, providing numerous examples of how the nasty wizard tormented him. Once again, when his peers tried to point out the inaccuracy of his memory, he not only refused to believe their arguments but sought revenge!

Patrick enjoyed scheming new ways to get even with his enemies, especially Mergan. He never meant to cause real harm, but one time he'd caught his teacher off guard and turned him into a nasty-looking troll. The humorless old wizard locked him in the basement and threatened to throw away the key! Patrick was terrified of the dark, and suffered from claustrophobia, so the ordeal was extremely traumatic! Mergan would always be his enemy and Patrick would treat him as such. One day he would get even!

Right now, he had to focus on getting out of his current predicament. "I promise you will not be disappointed!" he cried, trying hard to sound sincere. That was difficult because Patrick was quite certain he would *not* be keeping that promise.

He waited several agonizing moments, but finally Edna snarled, "I'll hold you to that!" Turning her back on Patrick, she snapped her fingers for the clan to follow and walked out the door. The wizards just stood there for a moment, staring at each other in shocked surprise. They'd never witnessed such leniency and were rather disappointed with their leader's odd treatment of the bumbling wizard. But they'd been commanded to follow, so with a shrug of their shoulders, they stumbled over each other in their haste to fall in line.

"Dodged another disaster, Trickster!" Patrick thought to himself, wondering for the first time if Mergan was onto something with that name. Watching the mindless sheep follow their leader out the door, he held his breath as Edna's high heels clattered on the concrete floor, growing fainter as she moved further away. Exhaling with relief when he finally heard only the beautiful sound of silence, Patrick hurried to his small room. Expecting Edna to change her mind at any minute, the young wizard hastily packed his bag, threw it over his shoulder and walked out.

"Good riddance to all of you, and with any luck, I'll never see any of you ever again!" he grumbled as he marched away from their encampment. Patrick didn't doubt the powerful wizards would seek swift and certain vengeance if he dared deceive them, but still hoped to keep his options open. With all the speed his short legs would allow, Patrick ran into the maze of tunnels winding through the wizards' forbidden land.

Chapter Eight

FINALIZING THE PLAN

Thanks to all their trips to the mines buried deep inside the tunnels, Patrick knew exactly where he was going and made good progress. Finally, he was greeted by a soft green glow. "I've reached my destination!" he exclaimed. "From this day forward, I alone will determine the fate of young Whitney and Edward!" With a satisfied grin he raced through the entrance and into the enormous cavern.

Hearing the waterfall well before reaching his secret hideout, he declared "My home for now!" and ran into the cavern. Shielding his eyes from the sudden brightness, the young wizard gazed at the beauty surrounding him. The glistening stalactites were his favorite, so he walked over to touch one that almost reached the floor and wondered how old it must be to have grown so long.

Patrick felt the kinks in his shoulders loosen as he walked toward the shimmering pond. "This place has always given me such comfort," he sighed. But there wouldn't be much time to relax. He'd heard the teenagers' panicked voices and knew they had fallen out of the portal and into the tunnels. He'd wandered these dark hallways every time he found the opportunity to sneak away and knew this area near the cavern extremely well.

Interestingly, the darkness didn't bother him as it normally did, and the narrow openings didn't make him feel claustrophobic.

He didn't know why that was but welcomed it. Though his previous excursions had only been temporary, the tunnels were his only escape from the clan.

Apparently, the explosion had not only dismantled the portal as Edna had planned, but it had conveniently opened a door leading to the very section of tunnels Patrick knew so well. They laid directly under the portal, buried deep below the towering mountains.

If events turned out as he hoped, the light from his cavern would attract their attention, and Whitney and Edward would come to investigate. It seemed like the perfect spot to wait for their arrival, and Patrick was more pleased than ever that he'd kept it secret from the rest of the clan.

Certain his time with the clan would eventually end in dismal failure, just like all the others, the trickster identified the tunnels as a quick means of escape and joined the wizards' mining operation. Patrick was deviously smart and easily memorized their preferred routes. He even had time to investigate the tunnels the clan rarely used.

To ensure they never suspected anything, he pretended navigation was too tricky for him. He looked completely lost all the time and mindlessly followed the others, making sure he complimented their adept skills often. Proud of his acting abilities, Patrick would look sheepish and embarrassed when they laughed at him.

His patience paid off when everything went as planned. They never had a clue Patrick was more than capable of finding his way through the maze. One memorable day they were short-handed and sent him to scout a new area and report back.

"We'll never see that one again!" one of them said, and everyone laughed as Patrick walked away. The clan had unwittingly given the young wizard a gift because that was the day he'd stumbled into this beautiful cavern. He'd kept it a well-hidden secret, returning only once before today. That scheme turned out to be pure genius on his part!

The huge pool covered most of the room and was so clear Patrick could see the rocky bottom far beneath the surface. The massive waterfall at the far end spilled from somewhere out of sight and was the source of light. Boulders and small pools of water glistened with light and brilliant colors as the waterfall tumbled over them on its journey to the pool.

Eager to soak his tired feet, Patrick ran to the flat boulder at the edge of the pool and sat down. Hurriedly removing his heavy boots, he gasped when his bare feet smacked the surface and splashed cold water in his face, drenching the front of his shirt.

The water moved around his tired feet in slow, leisurely circles, gently massaging each one and easing his worries. Patrick sighed and leaned back contentedly, watching the gentle waves cover the pool's surface in deep shades of purple and yellow. The colors were much like his beautiful Yagdian sunsets, which filled the exhausted young wizard with such joy, he closed his eyes. The day had been long and trying, and he fell asleep immediately, and began to dream....

Waking suddenly, Patrick blinked rapidly as he took in the scene before him. Rubbing the sleep from his eyes, the young wizard tried to remember why he was sitting there and wondered how long he'd been asleep.

"It couldn't have been too long, because I'm still sitting upright," Patrick murmured, vigorously shaking his tingling arms. Remembering his bizarre dream, the wizard frowned in concentration, knowing there was something important hidden in there. "Come on, think!" he murmured impatiently. "Who did I hear?"

Suddenly it came to him...Edna! He clearly remembered hearing the diabolical woman say, "We need spying eyes on that trickster *now*! GO!"

But that was impossible! How could he have heard her from so far away? Or had he just dreamed it? Though quite certain no one else had discovered his cavern, Patrick peered nervously over his shoulder and muttered, "It wouldn't hurt to stay extra vigilant, just in case!"

"I heard other voices too!" he thought to himself. "If it wasn't a dream, and if I'm correct in assuming no one else is near, the two chosen ones have arrived and will soon join me!" He'd promised Edna that he would figure out a way to entrap them and bring them to her. Whitney and Edward would be with the powerful leader very soon, and he would be back in her favor!

Anticipating a big reward and speedy rise in status, Patrick grinned proudly as he drew his feet out of the water and crossed his legs. Getting a glimpse of his reflection, the young wizard gasped in dismay and stood up. His hair was never perfectly groomed, but today it stuck out at funny angles and was matted and greasy. His bushy eyebrows were deeply furrowed with concern and those brilliant green eyes looked sad and disappointed. Once again, he'd been harshly judged by others, and found lacking.

Sitting back down, Patrick sighed and gently pulled out his only treasure. He watched sparks fly off the silky blue and silver tips of his magical feather as he spun it between two stubby fingers and allowed himself a rare moment of introspection. Wishing he could blame everything on Edna and her clan, he knew their plans had failed because he'd stolen her seer just when she needed it most, so the clan would not be returning to Yagdi, at least not as they'd intended! "Check another epic failure off the list!" he admitted grudgingly.

He'd never been cut out for those boring training lessons in wizard school. He struggled with rules in general, and that school had been more rules than fun. He hated Mergan's nickname for him but now had to admit it fit! He truly was a 'scheming trickster.' "What's the crime in having a little fun, even when it's at others' expense?"

Disillusioned by the cruel environment of wizard school, Patrick focused on his dream of becoming famous — a superstar within the world of wizards. That was the only thing that kept the disgruntled young wizard from growing weary and disenchanted. He would become legendary, no matter how long it took or how many he had to trample over to get there.

"What's a wizard supposed to do when he can't quite learn how to be a wizard?" he thought, looking at his reflection. "You're my best asset!" he murmured, reaching up to touch his big floppy ears. They danced when he moved and heard everything, giving him a huge advantage.

He'd stumbled on the ancient wizard clan by accident, but they were surprisingly welcoming. However, Edna knew of his reputation and insisted he must promise not to trick any clan members. He'd vowed to refrain from trickery, and everything had gone smoothly until he once again ignored his better instincts and 'borrowed' the powerful leader's seer.

Patrick was extremely curious by nature, so he'd discovered a great deal about the clan in a short period of time. He'd recruited a few spies willing to keep him informed as long as he continued to pay them generously. Through his informants, the young wizard learned that well over a century ago, Edna and her clan had been tried and found guilty of committing crimes against Yagdians resulting in banishment from their homeland, never to return.

They'd been conspiring their return ever since and had finally created a foolproof plan that pleased Edna. Hours before their victorious return, one of Patrick's spies took him aside and whispered excitedly, "They're ready to trigger an explosion that will seal that accursed alliance inside the portal!"

"Is that because the alliance caused their first plan to fail?"

Patrick asked. He'd clearly confused the informant, and hurriedly explained, "Your clan created Sylern and worked for many years planning for battle. The ruthless creature was to attack from several fronts and surprise the Yagdians before they'd established a defense."

"Edna's first mistake was assuming Yagdi's citizens wouldn't be prepared for a battle," Patrick continued. "If things had gone as she'd planned, the clan would've moved in and taken over after Sylern defeated the Yagdian army. However, the alliance, and a shocking number of courageous Yagdians, marched to war and defeated Sylern. Edna was dismayed she'd looked weaker than the Yagdian's make-shift army, and shocked when her first attempt failed."

"Ah but did it really?" his informant asked conspiratorially. Grinning at Patrick's frown of confusion, he continued. "Sylern still exists and will live only until he serves whatever purpose Edna has in mind." Shrugging his shoulders, he added, "She's quite ruthless you know. If Sylern had done his job, the plans we've discussed wouldn't have been necessary, but Edna always seems to have a backup plan."

"So, tell me more about Edna's plan to capture the alliance," Patrick encouraged, eager to hear everything before they were interrupted.

"That's a critical component. Her plan won't succeed if they can't nab the alliance first," his informant said, looking nervously up and down the hallway to make sure they were still alone. "She's worried that powerful group could interfere with our return and wants to put them all out of commission, particularly Traveller and Mergan. As you've no doubt heard, their skills are very impressive indeed. Once the alliance is trapped, Edna has an entire division prepared to rush in and grab 'em. Once we have 'em behind bars, they'll be powerless to stop us," he bragged. With an excited laugh, he leaned in and whispered, "Between you and me, Edna plans to leave the entire alliance here to rot, and no one will ever know what happened to them."

"But how will she know when the entire group is inside the portal?" Patrick asked.

"That's the beautiful part of her plan!" the informant said with obvious respect. "Edna keeps things close, but I'm rather clever at sniffing out mysteries. I discovered she has a seer and will use it to monitor their movements. Our ingenious leader will be alerted when the alliance leaves the celebration. That will allow her to track them until they enter the portal. That's when she'll set off an alarm, signaling her carefully selected assistant to pull the trigger on the explosives."

"Ah, that sounds foolproof indeed!" Patrick agreed.

"Couldn't be more solid!" the informant said as a door opened down the hall. Winking confidently, he turned and hurried away.

Totally on board with his old professor's fate, Patrick looked forward to mocking him through the safety of prison bars. But a hint of doubt crept in, spoiling his enthusiasm. "Was it wise to capture the alliance?" he wondered, hoping Edna and her inner circle had thought of every possible scenario. "If not, they could fail. Especially with Mergan and the alliance involved!" he muttered nervously.

Patience was not one of Patrick's virtues. His thoughts snapped back to the present as he grew weary of the self-examination. It was getting him nowhere, and he didn't want to feel guilty about anything ever again. The easiest solution to that problem was so simple; he'd just continue blaming others for his mistakes! With that settled, the trickster's mood shifted dramatically. Grinning mischievously, he tucked the feather back into his left shirtsleeve, stood up and stretched.

He really didn't care one way or the other about Whitney or Edward, or any other member of the alliance for that matter. Patrick just wanted to enjoy his reward for getting the kids to

'Queen Edna,' but if he could also exact vengeance on Mergan for treating him so poorly, that would be icing on the cake!

"It's time once again to show the world what this seasoned trickster has up his sleeve!" he said, pulling on his boots. "Vengeance will be mine!" he shouted excitedly. "I must prepare for their arrival!" But then he frowned, feeling an unexpected tug of concern. "If I don't play my cards just right, I may not have a future at all," he muttered. Raising his hand in the air, he yelled, "That just means I must be trickier than ever!" and raced from the cavern.

Chapter Nine

POWER OF A DREAM JUMPER

Whitney lay sprawled out on the boulder's hard surface, a large rock propping her head at an odd angle and her wizard staff gripped tightly between both hands. Although she appeared to be sleeping peacefully, the thirteen-year-old was balancing on a dangerous precipice between life and death. It would take a miraculous intervention to waken her!

Bobbing up and down on a gentle wave, the eerie gray world made everything look fuzzy and distorted. Her eyes fluttered occasionally when partial memories and vague images floated in and out of her sleepy mind, but nothing made sense or looked familiar. "I don't care," Whitney thought lazily. "I'm so comfortable."

A pleasant memory of her mom eased its way into Whitney's gray world, giving it a tiny spot of color. She smiled as Susan flipped pancakes, and sang their breakfast song, "Our house is a very fine house..." A disturbing concern interrupted the song, and she frowned. Her mom was worried about her! "But why?" she wondered fleetingly.

• • •

Randolph had no idea where the crazy idea came from, but he approached the tree murmuring, "My tiger's eye gives me clarity and my skeleton key has powers that go back to medieval times."

Spreading his arms over the spot the portal had once been, the dream jumper continued, "One of those powers is unlocking portals."

The ancient pine was so massive, he could only reach halfway around, so he made sure both the key and stone were touching the trunk before closing his eyes. "Let's test those powers right now," he said, and began murmuring phrases he'd never heard before.

"Well, I'll be!" Mergan yelled in surprise, recognizing the long-forgotten phrases of his youth. "What an ingenious idea, my dear Randolph!" he said excitedly, rushing to the opposite side of the tree. Leaning into the massive trunk, the wizard stretched his arms out as wide as they'd go, grunting with immense effort until his face was flattened against the tree.

"You're repeating a powerful transparency spell I haven't heard since I was a child in school! It's designed to make things clear that are not. I hope you don't mind my joining you. The spell might be twice as strong with two of us repeating them," he explained excitedly, latching onto the earth wizard's hands.

Randolph was shocked by his friend's reaction, but relieved to discover the nonsense words that had come out of nowhere had an actual purpose! The two wizards murmured the strange, ancient phrases until Randolph gasped, "I think I hear someone!"

"Hang onto me, Randolph! I want to keep our link. It appears to be very strong," Mergan grunted. The others crowded around their wizards and watched with rapt attention, as if simply being near would allow them to hear Whitney and Edward.

"Whitney, Edward, is that you?" Randolph yelled until he was out of breath and frustrated. "Just give me a minute!" he sighed apologetically.

Sylern had listened to him when he spoke forcefully. "Worth trying with the kids," Randolph murmured. Taking a deep, calming breath, he cleared his throat and commanded in a deep, authoritative voice, "Whitney, Edward, it's Randolph! You must say something to reassure us you survived the blast!"

Getting no response, he looked up and frowned in confusion. "Why are you staring at me?"

"Randolph, your voice!" Ellie gasped. "It's so deep and melodic, almost hypnotic!"

Her observation was unexpected, and Randolph started to respond when a soft voice interrupted. "Shh! I heard something!" he hissed, putting his head against the trunk once again.

Frowning in concentration, Randolph cleared his mind of everything so he could focus on Whitney. "I entered Sylern's world. I should be able to find Whitney and Edward," he muttered and felt himself drift away. He could no longer hear the waves on the shore or wind in the trees.

Somewhere between his world and hers, the dream jumper heard Whitney moan, "I don't want to get up yet!" Frightened for his two young friends, he followed the poor girl's weak voice and entered her nightmare.

Landing in a dark place, Randolph searched frantically until he found Whitney and gasped in dismay. His young friend was sound asleep, and her motionless body was bathed in an eerie greenish glow. "Is she okay, and where's Edward?" he worried.

"Whitney, wake up!" he commanded, and watched the poor girl groan and roll over, then flop an arm over her eyes. He couldn't let the chosen one slide back into her world of dreams. Sensing she might never return he urgently called her back. "Whitney, it's Randolph. You must open your eyes this minute!" Finally, he saw her frown and muttered hopefully, "Any reaction shows progress!"

"Come on, give me a break!" Whitney said tiredly. She had no energy to open her eyes but there was something vitally important that needed to be done. She just felt too groggy and confused to remember what it was! "Get up!" she told herself. And she did, but way too fast! "Oh, my head!" she groaned, putting her throbbing head in her hands as the room spun around her in dizzying circles.

"Why does everything hurt?" she wondered, feeling more pain as her brain slowly woke up. Suddenly, memories stirred deep inside, and she frowned worriedly, trying to bring them to the surface. "Ohhhh, now I remember!" she muttered as pieces of the puzzle began falling into place. She and Edward were heading home when the portal hijacked them.

"But where are we?" she cried out. "Mom will be awake by now. But I won't be there, and she'll worry herself insane!"

Suddenly she realized her best friend wasn't lying next to her! "Edward!" she screamed. He'd been unresponsive but still breathing when she'd fallen asleep. Disregarding the inky darkness that surrounded her, Whitney began crawling in tight, frantic circles, occasionally reaching out with her arms to feel into the dark places beyond her sight.

Swiping away fresh tears, the frightened girl sat back on her heels, defeated and lonely with no idea what to do next. She needed her friend's calm, thoughtful approach to solving problems! "Edward, where are you!"

Sighing sadly, she said to herself, "I may never know the fate of my friends! All I can do is hope they all made it safely through the portal before that awful blast!"

When the mind-numbing ache in her head finally lessened to a dull nuisance, she began taking in her surroundings. The little bit of light almost made her wish it was completely dark, because now she feared what might be hiding in the darkness.

"Edward, are you out there?" she cried in a raspy voice. But he didn't answer, and the silence terrified her even more. Attacked by a sudden fit of coughing, Whitney realized how dry her throat was, and she didn't have any water!

"Edward! Where are you?" she yelled again, then slapped her

hand over her mouth and stared nervously into the darkness. "Now you've done it, Whit!" she chastised herself. Thanks to her big mouth, if someone was lurking in the shadows, she'd just put out the welcome mat!

Shivering from the damp and cold, Whitney drew her knees up to her chin and wrapped her arms around her legs. She was afraid and alone and that strange voice wasn't making her feel any better! "Who's out there?" she cried, no longer caring who or what might be there. Drawing her legs closer, she wished with all her heart this was just a nightmare that would fade with the light of morning. But she knew better and whimpered, "Mom, I miss you, but please don't worry about me!"

Randolph watched Whitney's panic spiral to dangerous levels but couldn't help the poor girl. He wanted desperately to reassure her that she wasn't alone any longer, and that the voice she heard was a friend. But something was interfering, and he couldn't get through to her!

Whitney's plea to her mother was so raw, Randolph growled and dove deep inside himself, hoping to find a way to break through the barricade that kept him from reaching Whitney. Suddenly, the earth wizard felt an extraordinary burst of energy surging through his entire body, from fingers to toes.

Hoping he'd just smashed through the barrier, he walked closer to their young chosen one and urged, "Whitney, this is Randolph! I'm here with you, and it's my voice you hear. I want to tell your mother you're okay. But I can't do that truthfully until you prove it. Open your eyes and look at me!"

Whitney had been on the verge of falling back to sleep when that voice returned, demanding she answer. Giving up all hope of sleep, she opened her eyes cautiously, frightened by what she might find.

"Who's out there?" she cried warily, peering toward the glowing light like a deer frozen in the glare of headlights.

"My sweet young rockhound, this is Randolph. Can you hear me?"

"Randolph! Is that really you?" Whitney answered weakly, peering into the darkness once again.

"Oh, thank goodness!" Randolph yelled excitedly. Pressing his cheek firmly against the tree, Randolph shifted his eyes toward his friends and nodded. "I'm with Whitney, and she's talking to me!"

He heard their collective gasps but didn't waste time explaining because Whitney needed him. Transitioning back was much easier this time, so the earth wizard smiled reassuringly to the others as he watched Whitney wake up and heard her sweet voice grow stronger.

"Randolph, I feel so fuzzy headed! Is it really you? I'm thinking it must be! Who else would call me a rockhound? But I don't see you! Can you see me?"

"Yes, I can see you, Whitney. I'm right here with you. Unfortunately, in spirit only, at least for the time being. I can see you, and you can hear me, but my physical being remains on Ellie's Point with the others."

"I'm not surprised you found me, Earth Wizard," Whitney said proudly. "This is what you do so well! Maybe you can teach me how to 'see' you. But first things first, you woke me up, didn't you?"

"I think I did, yes," Randolph answered. "You appeared to be in a very deep sleep, and I was concerned I wouldn't be able to pull you out!"

"That must've happened when I hit my head on a boulder. I just couldn't stay awake. I don't know how long I was out, but you're my hero. You woke me up! I'm SO relieved! Did everyone make it out okay? Maybe you can help me locate Edward. He must've hit his head, because he wouldn't open his eyes, but he was breathing. He was gone when I woke up and now I can't find him! Just in case we lose contact, I'm somewhere in the portal. I'm okay, just scared and worried about Edward!"

Randolph wished he could carry the poor, distraught girl back to Earth, but that wasn't going to happen anytime soon. Trying to remain calm he reassured her the best he could. "Whitney, we're all fine and here at the portal on Ellie's Point. We're not going anywhere and will be waiting for both of you. We just need time to figure this out!"

"I'm so glad everyone's safe! Please find mom and TELL HER EVERYTHING! We have a strong connection that might help!" she pleaded.

Worried when her voice started to weaken, Randolph worked hard to keep her with him. "Whitney, can you hear me?" he asked.

"Yea, I just need a little nap," she murmured and fell back to sleep.

"Have a nice nap," he said soothingly. "But I'm going to return and wake you very soon, my dear girl!" he warned. "At least I can reach her. Maybe the others will have a solution to this mess!" he muttered to himself, easing his way back to Ellie's Point. Randolph dropped his arms, and turned away from the tree, shaking his head.

"My good earth wizard, what have you done?" Mergan demanded.

"Did you enter the portal?" Traveller jumped in.

"Are they okay?" Ellie and Aiden shouted at the same time.

Putting his hands up in mock surrender, Randolph said, "First, I did indeed find Whitney, but Edward is missing and she's worried to death about him and all of us! I reassured her we were fine, and as you'd imagine that was a big relief for our young chosen one. They're not in the portal, at least as far as I could tell. Whitney appears to be in a dark tunnel and there's a greenish glow coming from further down the passageway."

"Once again, you've proven there is more to you than meets the eye!" Mergan said, patting Randolph on the back.

"I've heard if you're quiet and patient, magic will show itself,"

Traveller said softly. Looking at both of her dear friends, she continued, "You two did something today that gives us hope! Thank you for that!"

Turning toward Randolph, she continued, "You, my dear earth wizard, will become our liaison. And I can't think of a more important role, and one that will be invaluable as we move forward. I just hope we can help them before it's too late! Let's try to reconnect again. I don't want Whitney to stay asleep. It sounds dangerous at this point!" She turned away before they could see her eyes glistening with sudden tears. Clearing her throat, she whirled back around and announced, "Let's get back to the tree! We have much to do!"

Sensing a sudden disturbance, she commanded, "Circle the tree, facing out!" Peering anxiously through the small pines, the bear saw Susan running toward them and dropped her guard. "Of course, Whitney's mother would sense something had happened to her daughter! And what better place to look than Ellie's Point?" she realized.

She couldn't appear to Susan in her true polar bear identity, not yet anyway. In a dazzling display of light, Traveller quickly transformed into the elderly woman named Ursula who Susan had met previously. The persona always served her well when she visited Earth.

Then she warned the alliance, "Susan will be here any moment! Aiden, you can NOT be a dragon, not at this moment!" she growled. "Ellie, please turn into your earthly form as a cat, and be quick about it, both of you!"

Squaring her shoulders, Ursula turned to face the wrath of a terrified mother. Sure enough, in no time at all, Susan erupted into the clearing. Blowing a stray hair off her very red face, she stopped to catch her breath.

Chapter Ten

DEMANDING ANSWERS!

Ursula watched Whitney's mother with keen interest and noticed she didn't seem the least bit surprised to see their group at the end of Ellie's Point. Quite the opposite, Susan stood with her hands on her hips, as if she'd geared up for an expected confrontation.

Looking furiously at each of them, her eyes sparked with anger when they landed on Ursula's wide brown eyes. "Where's my daughter?" she demanded.

"This is going to be tricky!" Ursula muttered to herself, acknowledging how alike Susan and Whitney were. Neither would settle for anything less than the truth! There were many ways to handle a distraught mother, but it was a challenge to figure out which would be most effective! Making the wrong choice could be disastrous, but Ursula shared Traveller's many talents, one being an astute ability to read emotions.

Squaring her shoulders, she said softly, "Susan, we have much to discuss!"

"Excuse me! There's no 'we' in this discussion because you're going to do all the talking!" Susan retorted with barely disguised anger. "If you know where Whitney is, spill it!"

The desperation in the poor woman's voice guided Ursula's next move. "Let's sit down," she said gently, grasping Susan's elbow and guiding her toward the trunk of a fallen tree lying on the ground.

"I don't need to sit to have this discussion!" Susan yelled, yanking her arm away.

Padding quietly to Whitney's mother, Ellie rubbed against her legs trying to help but couldn't manage to produce a purr of contentment. Susan stooped over and scooped their rescue cat into her arms. "Where have you been, Ms. Ellie? Have you seen Whitney? Can you tell me anything?" she cried, rubbing her face against Ellie's silky fur. "I think I'm losing my mind!" she sobbed. Hurriedly putting the cat down, she collapsed to the ground.

Dropping down beside Susan, Ursula pulled Whitney's mother in close, and rocked her back and forth as she cried. "I feel so lost, and I don't know what to do next!" Finally, Susan sat up and wiped her tear-stained face with the back of her hand. Blinking back the threat of more tears, she looked up at their concerned faces and pleaded softly, "Can you help me find my daughter?"

The longer she waited, the further away Whitney felt, and Susan needed answers! "Last night, in the middle of the night, my daughter called out to me in a dream! She sounded so lost and frightened. I searched the entire house for her."

On hearing this, the wizards and Ursula raised their eyebrows at each other but remained silent and just listened. Randolph was particularly intrigued that Susan had heard Whitney's voice and wondered if he might somehow use the girl's mother to help him reach her daughter. "They're so close, it makes perfect sense!" he mused, daring to hope Susan might be another valuable liaison.

"I looked everywhere! When I didn't find Whitney, I immediately called 911. Officer O'Neil came over right away, and searched the house and beach, but he didn't find her either. So, if any of you know anything about Whitney's disappearance, you need to tell me NOW!" she said, her anger rising again. "And if I'm not satisfied by your answers, I intend to call Officer O'Neil again to report she is still missing!"

As soon as Whitney's mother finished, they all started talking at once. Randolph finally commanded everyone's attention when he jumped up and grabbed Susan's hands and helped her to her feet. The others remained silent as their earth wizard guided Whitney's mother to the white pine tree. When Ursula and Mergan nodded for him to continue, he focused his attention on Susan.

Standing close to where the portal had once been, Randolph explained almost everything. He told her about all the events from the moment he'd met Whitney and Edward on the beach and travelled with them to Yagdi, to the battle, to Whitney's capture and finally losing them in the portal. He didn't mention wizards, polar bears, dragons, or panthers, figuring it was best to leave those possibly overwhelming details for later. Even so, Susan was struggling to comprehend everything she was hearing.

Ursula wasn't surprised to see the poor woman's shock. However, she was impressed that Susan had been able to calm herself and listen carefully to Randolph's entire summary of the last few days on Yagdi without interrupting. "Susan, Yagdi time is different from what you know here on Earth," the elderly woman explained gently. "All of this happened while you slept last night!"

Susan hadn't thought of the timing, but it was starting to make sense! She felt terrible! She'd been with both Whitney and Edward last night but somehow her daughter had slipped away, and she hadn't even known! "I should've heard my daughter leave and stopped her!" she moaned. "What kind of mother am I?"

Seeing her despair, Randolph knelt in front of her, grasped her hands and calmly but firmly said, "Susan, look at me! You are a wonderful mother, and you must hear this. These words came out of your daughter's mouth a short time ago. Whitney said,

'Tell mom everything! We have a strong connection that might help!'"

As those words sank in, Susan's resolve returned. "She's absolutely right! We need to try again, now!"

"I thought you might say that! And that brings me to another exciting possibility," Randolph said, squeezing her hand supportively. "You intrigued me when you said Whitney reached you through dreams. That sounds much like my gift. I can actually enter people's dreams. Based on what you've described, I suspect you might have the same capability. I would like to try something to test that theory."

Turning to Mergan, he asked, "Are you willing to do this once again, my friend?"

Mergan jumped up and raced to the tree. Stretching his arms around the trunk, he yelled, "How's this for an answer?"

"Just as I'd expected!" Randolph said grinning. Putting his stone in one hand and skeleton key in the other, the earth wizard leaned into the tree, and stretched his arms around the trunk. Then he grabbed Mergan's hand and held the other out for Susan. She followed their lead and quickly found their hands. Clutching each of them tightly, she asked urgently, "Now what?"

"We're linked! Now it's time to find our young Whitney!" Randolph said confidently.

Concentrating on Susan and Whitney, the two wizards murmured the phrases they'd used earlier. Desperately hoping to hear her daughter's voice, Susan closed her eyes and soon learned the phrases well enough to join in. But Whitney didn't respond. She'd sounded so far away and sleepy earlier; Randolph was growing increasingly concerned.

Suddenly, Susan gasped, "Is that you, Whitney?"

He feared it was just a mother's wishful thinking, but Randolph continued whispering his magical words. Suddenly, he too heard Whitney's sweet voice. "Randolph? Is that you again?" she asked softly.

"Yes, yes, Whitney it's me again, and I can see you!" he said, easily entering her world this time. "But I have help now!" and motioned for Susan to say something.

She stared at Randolph, wondering what he meant by "seeing" her daughter, but did as he instructed. "Whitney? Honey, can you hear me?" she asked hesitantly.

"MOM! Is that really you?" Whitney sobbed.

"Oh Whitney, everything's going to be alright!" Susan said, trying her best to sound calm and soothing. But it was so hard! Her daughter was alone and lost and she couldn't go to her!

"Mom! I'm okay, but I don't know where I am, and I haven't found Edward yet! I'm so worried about him! Are Traveller, Mergan, Randolph, Aiden, and Ellie all with you?"

Looking questioningly at Ursula, Susan said, "I don't know who Traveller is, but Ursula's here and so are all the rest!"

"That's good, mom," Whitney mumbled, remembering all that had happened in such a short time. "Ursula can tell you who Traveller is! But for now, I'm glad you have each other!"

Swallowing the bile forming in her throat, Susan's voice cracked, but she cleared her throat and continued. "We have each other, but you're all alone, and that's unacceptable to me! Trust me, we will find you, Whitney! In the meantime, we must stay in touch because I will literally go crazy if I don't hear your voice as often as possible. I'd feel better if you and Edward were together. I'm worried about him too! And I'll be seeing his grandparents later this morning. I'd love to at least be able to tell them Edward's with you!"

"You and me both, mom!" Whitney agreed. "And by the way, tell Aiden and Ellie to show their true colors immediately...no more secrets!"

Completely mystified, Susan looked over at their dog and cat, and wondered who her daughter could possibly be talking about. It sure seemed like they'd heard Whitney's message because they put their heads down and wouldn't look at her, almost like they felt terribly guilty about something. But that was too ridiculous, and Susan quickly disregarded it.

Whitney's voice started fading again and they had a hard time understanding each other, so Randolph said gently, "Whitney, before we lose our connection, can you tell us how you feel? Is anything broken or bleeding?"

"No, nothing but a few scrapes and bruises, thank goodness! My head was sore from hitting the boulder, but it's getting better."

That concerned Susan even more. Knowing any damage to her head could be extremely serious she asked, "Whitney, did you go to sleep after hitting that rock?"

"Yeah, I couldn't fight it, mom!" Whitney admitted. "Even though Edward tried to break my fall, I still hit pretty hard! I don't know how long I was asleep. I was dreaming about you when I heard voices. I think that's what jolted me awake!"

Looking gratefully at the two men, Susan said out loud, "We have Randolph and Mergan to thank for that!"

"I know! Those wizards are amazing!" she said sleepily. "Sorry, I'm really tired again."

Even as she tried to process this talk of wizards, along with all that she had heard from Randolph, Susan's hopeless rage and restless energy were again reaching the boiling point. But she needed to maintain control for Whitney's sake, so she closed her eyes in a herculean effort to calm down. When she opened them, her clear blue eyes held nothing but concern.

Ursula had been watching Susan carefully and shook her head in wonder. How could Whitney's mother do that? Her heart had to be breaking, yet she was able to tamp down her own fears and focus on helping her daughter. Clearly Whitney's brave heart had come from her mother!

"Whitney, do you have any idea where you are? Can you tell us what you see?" Susan asked as calmly as she could manage.

"Randolph has been down here and can describe what he saw too, but I'm somewhere in the portal! It's dark and I can't see more than a few feet. But there's a green glow from somewhere down the tunnel that gives me a little bit of light. If I can find Edward, we can do some more scouting and hopefully discover more."

Susan looked questioningly at Randolph, but he seemed distant and unaware of her or Mergan. "Odd," she thought, but she heard her daughter's voice grow weaker, and was desperate to keep their connection. "Whitney, let's sing our favorite breakfast song together!" and began singing. "Our house is a very, very, very fine house..." but stopped when her daughter didn't join in. "Whitney, are you still with us?"

"Whitney, answer your mother!" Randolph said, trying to maintain that commanding voice that had worked previously. But she didn't reply.

Randolph and Mergan dropped their arms and moved away as Ursula walked quietly to Whitney's mother. She leaned in so they were eye-to-eye, and said softly, "Susan, you are an unbelievable mother! I can see where Whitney got her bravery and determination. However, as you can well imagine, we have much to discuss! May I suggest we walk back to your house for some breakfast? I promise we'll come back soon!"

Feeling lost and so helpless, Susan slumped against the tree wearily and felt the rough bark scrape the skin on her back as she fell to the ground. "I can't leave her!" she cried, throwing her arms around the tree. Looking up through her tears, she found Randolph. "Did you somehow just see my daughter?"

Kneeling next to her, he answered, "I did, Susan. As I said, my gifts allow me to enter the world of others, and while I don't yet understand how or why, it seems you might be able to do the same, with a little coaching. In the meantime, we have good news to celebrate. You and I can hear Whitney, and we will become a lifeline between your daughter and her worried friends here on Earth." When her eyes teared up, he added, "Even if you can't see her until she returns, your voice alone has provided your daughter with much needed strength and hope, Susan."

Squatting down next to them, Ursula said softly, "I can only imagine how frustrated and frightened you must be feeling right now, Susan," and gently pulled her away from the tree. With Randolph's help, they lifted Susan until she was standing up.

Moving between Randolph and Susan, the elderly woman winked at the others waiting impatiently for news. "We have some amazing abilities among us, and I'm quite certain Randolph, and quite possibly Susan, will be able to speak with Whitney from any location. Whether they need to be touching to do so is yet to be determined. Mergan may be the missing link, but we'll experiment when we get to Susan and Whitney's house."

Guiding Susan away from the tree and off the peninsula, she continued in a soothing voice, "We must leave Ellie's Point, at least for the time being, so we can test my theory properly. I'd like to try various locations in and around your home, maybe places Whitney likes to spend time? Your home would be much more convenient."

Their house was in view when Susan stopped and turned hopeful eyes on Ursula. "I still don't understand what's going on, but I know several comfortable places we can gather. Whitney and I have spent countless hours in front of the fireplace, reading, talking, and puzzling. The deck is another favorite as well as the kitchen!" she said with a sad smile.

"I know the spot by the fireplace," Ursula murmured to herself, remembering the stormy evening she'd spent with Whitney and her mom. She'd sipped cocoa by the fire and pretended to be someone she wasn't! But she just grinned encouragingly at Susan and announced, "That would be a great place to start!"

Chapter Eleven

PERILOUS PASSAGE

ince they'd fallen through the portal, Whitney had slept more than she'd been awake. She was glad to be awake now and felt much more alert, but she was so lonely! "Where are you, Edward?" the frightened teenager muttered as she crawled on her hands and knees, scouring all the places illuminated by the strange green glow.

Her dark prison was cold and damp, and Whitney couldn't stop shivering. But at least she was doing something! Although moving around made her feel a little warmer, there just wasn't enough light to do a thorough search. Sitting back on her heels, Whitney vented her frustration. "I fell asleep with my hand on Edward's arm, so why isn't he right here, close to where I fell asleep? What if he's hurt and wandering around?" she cried, feeling her heart race all over again. "What do I do now?" Whitney moaned, wrapping her arms around her legs. She felt so lonely and had to find her friend, but the semi-darkness and absolute silence surrounding her was terrifying.

Searching for any kind of comfort, she thought "Well, at least I was able to talk to mom!" But her mind felt so foggy she questioned her own memory. "Or was that just a dream?"

Suddenly hearing a noise, Whitney's eyes widened. "What was that?" she gasped. Staying perfectly still, she held her breath and listened intently. "There it is again! Something's out there!

Edward," she hissed. "Is that you?" Losing her sight in the absolute darkness had enhanced Whitney's other senses. Her hearing was phenomenal, and her extraordinary gift of sensing the presence of others was magnified. She let her mind reach toward the sound, beyond the area she could see, trying to find Edward in the inky darkness beyond.

"I'd sense my best friend if he was there. If it's not Edward, who's making that noise?" she wondered, nervously looking for a place to hide. But it was too dark, so she grabbed a handful of rocks and crouched down low. "Like these pebbles are going to stop whoever's out there!" she grumbled.

After waiting tensely for what seemed like an hour Whitney finally tried to stand up, but she had been crouching for so long, her legs had gone numb, and she almost fell over. Shaking her legs out, and feeling the irritating tingles as blood returned, Whitney heard another sound and stopped to listen. Sure enough, it was the same sound she'd heard before, only a little louder this time, like feet shuffling on gravel.

It was coming right at her! Dropping to her knees once again, Whitney frantically grabbed two more handfuls of stones and held her breath as she waited. With nowhere to hide, and out of both patience and options, Whitney jumped up and screamed, "Don't come any closer!" Feeling ridiculously unprepared she drew her hand back to throw the small pebbles at her enemy.

"Whitney!" Edward yelled, running out of the darkness and into the dim green light. "You look scared half to death. I'm so sorry I was gone when you woke up!"

"Edward!" Whitney shrieked, dropping her pebbles and racing to her friend. In her eagerness she almost knocked them both to the ground! "You don't know how glad I am to see you! Where have you been? I thought I'd sense it was you, even in the dark, but I didn't! I woke up with a raging headache and couldn't remember anything for a while. Then I started seeing images and hearing a voice that brought everything back and..." noticing how tired his eyes looked, she stopped and stepped away. "I'm doing it again, aren't I?"

"Yep!" Edward said with a hint of a grin on his otherwise grim face. "Even in nowhere land, you sure do talk a lot, don't you, Whit?"

"Well, where were you?" she demanded again. "That was pretty rude, and I was so frightened for you!"

"I'm really sorry, Whit. When I came to, you were sound asleep, so I went on a little scouting mission." He noticed the gleam of hope in her eyes and quickly continued, "I didn't discover anything earth shattering. Here's the bad news. What we can see right here is as good as it gets. We landed on a boulder that lies on a path through a tunnel. There are green lights off in the distance that appear to be our only source of light."

"You're forgiven! I'm just glad you're here! And I might have an excellent piece of news! But what I'm about to tell you may have just been a dream, or me going crazy with worry. But if it's true, it was darn good, so here goes!"

She told Edward how she'd connected first with Randolph and then her mom. "Our Dream Jumper even found me. He could see me, but I couldn't see him! He said something about his 'spirit' being down here, but not his physical body. Strange, huh? Anyway, he told me everyone made it out of the portal just fine. If it wasn't all a dream, we need to find a way to reconnect, because they're worried about you, and we need to make sure someone tells your grandparents!"

"There you go, thinking about everyone else first! I love that about you, Whit! Anyway, that's incredible news and I hope it happened for real!" Feeling vastly more hopeful than he had minutes before, Edward grinned down at his friend and grabbed her hands. "We already knew Randolph was full of surprises! Your mom too? That's amazing! Let's just hope we can reconnect!"

Sobering quickly, he asked, "Speaking of connecting, have you tried using the little dragon Aiden and his parents gave us?"

"No! In all the excitement, I forgot about it!" she said with a frown, wondering what else she was forgetting. Dropping his hand, she dug in her pocket and sighed with relief. "Thank goodness, I still have it!" she said, pulling out her small trinket.

"I should've told you right away! Don't bother, Whit! I already tried...no go! They don't seem to have power down here, so we can't use them to contact our dragons," he groaned. "That would've been too easy! Looks like it's up to us, so we have to discover more of our hidden powers ASAP!"

"Exactly what I've been thinking!" she agreed. "We're on our own now and have to get ourselves out of this mess! I still have Mergan's gift," she added, looking down at her wizard staff. "It's gotta help, but only if I can learn how to tap into its powers better than I have."

"True! We have a lot to do. But we're together again." With a sly grin, he said, "I missed you too, Whit," coaxing her to sit down next to him. "And thanks for the apology. I'm glad you realize how important I am to you!"

"You heard everything I said?" Whitney asked, feeling her face heat up. "You really had me worried, Edward! I could tell you were breathing, but you never opened your eyes or said anything!"

"That's weird!" he admitted slowly. "I clearly remember every word you said! But you mentioned waking up with a headache. Is it still there and can you remember things, like that awful ride through the vortex?"

"I'm okay," she replied, "but it's all coming back way too slowly. I do remember that crazy ride, all too well! It happened so fast! I must have hit one of those huge boulders on the walls of the tunnel on the way down!" She winced when she touched the large goose egg on the back of her head.

Instantly concerned, Edward reached up and found the bump.

"Ouch! That can't feel good!" he said softly. "I tried to move us away from those nasty looking rocks, but it looks like I wasn't entirely successful."

"You got the brunt of our impact with that last huge boulder because you tried to shield me with your body! So, a better question is, how are you?" she asked, scrutinizing her friend carefully.

"I'm okay too. I reacted the same way I do when I crash my bike. As soon as we hit the boulder, I grabbed onto you and rolled us. We hit hard and flipped over a few times before we finally stopped. I don't remember much after that," he admitted. "Looks like it worked because we both survived. But that crazy ride reminded me of the virtual trip we took on Yagdi! My stomach didn't like it then and liked it even less this time!" he said, grabbing his stomach for effect.

"I know! Way worse than the butterflies in my stomach when I'm riding through the portal." Suddenly feeling deflated, Whitney held up her wizard staff, and pointed down the passage. "For lack of a better idea, how about we walk toward that light."

As they walked, a troubling thought came to Whitney. "Edward, a while before you finally came back to me, I heard some strange noises. Could that have been you?" Her friend frowned and looked confused, so she knew it hadn't been him, and that realization was frightening.

"Before you showed up, I heard the same sounds you made, like someone's feet shuffling on gravel. Only you didn't show up that time. No one did!"

Edward frowned with worry. "I don't like the sound of that! It definitely wasn't me. On top of that, I've been up and down this tunnel, and never saw anyone or anything else! But look," he said, trying to ease her fears. "We're together now, and we have each other's backs! We're a formidable team, don't you think?"

"You're right and I completely agree," Whitney admitted. "Maybe I just *needed* to hear footsteps earlier, hoping it was you."

Grabbing his hand, she said, "I so desperately wanted you to come back to me, Edward!"

Edward stopped and pulled her around to face him. "I won't leave you again, not down here, Whit!"

"I guess I just needed to hear you say that!" Whitney sighed gratefully. Then hissed, "Listen! Did you hear that?"

"Hear what?" Edward asked anxiously.

"I just heard something behind us. The same sound as before, like someone slipping on loose rock!"

"Nope, I didn't hear anything, but that doesn't mean you didn't. Just in case, let's pick up the pace a little. Maybe we'll ditch whoever, or whatever's stalking us."

Tripping over rocks they couldn't see, Whitney turned when she heard another yelp of pain, the latest of many from Edward. "That green light must be powerful to have reached us from so far away. We've been walking forever, and this feels like the hundredth time I've stubbed a toe!" he shouted in disgust.

"It must be magical!" Whitney reasoned. "The light I mean," she clarified, waiting for her friend to catch up. "Stop!" she said, grabbing Edward's arm. "There it is again!"

"This time I hear it! It sounds like water!" he said, walking faster. "I sure hope we can drink it because that's something I've been worried about!" he admitted.

The sound became deafening as they approached a bend in the tunnel. They didn't know what awaited them around the corner, so they held hands tightly as they cautiously inched forward.

Rounding the bend, Whitney and Edward skidded to a stop and stood there, gaping in astonishment. A magnificent waterfall towered above them, sending a kaleidoscope of colors cascading over the rocks, and into a shimmering pool. Dumbfounded by the beauty, Whitney stared in awe and whispered, "I think we just found the source of our light, and it's unbelievable! Those colors remind me of Yagdi's two stars and their magical sunsets. Was that just yesterday?"

Cringing when her whisper echoed through the cavern, she said quietly, "That was way too loud, especially since we don't know who or what might be watching!" Sinking to her knees, Whitney lifted her face toward the cooling mist. "That feels so good!" she sighed, and reached out her hand, inviting Edward to join her.

They sat there a long time, letting the refreshing mist hit their warm, grimy faces. "I know this is going to sound crazy. But I feel better just sitting close to this water, like it's connecting me to Lake Superior!" Turning toward Edward she leaned in, whispering "How can we be this close to so much noise and still hear something as quiet as a whisper?"

"In a strange way, everything you just said kind of makes sense," Edward said. "At one of our training sessions, Mergan shared something I'll never forget. He said natural elements, like this water, react differently to magic. They have a strong force of their own that most spells can't touch, and that power can be used in many ways, and for many different reasons. Maybe it's trying to soothe you, Whit!"

"Wow!" Whitney said. "That's amazing and worth remembering! If what Mergan said is true, we should try to figure out how to use that to our advantage." Shaking her head, she added, "Mergan's full of wisdom, isn't he? Trouble is, he knows it!"

"He sure does, and he never lets anyone forget it either!" Edward agreed, chuckling softly.

"Who would've thought we'd find something so incredible in this—what did you call it—Nowhere Land?" Whitney said, gently shoving Edward with her shoulder.

Chapter Twelve

AN OASIS

"There's a flat boulder over there," Edward said, pointing to a spot on the edge of the pool. "Let's sit on it for a while. My feet could use a soak!"

Whitney couldn't wait to touch the water! Yanking their shoes off, they put their feet in the water and were surprised when it started to bubble up through their toes and around their legs. Reaching into his pocket, Edward pulled out one of five precious granola bars and broke it in half. "You must be starving! I sure am!" he said, handing Whitney her half.

They ate quietly, but the food was gone far too quickly. Licking her fingers, Whitney said, "Now this is what I call 'bonus time!' Who would've thought we'd be enjoying a soak in a beautiful glowing pool next to an amazing waterfall in this 'Nowhere Land?'" she asked, leaning back on her hands.

"Earth to Whitney," Edward said softly, concerned when her expression suddenly turned dark and pensive.

Shaken from her troubled thoughts, Whitney turned to him and said, "Sorry about that! I was just wondering why us? I'm pretty sure we didn't arrive here by accident. So, what do you think will happen next?"

"I've been thinking the same thing. Your guess is as good as mine!" he answered grimly. "I wish we had a crystal ball so we could see what's coming. But I'm not sure we could do anything about it even if we knew. I get the feeling someone, or something else is pulling all the strings." Nervously dragging his hands through his hair, he added, "I just hope whoever or whatever they are, they're friends!"

"Friends don't pull you away from those you love!" Whitney shouted angrily, then looked at him apologetically. "I'm sorry, Edward. I shouldn't scream at you, but I can't vent my frustration on the true culprit!"

"You're right, and I get why you're frustrated. I am too! But even good friends can behave strangely when they're desperate or frightened."

Whitney smiled at her friend with renewed appreciation. "How do you even think that way? You can always look at a situation from so many different perspectives. I've been so fixated on us, terrified we'll never make it out of here!"

As she watched the tiny drops of water tumble over rocks and disappear under the surface, Whitney pulled her legs out of the water, and curled them underneath. "Maybe someone is trying to keep us out of trouble, or maybe what happened was just some crazy accident!"

Tearing his eyes away from the pool to look at his friend, he said quietly, "Look, I know this whole side trip is unexpected. It feels like we've been hijacked, and yea, that's scary! Let's just try to keep an open mind but stay vigilant." Then he grinned and said, "How's that for a plan?"

"Perfect!" Whitney murmured, rolling her eyes. Staring into the water sullenly, she began to feel guilty. Her dark mood had to be affecting Edward, and that wasn't fair!

"I'm sorry, Biker Boy!" she apologized, turning to face him. "I guess everything that's happened to us this summer is finally catching up to me. I'm devastated that we didn't make it home to mom and I feel helpless to do anything about it."

"Believe me, I get it, Whit! We've been through a lot, but I think it'll make us stronger," Edward said hopefully.

"Thanks! I know you get me, and that means a lot! If all of this makes us stronger, I guess that's something," Whitney admitted, following his gaze back to the pond. Its shimmering colors were mesmerizing, and soon their jumpy nerves disappeared.

Whitney's terrified gasp shattered the peace and quiet. Whipping his head around, Edward was shocked to see his friend's face contorted in anguish. He grabbed her arm and tried to turn her to face him, but she stubbornly refused to budge and wouldn't take her eyes off the pool.

Whitney looked like she'd seen a ghost! Edward watched his friend turn disturbingly pale and pant frantically. "Tell me what's going on, Whit!"

Wriggling out of his grasp, she jumped up, but continued staring into the water. He watched her hands clench nervously, and her arms stiffen as she stared at something under the surface that he couldn't see. Suddenly, she dropped down and covered her face with her hands and started crying.

"Please tell me what just happened. I can't help you if I don't know what's wrong. Don't lose it now, whatever you do! I need you too much!" he pleaded, pulling her gently toward him.

Wiping her eyes with a shirt sleeve, she turned to her worried friend. "You need me, huh? I like hearing that! But right now, I don't think you need me nearly as much as I need you! I'm so sorry! I know it seems like I'm saying that a lot lately, but I really can't explain what just happened!"

Edward watched Whitney carefully as she turned to gaze out over the pool again. He was relieved to see her shoulders relax and her breathing slow down; in some strange way it almost seemed like she was drawing strength just from being near this pool. He waited for her to say something, but after several minutes of silence he grew impatient and was ready to demand answers.

Finally, she sighed and looked at him, saying, "You won't believe what I'm about to tell you because I find it hard to believe myself."

Her voice quivered just a little and Edward saw tears glisten in her eyes, but he stayed quiet.

"I saw a reflection of someone's face in the water," she whispered. "For thirteen years, I've looked at my mom's photos of dad, and that face looked like my father!" Seeing Edward's look of confused concern, she buried her face in her hands, and cried out with frustration, "I know! Crazy, huh? My mind knows it can't be, but my heart saw my dad!"

Whitney's sadness was killing him, so he grabbed her hands, saying "Whit, look at me! Like you just said, we've been through a lot in a short period of time! You're exhausted and scared. Maybe your eyes are playing tricks on you. I wouldn't be surprised if you feel like you need him more now than you ever have before and wish he was here with you."

"What you say makes perfect sense," Whitney admitted quietly, turning back to the calming waters. "So why do I keep thinking it really was my dad?"

• • •

"Because I imagine that's who you just saw, Whitney."

"Who's there?" she gasped, jumping up and whirling around to confront the intruder.

By the time Edward leaped up and reached for her, Whitney was already running toward the rock wall behind them.

"There's someone standing right there," she yelled, pointing to the wall. Turning back, she stomped her foot angrily, and screamed, "I don't know who or what you are, but you can't be my father. Stop playing this cruel game. It isn't funny at all!"

"What happened? Whitney's acting crazy!" Edward thought. He raced up to her, grabbed his friend's shoulders and spun her around yelling, "Whitney, look at me! Tell me what you think you see!"

"THINK I see, Edward?" Whitney shot back. "I'll tell you what I THINK I see...I THINK I see my father!"

Dropping his arms, Edward stared at Whitney in complete shock, not sure how to respond.

"Yeah, you heard me right!" she continued, irritation oozing out of every word. "At least, I see something that's working hard to look like my father," she said angrily, pointing toward the wall.

"Whit, I don't see anything but a rock wall," Edward said cautiously, trying not to upset his friend any more than she already was.

"You really don't see anything standing against that rock wall over there?" she asked, suddenly realizing what he was saying, and mystified by his response.

"No, Whit. I don't," he answered honestly.

"He can't see me because I don't want him to," the stranger said petulantly, raising his hand in the air to spin a feather between his fingers.

Whitney watched the stranger warily, wondering if that feather was some kind of weapon. "Edward, I wish you could see all of this!" she cried then gasped as a chilling child-like voice interrupted her.

"I have the power to go places without being seen, at least most of the time, and with the proper motivation, I can even become the person you'd most like to see, and apparently that's your father, Whitney." Grinning proudly, the strange creature bowed low, and swept his arm out to the side dramatically.

"You don't know anything about my dad!" Whitney shouted angrily, taking several steps toward him.

"That's very true, but I'm happy my little impromptu show turned out as I intended, because that's not always the case. I'm working on that! My skills are unpredictable, so who knows what will happen next? You and Edward are here alone, all because I made a BIG mistake! But now the three of us can have some fun!" he sang and began to dance.

"How dare he pretend to be my father!" she thought. More angry than afraid, and tired of his shenanigans, Whitney put her hands on her hips and glared at her tormentor. "Fun? You call this fun? Are you kidding me? We're in this mess because of you!"

"Sadly, yes," he admitted, and stopped dancing. "Or rather, sort of. It was the wizard clan's scheme. They intended to capture your entire alliance, but I messed it up. I'm sorry you almost died!" he said, putting his head down in feigned shame. "I guess that part is my fault!"

"Wait! Did you just say Wizards? What wizards?" she asked nervously, suddenly feeling those familiar tingles on the back of her neck.

Crossing his fingers behind his back, he fed the girl part of the truth. "There's a wizard clan down here. They're all business, and not much fun, so I left. I'm happy to have found you! Will you be my friends? I don't have anywhere else to go but here!" he said sadly, wiping fake tears away. "Maybe we can help each other get out of here, that is, if you give me enough reason to do so! Edna was planning to capture your entire alliance so they couldn't interfere with her 'victorious return to Yagdi.' They may be looking for you as we speak!" he taunted.

Whitney gasped and stared at Edward. He frowned and raised his arms. "Now what, Whit?" he asked.

"Tell ya later!" she mouthed.

"From what I learned Edna's clan was banished over a hundred years ago. Talk about long-term planning!" he said with a frown.

"This joker's mood swings so wildly, I can't predict what he's going to do next, and I don't believe a word that comes out of his mouth!" Whitney muttered to Edward. She wasn't at all surprised when the silly imp turned on a dime and looked at her mischievously.

"Looks like you're trying to tell your friend what's going on, and I have to say, I don't think he's buying it," he said. "That's too bad for you. Maybe I'll show myself one day and we can talk 'til we're blue in the face. Anyway, I'm so happy not to be alone anymore! That's something, isn't it?" he added hopefully. "But I truly didn't mean for either of you to die!" he said, sad once again.

"But we almost did, didn't we?" she chastised him, suddenly feeling like his mother.

"Stuff happens. Nothing we can do about that now, is there?" he pointed out gleefully, then started dancing again.

"Hold on!" Whitney shouted, wanting more information. "Be serious for one second and explain what you meant by this wizard clan. They're somewhere down here? And they wanted to capture our alliance? And who is Edna?"

"Too many questions, little girl! Didn't your mother teach you manners? Maybe they'll be answered but, then again, maybe they won't!" he chirped happily. Then he grinned and began to twirl, faster and faster until he was just a blur.

Angry at his outrageous assumption her mother was anything less than perfect, Whitney stomped her foot and started to answer, but he interrupted.

"And your friend Mergan was the worst! Talk about a task master! We didn't see eye to eye either!" He finally stopped twirling to cross his arms and pout.

"Wait! You know Mergan? How?"

"I do indeed," he said, eyeing her wizard staff. "Did he by chance give that to you?"

Putting it behind her back, Whitney glanced at Edward and eased her way toward him. She didn't want to show it, but suddenly the intruder had gone from bizarre to frightening. She needed to distract him before he realized she was scared, so she answered using the same cryptic nonsense he seemed to enjoy. "That's for me to know and for you to probably never find out! But I might share more if you tell me how you know Mergan."

"Could be a fun swap of tales someday, we'll see!" he sneered with a huge grin, enjoying their bantering.

Snapping his fingers suddenly, he said, "I almost forgot something the two of you might find important! If you remain near the waterfall, you'll be protected until we meet again. How's that for a peace offering?"

Edward noticed Whitney's frown and saw the way she gripped her wizard staff tightly by her side, so he moved in protectively.

"I might indeed let your friend see me next time!" the intruder added mischievously. And with that he simply disappeared.

Exhausted by his frantic energy and confused and frightened by the strange creature's cryptic messages, Whitney turned wide eyes on Edward just as her legs gave way.

"Whit, what's going on?" he gasped, reaching out to grab his friend before she fell to the floor. Her face was so pale, and she looked so frightened, but he didn't know how to help because he still had no idea what she'd just seen.

Finally able to speak, Whitney said, "Edward, I know you just heard a very strange, one-sided conversation, so let me fill you in on the rest. There's someone here with us! I'm not sure who or what it is, and I truly don't know if his intentions are good or bad, but he frightens me! He promised he'd be back and said he might allow you to see him next time! He talked about a wizard clan living here in the tunnels and how they tried to ambush our entire alliance because they're planning to invade Yagdi, and he warned me they may be looking for us."

"Wizard clan?" Edward said skeptically.

"Yes! He *said* he left them because, and I quote, 'they weren't very fun,' and claims he just happened to end up here. But it just seems too coincidental that we end up in the same cavern. And get this! He says he knows Mergan!"

"Whaaat? How?"

"He talked so fast and trying to get information from him was flat-out ridiculous. He claims he messed up this so-called wizard clan's plot to kidnap our alliance!" With a pained look, she added, "I honestly don't know what to believe."

"Whitney, help me sort this out," Edward mumbled, shaking his head. "Believing all of this takes a giant leap of trust, because I didn't see or hear anything. Do you understand what I'm saying?"

When she nodded, he continued cautiously, carefully considering his words. "If I don't believe you, that means I think you've lost it, and I don't want to go there!"

With a frustrated sigh, Edward looked down and considered his options. Finally, he raised his head and stared at her for so long Whitney began to squirm.

"Whit, I don't like the idea that some wizard clan, or even worse, some unknown creature brought us down here, but it sounds like you sort of get him! I trust *you* with my life, and you're pretty good at figuring people out, but you'll have to give me time to think about this. From what I heard you say while you were talking to this invisible creature, I don't see how we can trust him. Period, end of conversation. If he stays near the cavern, we'll have to figure this out together!"

Edward shook his head and sighed. "You've always been there for me, and I admire your courage, your strength and crazy sense of humor. Even more, I just can't believe you've lost it, so I won't. Whatever comes next, I'm with you!"

"Ditto to all of that!" she cried, jumping up to give him a huge bear hug. "We can do this!" she reassured him. Pushing her best friend out to arm's length, she continued, "But we must figure out how to partner up with someone very strange, who we know nothing about, but seems to be full of lies and tricks! We'll have each other's back if things get crazy."

"Always!" he responded with a grin, pulling her down to sit beside him.

"Ah!" Whitney sighed, letting her bare feet sink into the water. "This pool really feels magical!"

Chapter Thirteen

A NIGHT VISITOR

The strange creature didn't reappear, so Whitney relaxed and talked quietly with Edward until she nodded off and almost fell headfirst into the pool. "I think it's time to call it a day!" she murmured with a big yawn.

Using their backpacks as pillows, the teens curled up on the rock's smooth surface and were out immediately. Thanks to the soothing sound of the waterfall, they slept peacefully and uninterrupted for several hours.

Whitney woke suddenly. She yawned and stretched lazily, then gasped and bolted upright. "What if he's in here, hiding?" she muttered, peering nervously into all the dark corners and crevices. Her anxious gaze drifted over the surface of the pool, then toward the rock wall where he'd stood not hours before.

Satisfied nothing was lurking nearby, Whitney sighed with relief and looked over at Edward. He was still sound asleep, but he'd shoved his backpack aside and his head was now resting on a small rock. He looked so uncomfortable! But she wisely decided to let her friend sleep in peace.

As she was plumping her backpack, getting ready to lay back down Whitney felt the familiar goosebumps and warning tingling on the back of her neck. Determined to find out if something was out there, Whitney scooted on her stomach to the edge of the pool and cautiously peered over the edge. There was the intruder, staring up at her from under water! With a quick, mischievous wink, he disappeared.

Covering her mouth to stifle a scream, Whitney scrambled away, crawling backwards until she felt her backpack. Pulling it in front of her like a shield, the teen kept her eyes glued on the water as she crossed her legs and waited for him to return.

"I wish my stones still worked! They'd warn me if that character was skulking around!" Whitney muttered, clutching her staff close. "We can't use our tools, and our abilities seem to be blocked, but I'm keeping all of them close, including my wizard staff. Edward and I are good trouble-shooters. We'll find a way! At least my internal warning system worked!" she sighed, grateful for that small favor. Wondering why the strange elf-like creature had triggered it, she drifted off to sleep.

• • •

The next thing Whitney knew, someone was rudely shaking her out of a deep sleep. "Just a few more minutes, mom," she groaned and rolled over.

"I'm not your mom, and we don't have a few more minutes!" Edward growled. "Wake up, sleeping beauty!"

With an irritated groan, Whitney rolled onto her back and screamed! Edward and the creature were standing over her with very different expressions. While her friend frowned in irritation, the unwelcome intruder's rather wide face was smiling pleasantly.

"What's going on?" she yelled, jumping up.

"It's all good, Whit. Calm down!" Edward said softly. Pointing his thumb toward the figure standing next to him, he continued, "I woke up and found this guy sitting next to you. Patrick says he doesn't have all day and you need to wakey wakey so we can have a serious conversation!"

"Not so sure about that serious part," she said skeptically. "But you can actually see him now?"

"Yes, I decided to honor Edward with my presence," Patrick quipped.

Rubbing the sleep from her eyes, she looked curiously at their short, rather disheveled new acquaintance and asked, "So your name's Patrick, huh?"

With a big grin, he clapped his hands together excitedly and announced, "My friends call me Pat, and I consider you friends."

"How can you say that?" Whitney demanded. "I don't know you, or your intentions well enough to call you a friend."

"I get that a lot!" he said with a frown. "My behavior confuses everyone, but I can't seem to help myself. I'm a spontaneous kind of guy. I can't control much of anything, but sometimes things work out beautifully!"

"Now that sounds like the truth," Whitney said. Then she looked at Edward and asked, "What do you think? You're much better at judging people than I am."

"The truth? Right at this moment, I think he's telling the truth," Edward answered, staring at Patrick long enough to make the strange little man squirm and avert his eyes. "But don't underestimate us Patrick, er, Pat, if that's your real name. I can usually tell when someone is lying. And Whit's no pushover either! Neither of us tolerate liars. And no more sneaking around or disappearing on us!"

"Will you kick me out like the wizard clan and Mergan did?" he asked pitifully.

Noticing the discrepancy immediately, Whitney asked, "I thought you said you left them, Patrick."

"Well, there are two sides to every story," he said cautiously. "But I don't feel like answering questions right now."

"I want to hear more about Mergan, but more importantly, we need to get home. Whitney says you might help us do that, Pat?"

Edward was still skeptical but given their plight he didn't want to alienate a possible ally.

"Depends on where home is," Patrick answered, sounding somewhat sincere.

Whitney was feeling less patient and growing tired of Patrick's games. "We were in the portal heading to Earth from Yagdi when it broke! Got anything more to say about that?"

"I guess you could say you're here because of me. But I already told you, I didn't mean to do it, and I certainly didn't intend to break the portal! It was the wizard clan who wanted to capture all of you! Now, I'm the bad guy, and we better stay clear of them!" With a grimace, he admitted, "That was the latest in a lifetime of mess-ups!"

Whitney watched Patrick's embarrassment turn mischievous, like something flipped inside his brain. "So, you want to get back home, eh? Hmmm, let's see now. Just how badly do you want to return to Earth, and what do I get for helping you?" he asked with a devilish grin.

"Uh-oh," Whitney said looking at Edward. "I think we've lost 'honest Pat.'"

"Yeah, and I don't think we'll get anymore straight answers. I don't trust him!" Edward growled, turning back to Patrick with a frown. "Tell us how and why you want to help us."

"Maybe, if you're nice to me!" Patrick pouted. "Be careful not to demand too much from me without giving something back," he warned, eyeing Whitney's staff with great interest. Then, with a dizzying twirl, he disappeared once again.

Whitney gasped and took a step back. "That was just wrong!" she huffed. "I wish there was some way to keep him from doing that disappearing thing anytime he wants!"

"There's a lot I'd like to change about that nut case!" Edward agreed. "But if he can get us out of here, that might be reason enough to play along. 'Keep your friends close and your enemies closer,' and all that! But it's risky. I'm pretty sure he'll be back, so we need to keep our eyes open. That tricky guy could cause real serious problems for us."

They sat in silence for a while, pondering all they had heard from Patrick and wondering what might happen next. Finally, Edward spoke up.

"Unfortunately, we can't run away from him, so maybe scheming with him is our best bet! But right now, I'm thirsty and starving, so let's get some water and share a couple bites of a granola bar. We should look for something to eat. Patrick has to eat too, so maybe he can help us find something. I'm not holding out much hope, but it's worth a try. We just have four granola bars left!"

Filling her water bottle, Whitney asked, "Do you think we'll really be safe here, or is that just Patrick playing with us?"

"Who knows?" Edward sighed, shrugging his shoulders. "There's a lot we need to learn, and fast! Is there really a wizard clan down here, and did they really intend to grab our alliance? If that's true, I just hope they don't know we're here, at least not until we find out more! Unfortunately, that brings up another problem! I'm not convinced Patrick won't spill the beans for some sort of reward!"

"You're right! Patrick could easily be a spy. I think he'll do whatever benefits himself the most. That means, we need to convince him we have more to offer than anyone else! I hope Randolph reaches out to us soon! And since Patrick's mentioned Mergan, more than once, we should ask our wizard friend if he knows our visitor. He might be able to answer a lot of our questions!" Whitney said, screwing the lid back on then tossing the bottle into her backpack. "Maybe Traveller's right, and all things happen for a reason. If that's true, I can't wait to discover why we were kidnapped, and why Patrick's hanging around us!"

"Agreed!" Edward said, tossing down more water then refilling his Yeti. Making sure the cap was tight, he threw it into his backpack and stood up.

"We're an amazing team! But now more than ever, we really need to uncover the powers that are still buried within us!" he said grimly and put his hand out toward Whitney.

"I hate this!" she cried, grabbing his hand and pulling herself up.

"What part?" Edward asked softly. "Falling into the tunnel and crashing into a boulder, or the bizarre creature we can't trust who seems to have adopted us?"

"I hate all of it!" she moaned. "I hate what this is doing to us. You, me, my mom, your family, and our entire alliance. We need to figure out how to get home. But I agree with you," she added, with a look of grim determination. "Our top priority must be expanding our powers, and we needed to do that like yesterday!"

Chapter Fourteen

JOINING FORCES

Anxious to connect with Whitney again, and hoping Ursula was right, Susan hurried to lead her group back to the house. They were getting close when they saw two figures walking along the beach. "That's rare to see someone on the beach this far from town so early in the morning," Susan muttered, squinting to get a better look.

"That looks like Edward's grandparents!" Ursula said, raising her eyebrows at Susan.

"Oh boy! I didn't expect them this early!" Susan answered. "Now what do we do?"

"May I suggest we start by trying to act normal?" Mergan said. "We all know each other, so no introductions should be needed. But we do need to come up with an explanation as to why we're strolling along the beach at six in the morning."

"That's easy!" Susan said. "I was so worried about Whitney I called Jerome and Cathy before dawn to see if she was with them. Just before we hung up, I told them I was headed out to Ellie's Point!" Their curious expressions begged for further explanation. So, she shrugged her shoulders and said, "They were going to look for the kids at their campsite, then come over for coffee so I wouldn't be alone."

As they drew closer Susan shook her head, and mumbled, "They're running toward us, and those two never run. We know they didn't find the kids, but they must have something important to tell me! How much should we tell them?" she asked hurriedly, while keeping her eyes on their quickly approaching friends.

"Good question, and something we should all agree to right now," Randolph said. "You know them best, Susan. What do you think?"

"We need to tell them, but given what I just went through, we must do so very carefully," Susan said slowly. "We can't keep them in the dark, especially since they're going to be worried about Edward!"

"Agreed!" Ursula said. "We'll take our cue from you, Susan. How's that?"

Susan nodded uncomfortably, just as Jerome and Cathy ran up.

They were breathing so hard neither of them could put together a complete sentence. But they managed to hug Susan before Jerome bent over to put his hands on his knees, and Cathy leaned onto his back.

"My, this is a surprise!" Cathy said, standing up and looking at everyone.

"How are you holding up, Susan? Any word from Whitney?" Jerome asked, taking Susan's hands in his.

"Yes and no," Susan answered, glancing toward Ursula. "We uncovered some new information, but it's all very complicated and I've been on my feet for hours. Can we discuss this sitting down?" she pleaded, squeezing Jerome's hand gratefully.

Cathy and Jerome eyed Susan with obvious curiosity, but Edward's grandmother just said, "You must be out of your mind with worry Susan! Of course! We should sit down! I'm just glad we have each other to lean on," and pulled her friend in for a hug, raising her eyebrows toward Jerome.

That was enough to bring Susan to tears again. "We'll be able to figure this out together, Susan." Cathy said softly, rocking her back and forth, much like Ursula had done earlier.

Wiping her face with the back of her hand, Susan tried to smile. The expression was so like young Whitney, Ursula had to look away before anyone saw her own tears.

Jerome shook hands with Mergan and Randolph while Cathy hugged Ursula. When Edward's grandma bent over to pet Aiden and Ellie, Ursula shook her head, warning them not to transform, at least not yet. "Why don't we do as Susan suggested and go up to the deck for some coffee? We can talk there."

Flapping its tiny wings excitedly, a small yellow bird waddled up to Susan and jumped up and down until she bent over and scooped her up. "Meet Looa, our little rescue bird. She was quite comforting when I was beside myself with worry. So much has happened, it's hard to believe that was just last night!" she added, shaking her head sadly.

"Nice to meet you, Looa. Thank you for being such a dear friend to Susan," Ursula said, reaching out to pet the small bird. "Everyone will soon discover our little secret," she thought as she climbed the long stairway to the deck perched high on a bluff overlooking Lake Superior.

When they were all settled, Cathy turned to Susan and filled her in on their trip to the campground. "There was no sign of the kids at the trailer, but we found tons of strange looking footprints all over the campground, especially around our campsite. And get this, the door to our camper was wide open! I went inside, expecting to see everything torn apart, and was surprised to find nothing out of order. But I made sure the door was good and tight, and locked it. Who knows what kind of strange critters could find that a perfect spot to hibernate!"

"You never know what you're going to find in the woods, do you! Can you describe the prints?" Ursula asked, stealing a glance at the two wizards.

"They were all the same size and looked human but way smaller," Jerome noted. "Those footprints had toes on 'em! That means they were running around barefoot. If you ask me, the whole thing seems pretty odd!"

"That is intriguing," Randolph said. "I can't imagine what that could be."

"If you wouldn't mind, I'd love to go out there with you later. I know a thing or two about animal prints. Maybe I can help solve your mystery," Mergan offered. "We can bring the canine and feline along to help us track the prints," he suggested, looking toward Aiden and Ellie who'd lifted their heads and looked at him expectantly.

"They act like they understand you!" Jerome laughed. "Anyway, you just say the word, Mergan!"

It was still early, but it looked like it was going to be a beautiful late-summer day. The temperature was climbing, and the deck was bathed in bright sunlight. "Clouds and rain would suit my mood better!" Susan thought as she and Cathy opened the large red umbrella.

Susan, Ursula, and Cathy sat at the table, with Looa settled comfortably in Susan's lap. As they talked quietly, Aiden and Ellie moved under the table, circled a few times then collapsed onto the deck and promptly fell asleep at their feet.

Clearing his throat, Jerome asked, "What can we do to help, Susan?"

"We were just talking about that," Susan answered, sneaking a quick glance at Ursula. When her friend nodded, she continued. "You both must be worried about Edward too."

"That's a nice opening to our much-needed discussion," Ursula said.

"Wait just a minute!" Cathy said, looking at her friend. "I know Susan's worried, and you've hinted there's more information coming, but we've chatted long enough. We must inform

Russell, Laura and Mallory that Edward is missing. They need to know what's going on. And it may even be time to call the police!" Cathy said, pulling out their cell phone.

"Let's finish our conversation before you do that," Ursula suggested quickly.

But Jerome frowned and stood up. "I think it's past time, Ursula. Make your call, Cathy," he said stubbornly.

"Trust me, there's a reason!" Ursula said in a deep, commanding voice. "Can you wait just a bit? I promise this won't take long."

Mystified, and a bit dazed, Jerome and Cathy looked at each other and shrugged their shoulders.

"I guess we can wait. But let's hurry!" Cathy said, putting her phone back in her pocket. "While we were out, we stopped at the bakery and picked up some fresh doughnuts. I'll bring them out," she said, grabbing her coffee cup and motioning for Susan to follow her into the house.

"Put your tongue away, Mergan! We're all hungry but drooling isn't allowed!" Ursula hissed, keeping her eyes on the two women walking into the house.

As soon as they were in the kitchen, Cathy whirled on Susan with a worried expression. "Something's going on here, and I need to know what that is, especially if it involves Edward! Now please explain to me why I shouldn't call his parents immediately!"

"It won't help!" Susan sobbed, dropping into a chair. "I want to tell you and Jerome everything, but I don't know where to begin!" and looked up just in time to see Jerome fly through the door with the rest on his heels.

"Begin at the beginning, Susan!" Jerome demanded. "If Edward's in trouble, you need to tell us everything you know, and right now!"

Susan could relate to their distress and pleaded to Ursula, "This is going to be difficult. Can you help me?"

"I'll do my best, Susan," Ursula agreed, looking first at Cathy then Jerome. They were decent people who cared deeply for Susan and Whitney. But they were afraid and lashing out at the wrong person. She wanted to ease those fears, but what they were about to hear would be difficult in so many ways.

"First of all, Susan is absolutely right. Calling Edward's parents, or the police for that matter, will not help us find your grandson or Whitney. We have much to share, but there is still a great deal yet to uncover. Shall I begin at the beginning?" she asked, sitting down next to Susan.

"That sounds like a plan!" Jerome said angrily. Looking at Susan, he added, "I can't believe you held out on us!"

"I didn't mean to!" Susan began but Ursula interrupted.

"May I suggest you both sit down so we can discuss this like civilized human beings? And let's keep our focus where it belongs. On the kids!"

"Jerome let's sit down," Cathy prompted her husband, eyeing her friend warily.

"This is an unbelievably difficult situation. Susan just discovered what happened to Whitney and Edward not two hours ago, and as you can tell, she's still adjusting. She is struggling with fear and anxiety over her daughter just as you are over your grandson. I fear you will need all the support you can get until we bring them home, so please don't blame her for any of this!"

"How dare you suggest what we should or shouldn't do!" Jerome bellowed, still refusing to sit down.

"We're not the bad guys here!" Mergan started, but Ursula grabbed his arm saying, "I can see how concerned you are, and you have every right to be. We can't pretend to feel the depth of emotion you both and Susan must be struggling with. However, I can assure you, we all care deeply for both of your children. Now, Jerome, if you'll please join us at the table, I'd like to begin at the beginning," Ursula suggested in the deep resonating tone most found impossible to refuse.

Jerome frowned and started to say something but decided against it and sat down next to his wife.

Just as Randolph had done so well with Susan, Ursula explained everything. She told Cathy and Jerome that she and Mergan, along with Ellie and Aiden, were from Yagdi, and that the portal between their worlds lay hidden in the ancient Michigan pine tree at the end of the peninsula. She explained how Whitney and Edward were chosen ones with extremely unique talents, and even shared how Susan's husband Stan had those same skills.

Ursula admitted she'd fixed the mountain bike competition so Edward would be close to Whitney, knowing they could help each other sort through all the sudden changes they would experience together. She described how the Yagdian alliance needed their talents to save their world from an evil enemy and detailed the kids' frantic departure in the middle of the night, and the events during the war itself. Looking apologetically at Edward's grandparents, she confessed the footprints near their trailer had actually been creatures sent by their enemies to capture the kids.

Ursula very carefully revealed the kids were now trapped in the portal, and this group of family and alliance members needed to help them get out and back home. Finally, she explained Randolph's unique dream jumper skills and how he was able to speak with Whitney and Edward, and helped Susan do the same.

Squeezing Susan's shoulder, Ursula got up from the table and filled a glass with water then took a long drink, trying to clear the uncomfortable bile filling her throat and chest. When she was done, she looked around the room. Jerome and Cathy looked shocked, but no one said a word for a very long time.

"You just heard this too?" Cathy finally asked, turning to Susan.

"I did, and I must admit it's a lot to take in! I'm still struggling to believe it myself," Susan admitted, gauging her friend's reaction.

"That's an understatement!" Cathy said in a shaky voice. Gripping her husband's hand, she looked warily at the people she thought had been her friends, but now felt like dangerous strangers.

"This is all too much!" Jerome interrupted, shoving his chair back. "How can we believe such nonsense?" Standing up, he pulled Cathy out of her chair. "We need to leave immediately and call 911!"

"There's no point!" Susan insisted softly, looking sympathetically at her two friends. "No one on Earth can find our kids. We must trust these people to help us because there's no other way!"

"That's impossible!" Cathy sobbed. "How can I trust these people when everyone sitting here suddenly terrifies me?"

Unable to contain himself any longer, Jerome whirled around to confront the entire group. "Why didn't anyone tell us Edward was involved in all these strange activities with bizarre people?" Leaning threateningly toward Ursula he growled, "You brought our grandson halfway around the world, and we had no idea! What are we supposed to tell his parents? We were responsible for their son!"

Without waiting for an answer, Jerome threw up his hands and walked angrily to the door. Yanking it open, he stormed out, letting the heavy door slam behind him. Cathy got up quickly and followed him onto the deck.

Hearing their voices go quiet, Susan looked nervously toward Ursula.

"They'll be back soon, dear. Let's just give them time. As you well know, they have a lot to process."

They did come back in. Jerome stood with his arms crossed, staring accusingly at everyone while Cathy sat down across from Susan. "You're a mom too. How do we get through this, Susan?" she cried, her voice quivering as she battled powerful emotions.

"I don't know!" Susan answered honestly. "Our kids are in

trouble, and we can't get to them!" Tamping down her own fears for the moment, Susan grabbed her friend's hands and whispered, "I need you and Jerome. Losing you as friends right now would be horrible, but you must do what works for you. If I had my wish, we'd be together as much as possible, for support if nothing else."

Cathy nodded. "I'm sorry, Susan. I know this isn't your fault. But I can't forgive the other adults in this room," she added angrily, looking at Ursula, then Mergan and Randolph. "I'd like to know what right you had to put our kids in danger!"

"You sound much like me two hours ago!" Susan admitted with a sad smile. Looking toward Ursula, she added, "She says there's more to Whitney and Edward than we ever imagined."

Squeezing Cathy's hand, she looked at Jerome and added, "Our kids followed their brave hearts, and I believe the three of us might have behaved similarly."

The room got deathly quiet as Cathy sat down next to Susan and wrapped her arms around her. Blinking tears away, she whispered softly, "I'm so sorry to hear about Stan. I knew he'd passed, but I can see it's just as fresh and devastating now as it must have been thirteen years ago, dear friend!"

Clinging to her like a lifeline, Susan cried, "We can do this together," over and over, trying hard to believe her own words.

Rubbing his whiskered face nervously as he watched his wife and Susan, Jerome ran a hand through his disheveled hair then turned to Ursula with eyes full of anguish. "To believe your story, and trust all of you is taking a mighty leap of faith! And how can we be expected to put on brave faces when we're broken inside?"

"Oh Jerome!" Cathy sobbed, rising to go to her husband. "We must follow Susan's lead and trust these people to help us bring our grandson and Whitney home. No one expects us to pretend we're not worried and afraid!" she said soothingly, laying her cheek against his soft cotton shirt.

Holding his wife close, Jerome looked at their concerned expressions and his face softened. "We'll work on trusting you to guide us to a successful reunion. Cathy and I want to help, but we don't know how! We want to understand, but that's going to be difficult."

"That is the crux of the matter, is it not?" Ursula said softly, standing up.

"You've just described what we're all struggling with so beautifully. May I suggest we start from there? We can share what we know, learn from each other, and develop a plan of action together."

"That sounds like a good beginning, doesn't it dear?" Cathy whispered, looking up at her husband.

"I can't promise to hold my anger or my tongue in check all the time because that's just not who I am!" Jerome declared. "But sharing what we know and developing a plan together sounds like something we can all live with!" He turned to Ursula, admitting "You seem to have remarkably good sense and I feel like you understand what we're going through. I'm glad you're here!"

Surprised at the unexpected compliment, and relieved Jerome had accepted her presence, even after all he'd heard, the Yagdian smiled and said, "I try. Sometimes I can help while other times I cannot. In all honesty, I can't promise miracles, and the road ahead will be bumpy. There will be plenty of obstacles and frustration. However, if we remember we're all united in helping the kids, and can look to each other for guidance and comfort, it might help soften the difficult moments!"

"You nailed it, Ursula! The tough part will be getting through those difficult moments without hurting each other in the process. I for one will keep that in mind moving forward," he promised with a rueful smile.

"That's all anyone can ask," Ursula agreed. Looking toward

Randolph and Mergan, then Ellie and Aiden, she added, "The five of us have some pretty remarkable powers of our own."

"You just admitted to having powers, and that jogs my memory," Susan said, looking curiously at Mergan and Randolph. "Whitney said three things that sounded kind of funny at the time. She called the two of you wizards." When they both coughed and averted their gaze, she raised her eyebrows, saying, "It looks like there are more revelations to come!"

"She also said you would explain Traveller to me, Ursula," to which the elderly woman simply nodded. That would have to suffice for now, but Susan wouldn't let it go much longer without explanation.

Finally, she looked down at Aiden and Ellie. "And, Whitney very clearly demanded that these two furry critters show their 'true colors.' At the time, I thought they acted as if they'd understood her. Does that make any sense? Does anyone have a clue what she meant by all these strange statements?"

Relieved that the mood in the room had turned from anger and sorrow to hope, Ursula nodded encouragingly. "Those are all very astute observations Susan, and I believe they'll all be answered in due time. However, let's first try to contact Whitney and Edward again." Linking arms with Cathy and Susan, the three strong women walked out of the kitchen and onto the deck together, and the rest followed close behind.

Chapter Fifteen

A BRIDGE BETWEEN WORLDS

"I hope this works as I suspect. What do you think, Earth Wizard?" Ursula asked, turning toward Randolph. "Should we try to reach our chosen ones from the comfort of Whitney's deck?"

Uncomfortable in the spotlight, Randolph squirmed in his seat, wondering how to answer that question.

Coming to his rescue, as she so often did, Ursula explained, "Randolph is a dream jumper and has amazing talents that allow him to do extraordinary things. We would be wise to let him guide us forward."

Still feeling confused and skeptical, Jerome and Cathy looked back and forth between Ursula and Randolph before Cathy finally asked, "What do you mean by dream jumper, and what remarkable abilities are you talking about?"

"I promise you will know everything in good time," Ursula said in a soothing voice that captured and held their gazes.

Susan saw the remarkable transformation in Edward's grandparents immediately. As Ursula's soothing voice droned on, they both visibly relaxed. She noticed their eyes stopped darting back and forth and their hands no longer shook. Although she understood the need to take things slowly, Susan didn't have Ursula's patience, not with her daughter's life threatened. "Randolph's abilities allowed us to speak with Whitney earlier today."

"Explain how you spoke with Whitney," Cathy said anxiously.

Trying to follow Ursula's lead, Susan took a deep breath and worked hard to remain calm while keeping a watchful eye on both grandparents.

"Randolph used a special stone and an old skeleton key. Then he, Mergan, and I wrapped our arms around that ancient Michigan White Pine tree at the end of the peninsula. You know which one I'm talking about, don't you? This will be almost impossible to believe," she warned, "but please try."

Thinking of her daughter lost and frightened threatened to undo her, but she bravely continued.

"These people knew our kids were lost somewhere in that portal, and Randolph figured out a way to enter it and speak with Whitney," Susan explained in a husky voice filled with grief.

Through her own shock, Cathy sensed Susan's extreme sadness and grabbed her hand and nodded. "Continue when you can, Susan," she encouraged softly.

Ursula noticed Susan relax a tiny bit and smiled gratefully at Cathy, acknowledging her kind gesture.

Taking a deep breath, Susan admitted, "I haven't learned everything yet either, but I know Randolph's abilities are the key to communicating with our kids, and that's the most important thing right now, wouldn't you agree?"

At a loss for words, Jerome and Cathy stared at everyone in disbelief. Ursula saw how Cathy's hands fluttered in her lap and little beads of sweat appeared on her forehead. She saw the poor woman's face become pasty white, while Jerome kept swallowing and reaching up to swat away something she couldn't see. Sensing it was time for another gentle intervention, she said softly, "Jerome and Cathy, can you look at me for a minute?" and waited until she had their full attention.

Mergan and Randolph knew what was coming next and leaned forward in their chairs, hoping their friend could help the distraught couple. Ursula, otherwise known as Traveller on Yagdi, was very powerful and capable of probing minds. Their friend could quite possibly remove the frightened grandparents' fears and encourage both to accept and even welcome the impossible.

"We are going to speak to the kids right now. We won't be able to see them, but Randolph will and can describe everything to us later. I don't know how it's possible, but Susan can speak with Whitney while connected with our dream jumper. I don't know if the rest of us will be able to hear them first-hand. We may have to rely on our liaisons for updates.

"You must remain calm and reassuring, for Susan's sake. I can tell how much you love your grandson, and Whitney too. We must reassure them everything will be okay," Ursula said very quietly. "That isn't a lie by any means, because I'm confident we'll find a way to bring them home."

Both grandparents were calming down as she talked, but Ursula still proceeded cautiously. "This was all very shocking to Susan too. But she kept her cool under very trying circumstances because Whitney and Edward needed to hear her voice. I know it's asking a lot of both of you, but Susan must be surrounded by strong and supportive friends. Can you try to do that, for Susan and the kids?"

Jerome and Cathy stared at Ursula for quite some time without saying a word. Turning to look at each other, they seemed to reach an agreement and nodded.

"Edward and Whitney can count on us, and we'll do anything and everything to help! So, don't worry about us any longer. Let's focus on the kids!" Jerome answered gruffly, trying to tamp down his fear for what the kids must be going through.

Witnessing the miraculous transformation, the two wizards looked at each other in amazement. "I taught her everything she knows!" Mergan said with a grin.

Randolph smiled good-naturedly, then frowned and turned to

Ursula. "This setting is very different, so I'll need a little guidance. We linked hands before, should we do that again?"

Looking at Susan, Ursula explained, "As I've said, your home is a special place for Whitney. Although untested, if my theory proves accurate, we should be able to connect with your daughter anywhere. However, I believe the closer we are to your house, and its special connection with Whitney, the more likely we are to succeed. We were successful at the portal, and I feel we will be here as well. How about we remain seated and attempt to do this without a physical connection? If it doesn't work, we'll make changes. How does that sound?"

"It all sounds reasonable. Let's try!" Susan answered, getting up to scoot Mergan over so she could sit between the two wizards. "I'd like for the three of us to connect, at least this first time here." Turning eager eyes on Randolph, she winked excitedly. "Dream Jumper, let's find our kids."

Cathy reached for her husband and looked from Susan to Mergan then nodded at Randolph. "Please find Edward for us. I need to call his family, and if I can tell them he is alive, it will give them much-needed hope."

"I'm not sure I'll even need these," Randolph admitted, pulling the stone and skeleton key out of his pocket.

"We had the stone between our hands last time," Susan remembered, her expression turning hopeful. "Maybe it'll bring us good luck again!" Nodding solemnly, Randolph placed the stone between their hands and held the skeleton key in the other.

He'd just begun his magical chant when Susan gasped and looked down. Following her gaze, Randolph noticed the stone was glowing brilliantly between their fingers. "Up to now, it's only done that in my hand, and not every time," he admitted. "It appears to be reacting to our connection, Susan."

Settling in once again, he started his chant, and Mergan and Susan joined in, then he heard Ursula's deep voice and smiled, thinking "This is a very strong group, and one I hope will draw the kids in."

Stealing a sideways glance at Edward's grandparents, Susan noticed they were both staring at Randolph hopefully, but his deep, authoritative voice lured her back to the task at hand.

"Whitney and Edward, this is Randolph. If you can hear my voice, please say something," he commanded, hoping the tone of his voice would capture their attention.

Cathy had been holding her breath in excited anticipation, but when nothing happened right away, she grew nervous. "Is this supposed to work every time?"

"We've only done this twice, and never from here. Therefore, may I suggest we stay patient for a little while longer," Ursula said softly. "How about we try it this way. Susan, you try calling the kids while Randolph, Mergan, and I continue chanting."

Nodding his agreement, Randolph resumed his sing-song chorus of nonsense words, and Susan said anxiously, "Whitney and Edward, are you there? Please answer me!" she cried, over and over. "We're all here at our home, Whitney. Edward, your grandparents are with us." Trying not to lose hope, she cried out in desperation, "Please say something!"

Susan began to cry softly when they didn't answer. Equally disappointed, Cathy looked at her friend sympathetically and squeezed her hand. Ursula stood up and was ready to suggest they try later when Susan suddenly gasped, "Wait! I hear something! Edward, is that you?"

"Grandma, grandpa?" he shouted.

"They can't hear you, Edward. Apparently, Randolph and I are the only ones who can." Nodding toward Cathy and Jerome, she added, "We promise to relay everything word-for-word!"

Edward's grandparents sat there, staring at Susan, shocked and bewildered. Putting his arm around Cathy, Jerome leaned toward Susan and said, "Can you tell him we're glad he's safe, and we will do whatever it takes to help him and Whitney?"

Susan quickly and accurately repeated his words to Edward. Suddenly realizing Randolph had been quiet, she looked over and gasped. His face had no expression; it was as if he was dreaming with his eyes open. Then she heard his voice, but it sounded as if he were right next to Edward.

"Susan, please explain to everyone that I'm right here looking at the kids. They're both alive and well and quite chipper. Edward, I must add it's wonderful to see you, and Whitney you look and sound much more energetic than just a short while ago!"

"I'm much better now that Edward's back!" Whitney admitted.

It was hard to speak with the kids while sharing everything with the group, but Susan was giving it everything she had. She wasn't the only one worried about the kids, and understood how frustrating this had to be, especially for Cathy and Jerome.

"Whitney, it's so good to hear your voice!" she said.

"You too, mom! Are you all okay?" Whitney asked.

"You and Edward are the ones lost somewhere and you're asking me how I am? How like you!" Susan cried but hurried to ease their concern. Nodding toward her friends, she said, "We're all fine, but crazy with worry about both of you! Whitney, you sound out of breath, like you've been running. Tell me the truth, you're both fine?"

"I was down by the pool getting water and ran up when I heard you," Whitney explained.

"Whitney, Randolph here again. I'm here in the cavern with you. I wish we could see each other, and that's something I'd like to work on. We'll have to see if your skills are developed enough to find a way to see me."

"None of our skills work down here," Whitney moaned. "The same goes for my staff, my stones and our tokens from the dragons. I got that familiar stranger-danger warning on the back of my neck, so I know that still works, but that's the only thing. We need to figure out why our other powers aren't working, so if any of you have any bright ideas, I'm all ears!"

"Hold it!" Susan cried, "What do you mean by your neck warning you? Does that mean there is danger nearby? Spill it, daughter of mine!"

That made Mergan sit up and take notice. "Randolph, will you please stop the chit-chat and listen! I must find out what danger triggered Whitney's warning and we need to be quick about it!" he demanded.

Picking up on his friend's urgency, Randolph asked, "Do you know what triggered your warning, Whitney?"

"We have a visitor that literally pops in and out when it suits his fancy. Honestly, he scares me a little, but Edward and I have each other, and that helps a lot! He calls himself Patrick and says he's a wizard. He might be harmless, but we don't trust him!"

"Harmless if you don't include the fact that we're in this mess because of this guy!" Edward interjected.

"Yeah, he's a trickster, and we never know what to expect!" Whitney agreed. "He claims he might be able to help us get home, but only if we can give him something in return!"

"He says there's a wizard clan down here in these caverns, and that he left them because they weren't fun," Edward chimed in. "In fact, he mentioned Mergan. He said Mergan kicked him out of the wizard academy years ago!"

"And get this!" Whitney added. "This joker says the wizard clan meant to kidnap our whole alliance, but he messed it up. That's why we ended up down here without the rest of you."

Randolph was extremely worried and hurriedly relayed what the kids had said.

"HOLD ON JUST ONE MINUTE!" Mergan shouted, shooting out of his seat to pace nervously, deep in thought.

"Oh no!" Susan exclaimed. "What's happening!"

"Mergan, sit down and calm yourself before you get every-one all riled up!" Ursula said firmly, watching everyone's surprise turn into concerned frowns.

"Sit down, woman? You want me to sit down when I've heard the worst news possible? I think not! Apparently, you don't remember the young, no-account wizard who turned me into an ugly troll!"

"Ah yes!" Ursula said with a frown. She remembered the little imp all too well and it worried her to think he'd found Whitney and Edward! Their chosen ones were intelligent and capable of many things but trying to match wits with that scheming trick-ster would be difficult indeed and could have devastating results. Without saying a word, she nodded at Mergan then stood and walked over to the rail to gaze out over the lake.

Susan could feel her concern escalating. First Mergan and now Ursula! Something was going on, and she needed to find out what it was! "Mergan, while I'm still connected to the kids, can you please explain yourself and let me share whatever is both-ering you. We all need to know if our kids' lives are in danger!"

Flustered and working hard to control himself, Mergan wisely calmed down so he could focus on the kids. "Susan, listen to me carefully, and share everything I say. They must tell me everything they've learned about this fellow Patrick! Make them describe what he looks like; does he have any funny mannerisms, how does he talk? How exactly does he disappear? In other words, tell them to assume everything they've heard and seen, as well as their reaction to this intruder, is important and not to leave anything out!"

Concerned over Mergan's distress, Susan shook off her own fears and relayed everything to the kids, with Randolph helping.

"You go first!" Edward mouthed, pointing to Whitney.

"Thanks a lot!" she hissed but shrugged her shoulders and cleared her throat.

"Mom, Randolph, whoever's listening right now, we'll share everything we know. Patrick showed up yesterday. After Edward and I found each other, we followed a faint greenish glow that led us to the cavern we're in now. We were soaking our feet in the pool when a face appeared under the surface of the water."

Hesitating briefly, she sighed and added, "Mom, it was pretty creepy because the face looked like dad!"

Whitney heard her mom gasp and moved on quickly. "We didn't know he was a wizard because he doesn't look at all like Mergan, or Randolph either for that matter. He's not tall and lanky, but way shorter than both of you. He actually looks a lot younger too!"

"Edward couldn't see him the first time he showed up," she continued. "Lucky me! I saw him right away! Patrick says he decides whether to let people see him depending on his mood, and he admitted that he made himself look like dad to me! This strange wizard, if that's what he really is, seems quite unpredictable, way too immature, and pouts a whole lot!"

"There is *some* truth to what he says *sometimes*. For example, I believed Patrick when he claimed he studied under Mergan a long time ago. He seemed honestly bitter and resentful as he described how Mergan constantly punished him!"

"For some reason, we sort of believe the joker about a wizard clan being down here somewhere, and that worries us. We're staying vigilant and will be taking shifts to sleep. He gave up a lot of information, but we suspect he has a hidden agenda. We just don't know what it is. He said this so-called wizard clan was planning to attack Yagdi, but he blew up their plans at the last minute, after they'd waited a century to return!"

"The second time he joined us, Whitney was still sleeping, but I saw him for the first time," Edward said. "I didn't like the way Patrick was sitting so close to her, and I noticed our little guest was inching his way toward the staff Mergan gave her. That's when I woke Whitney up, and we double-teamed him with a boat-load of questions."

"We did learn that the more we grilled him, the less inclined he was to answer our questions. When that little wizard decided he'd had enough, he leaped up and twirled so fast he became a blur, then disappeared altogether," Whitney added before pausing to sip some water. "Oh, and by the way, I agree with Edward. He really does seem way too interested in my staff! Anyway, that's all we can come up with, so now it's your turn. Does Mergan know this character?"

Chapter Sixteen

AN OMINOUS WARNING

Between the two liaisons, Mergan was satisfied he'd gotten all the information needed, but didn't like what he'd heard. "Tell Whitney her details are quite impressive, and helpful indeed! Do I know this clown? You bet I do!"

Lowering his voice, he then spoke grimly to Susan and Cathy, "I don't want anyone to worry more than they already are, but that wizard's no good and we would all be wise to keep that scoundrel at arm's length!"

Feeling her own concern escalate, Susan relayed Mergan's message to Whitney and Edward and then asked, "Are you somewhere safe? And can you tell me how on earth that creature could possibly look like your father?"

"Patrick seems quite good at changing his appearance, and can look like someone we care deeply about, or someone who's on our mind. I have to say, it really threw me! But it's okay, I had a good cry and Edward was really supportive. I got angry the trickster would do such a cruel thing, and now, after what Mergan said, we're more determined than ever to figure out his true motives!" Edward nodded in agreement.

"Whitney, you understand yourself so well, and your ability to see what motivates others is a gift that might help you. You make me so proud, and I'm glad you're not alone! Promise me you'll both stay safe until we get you back home!"

"I love you too, Mom," Whitney said, then tried to reassure everyone. "We feel somewhat safe here by the water. In fact, Patrick told us we'd be safe if we stayed in this cavern. He claimed it was a peace offering, but honestly, we don't know what to think. He comes and goes at will, and there's nothing we can do about that, at least nothing we've thought of yet. Anyone have any ideas we could try?" she asked hopefully.

After Susan's detailed relay, Ursula looked at Whitney's mother, then Cathy and Jerome apologetically, and said, "We understand their powers aren't working. However, ask Edward if he's tried creating a dome. If he can do so, it might prove useful, both for safety and to keep our conversations hidden from prying ears."

Susan had no idea what this dome might be, but quickly shared Ursula's suggestion.

"That's a great idea! Mind if I try it right now while we're connected?" Edward asked eagerly.

When Susan shared Edward's eagerness to give it a try, Ursula smiled and said, "Tell him, by all means, and we'll wait for his report!"

"Go Edward!" Whitney screamed and started cheering when it worked. Susan and Randolph gave everyone a thumbs up which caused Ursula to stand up and cheer, joined by Mergan. Cathy and Jerome weren't sure what they were cheering for, but they knew it was big and joined in! Leaning toward his wife, Jerome hissed, "Add that to our growing list of questions!"

"Please tell Whitney and Edward to keep that dome around them at all times, and only remove it when they want to move about. Make sure they understand that!" Ursula said.

"We understand and completely agree!" Edward assured them. "We already feel much better! If Patrick's truly our ticket out of here, the challenge will be staying safe while we act like we're becoming friends, and that's not going to be easy!" Brightening a little, he added, "Hey, tell Mergan I told Whit what he said about water having its own magic. We're wondering if we might be able to capture some of that moving forward. We'll take all the magic we can get!"

Hearing what Edward said, Mergan grinned proudly. "Reassure the kids I'll look into that, and I'm glad Edward remembered. It could prove important indeed! Tell them I applaud their instincts! They must be very wary of Patrick. As I remember more, I'll be sure and share what I know with them. The more our kids know about him, the safer they'll be!"

This time it was Randolph who shared Mergan's answer, then asked the question that had been nagging him since he'd heard Patrick had been with an ancient wizard clan. "You just said Patrick was booted out of a wizard clan down there, and they'd intended to kidnap all of us. Do you believe him?" he asked anxiously.

Detecting the worry in her friend's voice, Whitney jumped in. "We're not sure, Randolph. There's no reason not to believe him, but there's no proof, and we haven't decided how to proceed. We'd like to poke around and learn more. He did say we'd be safe if we stayed here in this cavern. We're not sure if that's the truth either! But you sound worried. What's bothering you?"

"Something you told us earlier has me thinking," Randolph said, looking worriedly first at Susan, then Cathy and Jerome. "Oh, I may as well spill it. As soon as you mentioned a clan of wizards down there, I thought of my distant relatives. I find it quite possible that one or more are knee deep in this mess."

Whitney's mom and Edward's grandparents looked so shocked, he shrugged his shoulders and said, "It looks like there's going to be a lot of explaining to do on this end when we're done talking, young ones. However, I do have an idea. I have a bunch of boxes in my basement filled with generations of family photos and heirlooms. I might be able to uncover something of importance down there."

Growing more intrigued by the minute, he finished excitedly, "I'll get on that immediately! Meanwhile, Whitney and Edward, much good information has been shared today, the best being you are both together and healthy. We all miss you terribly, but each time we talk I feel more optimistic. We will come up with a plan and have you home in no time!"

Looking over at Susan, he added, "Whitney, your mom is one of the strongest women I've ever had the pleasure to meet, and I plan to have a long, wonderful relationship with both of you. And Edward," he continued, winking at Cathy and Jerome, "your grandparents have become a very important support system for Susan. I'm amazed at how much they all care for each other, and I know each of them will do anything to help the two of you get home safely. You are extremely lucky to have them in your lives, kids! One final thing you should know, Edward. Your grandparents intend to call your parents and sister today. Is there anything you would like for them to say on your behalf?"

Randolph and Susan heard Whitney mumble something, then Edward said in a very subdued voice, "Just tell them I love them and miss them, even Mal!" he added with a grin. "But I don't want them to worry. Are you sure that's a good idea?"

Randolph posed the question to Jerome and Cathy, and their response was immediate and heartfelt. "Tell Edward we've thought about that, and tried to look at it from his parents' perspective. They'd be horrified to find out we'd kept this from them, so our vote is a most definite yes. We need to tell them everything! Believe it or not, I think it's the kindest thing we can do!" Jerome said vehemently, as Cathy nodded in agreement.

"Edward, that's a resounding yes from your grandparents," Susan said. "They feel strongly about telling your parents and Mallory. Is there anything more we can do for either of you?"

"Mom, just knowing we can connect now, and pretty easily too, gives me hope and the courage to do whatever it takes to get us home! I love you so much!"

"Me too," Edward said. "Whitney speaks for both of us! We're both going to look hard and deep to find the powers still hidden inside each of us!"

Nodding his approval, Randolph shared their plan. "Tell them that's where their true strengths reside!" Ursula announced. Susan couldn't have agreed more, and looked at her new friend with renewed appreciation.

Edward thought of one more problem. "By the way, we're going to see if Patrick can help us find food. He seems to know his way around here! We have plenty of water now, and that's a huge relief, but it would be great to have something besides granola bars to eat!"

When Susan presented their dilemma to the group, Jerome answered immediately.

"I know this stuff from teaching college-level biology and botany. There's much nutrition to be found in nature. Tell them to check the edge of the water!" Jerome suggested, muttering, "I wish I was down there to help!" Then he snapped his fingers, adding, "Tell them if they find something that looks interesting, describe it to me, and if it sounds familiar, I'll let them know if it's good or bad."

Although his grandpa's offer was well intended, and probably made him feel somehow connected to them, Edward knew that wouldn't work. "Can you tell gramps thanks a lot! In the meantime, we'll see if Patrick can offer any suggestions."

Mergan suddenly remembered something vitally important and held up his hand for quiet as he looked at Randolph. "This is crucial information. Tell them it's been ages since I saw Patrick, but the rogue was quite a handful, and old memories are returning. They're right about his crazy mannerisms. I remember they seemed random at first, but after a while I noticed a pattern. As I remember more, I'll keep sharing. But for now, tell them to beware of the feather he keeps in his shirtsleeve. If that's still on him, it holds magic, and allows the little wannabe wizard to do things he wouldn't otherwise be able to do."

They both promised to be extremely cautious moving forward, especially when it came to their safety and protecting Whitney's staff.

"Remind Whitney her staff cannot be taken from her. That's impossible. But I gave that little trickster his nickname for a reason. He may try to convince Whitney to hand it over by coming up with something quite believable. I can't say this strongly enough, tell them not to believe anything he says and always make him prove his claims. They just can't trust him!"

The kids agreed with everything Mergan said, but knew him well, so Edward told Randolph and Susan, "Make sure he's truly done talking, because that head of his thinks a million steps ahead!"

Grinning appreciatively at their depiction of him, Mergan added, "There is one more thing that might help. Tell the kids to ask Patrick about Mergan's dungeon and goad him into explaining why he found himself so frequently locked up in it! I don't think it'll be a welcome topic, but it should remind him that I am helping them. End that conversation by telling him *I will never allow Patrick to hurt one hair on their heads without suffering severe repercussions!*"

Susan nodded grimly and shared his warning.

"Mergan, Randolph, why don't we go to the kitchen and prepare lunch and let Susan and Edward's grandparents have some private moments with Whitney and Edward," Ursula suggested, standing up and leading them away.

Grateful for the opportunity to spend extra time with their

kids, Susan and Edward's grandparents made the most of their private moment.

"We're with you in spirit!" Susan finally said through fresh tears. "You're not alone anymore." Looking at Jerome and Cathy, she continued, "Promise us you'll take good care of each other until we get you home. Although we hate to say good-bye, we should get back to the others and start formulating a plan!"

"Okay," Whitney and Edward agreed.

"We promise to be careful, Mom!" Whitney continued. "Like I said, it feels good knowing we can connect so easily. Bye for now."

Susan, Cathy, and Jerome sat in silence until Whitney's mom said softly, "I have no appetite whatsoever, but I have to admit whatever those three dreamed up smells wonderful!"

"We need to call Edward's family first, and believe me this won't be an easy conversation!" Cathy said. "We'll join you later."

"Which of you do we have to thank for this amazing meal?" Susan asked as she sat down.

"All three of us!" Ursula answered. "We opened your refrigerator and cupboards and got creative. When we're done, we have some plans to discuss!"

"Yes, that's true," Susan said slowly. "But I believe there's information about each of you we need to uncover first. Maybe we can start with someone named Traveller?" she said, winking at Ursula. "And I believe I also need to learn more about the two of you!" she said, lifting the tablecloth, uncovering Aiden and Ellie who were positioned under the table and ready to beg. "Whitney said you must reveal your 'true selves' today!"

Without looking at her, each one turned to look at the other, then stared silently down at the floor.

Chapter Seventeen

TRUTHS REVEALED

Susan and Ursula stood at the rail with their faces turned toward the sun. "Cathy and Jerome should be joining us shortly. They had to call Edward's parents and sister, and I don't envy that conversation!" Susan said, her eyes closed.

"No, that won't be easy!" Ursula agreed quietly.

"This weather is unusual for late summer in Michigan's Upper Peninsula," Susan mumbled distractedly as she gazed out over the broad expanse of sparkling blue water. "If only our lives were as calm as Lake Superior is today!" she sighed sadly. "I honestly don't know how much more of this I can take!"

"I'd bet everything I own you can and will do whatever is necessary to bring your daughter and Edward home safely," Ursula answered, trying to sound confident for Susan's sake. But it was a struggle! Her heart was breaking for the kids and their families, and she'd never felt so helpless in her very long life! "Maybe Susan needs to hear that I, too, fear what lies ahead," Ursula thought.

Placing her hand over Susan's, Ursula quietly admitted, "I understand, Susan. I feel lost too. I struggle with uncertainty and wonder how best to proceed. You must know I care a great deal for those two teenagers and would trade places with them in an instant if it meant getting them home!"

Smiling sadly, Susan squeezed her hand reassuringly. "I know how special Whitney and Edward are to you. But I wish things were different. I wish they hadn't gotten involved in your war. And I'm sorry, but I have to say it! I wish she'd never met you!"

"I thought that might come up," Ursula said sadly. "You're right, and I wish it hadn't come to this! Although, I too must admit something. I feel so honored to have met Whitney and Edward, and their families. You are all remarkable human beings!"

"You know, there's something about you that gives me hope, Ursula. You are clever, strong, and an obvious leader. In addition to all of that, you appear to be extremely powerful. If anyone can pull this off, I know you can! Now, let's get to that planning and unveil who everyone really is, shall we? No more secrets! We're in this together!"

Ursula pulled Susan in for a hug and whispered, "You are truly worthy of being a member of our alliance, Susan. You're right, there will be no more secrets, from this afternoon forward, but we must wait for Cathy and Jerome to join us."

"Speaking of," Susan said, pointing to the beach.

Anxiously drumming her fingers on the rail, Susan watched her friends slowly climb the long, winding stairway. "Is everything okay?" she prompted as soon as Jerome and Cathy reached the deck.

"Give us a minute!" Cathy huffed, putting her hand on her chest, and breathing hard. "We just talked to Mallory," she finally said, sagging against the rail next to Jerome.

"The news was disturbing to say the least! Our granddaughter's staying with a good friend while Russ and Laura are on a two-week fly-fishing trip in the backcountry! They left two days ago and can't be reached until they return! New Zealand has only spotty cell service in any of its cities, and none whatsoever in the country."

"Russ has wanted to do this for a very long time," Jerome stepped in. "But the timing couldn't be worse! Mallory's distraught that her brother's missing and insists on joining us immediately! We tried to get more details, thinking there had to be some way to reach Edward's parents. Although Mallory admitted she hadn't been the least bit interested in fish or uncivilized places and couldn't remember much, she was emphatic that her parents couldn't be reached. Her account definitely lacked details, but our granddaughter was quite creative in her description. She said, and I quote, 'Mom and dad hired some dude in a cowboy hat to fly them over the mountains to a smelly, fish-infested trout stream too far from coffee houses and WiFi."

"Mallory is alone and too worried about her brother to stay so far away!" Cathy sighed. "We can't reach her parents or the pilot, so what should we do now? I feel terrible, like we're withholding information from them!"

"Now, now! None of this was expected, nor is it your fault!" Ursula soothed, steering them both to the table. "Let's sit down and figure this out together."

"Do you think it's wise for Mallory to come on her own?" Susan asked gently, looking first at Cathy then Jerome.

Edward's grandparents exchanged glances, then Jerome said, "You haven't met our headstrong granddaughter yet, Susan! She'll find a way to get here, whether we help her or not. Of course, Cathy and I promised we'd pay for her airfare, so she's searching for the flight that will get her here quickest."

"She'll be calling soon with flight information," Cathy added.

Hearing Jerome's description of his granddaughter as he and Randolph walked out, Mergan grinned and said, "Headstrong you say? Sounds like my kind of person! But Randolph and I missed the first part of your conversation. Why won't Mallory's parents be with her?"

Cathy sighed and told them everything, including Mallory's description of their flyfishing trip.

"That's a shame about Edward's parents! What terrible

timing!" Randolph said sympathetically. "You must both know it's not your fault they can't be reached!"

"I know, but we still feel terrible, and it's hard not to worry about the consequences!" Cathy moaned, stealing a glance toward her husband. "Our son is quite explosive! Wouldn't you agree Jerome? Russell is very quick to jump to judgment, and it will be extremely difficult to explain all of this, especially after-the-fact! Let's just hope we bring our kids home before they return!"

"I believe that's something we can all agree on!" Susan affirmed. "In the meantime, all we can do now is wait for Mallory to call with flight information. While we're waiting, let's have our friends reveal some mysteries. I still have so many questions about how all this happened in the first place!"

Ursula turned to her alliance and declared, "It's time we show Susan, Jerome, and Cathy who we really are! But may I suggest we move out to Ellie's Point where we'll have a better chance for privacy? At any rate, I'm quite certain this deck wasn't meant to hold my weight, or Aiden's either for that matter."

Noticing their dumbfounded expressions, she smiled reassuringly. "We agreed the time for secrets and half-truths is over! You know about our alliance, and your kids' crucial involvement in it. You know they bravely fought in a war alongside us and many patriotic Yagdians. Although Whitney and Edward have many outstanding talents, their appearance doesn't change when they use their skills, nor will it ever!"

"However, I can't say the same about myself, the two gentlemen standing beside us, nor the dog and cat who look eager for a walk. Our appearances will change quite dramatically when we transform into Yagdians. That will be especially true for me, Aiden, and Ellie. I'll let you decide how different these two gentlemen appear when they reveal themselves."

"This is all quite intriguing, but I have to admit you're frightening me a little," Cathy said, staring around the circle.

"I agree!" Susan said emphatically. "But I'm more comfortable with all of you now, and my curiosity is stronger than my fear. I'm in!"

"Should we bring something to defend ourselves with?" Jerome asked, still not convinced he could trust these people.

"You certainly could," Ursula chuckled. "But I assure you nothing would stop us if we wanted to get to you." Seeing their shocked expressions, she added. "That revelation should be comforting because our ferocity will be directed only at our enemies, and I think you'll appreciate having us as allies even more once you see who we truly are!"

Recovering quickly, Jerome took his wife on one arm and Susan on the other and said, "Lead on!" but they were stopped when Looa blocked the stairway, leaping up and down until Susan relented and reached down to pick her up.

"Looks like we'll have one more with us!" Susan said, smiling down at the small bird.

Their walk took less than a half hour, but there were no clouds in the sky, so the pitiless sun beat down on them until they passed through the circle of pines and into the comforting shade at the base of the ancient Michigan White Pine. Mergan and Randolph took their hats off and fanned their faces while everyone found stumps and fallen tree trunks to sit down on.

Walking to the massive trunk, Susan rubbed a hand reverently over the rough bark and lowered her head as if listening. Then she sighed and said softly, "Whitney and Edward, you're in there somewhere and we're going to find a way to get you home!"

"What now?" she asked, turning to the rest.

"First, let me remind you these revelations will shock the three of you, but none of us are the least bit threatening. We're all members of 'Team Whitney and Edward!' Now, gentlemen first! Please show these honorary alliance members who you truly are and be quick about it!" Ursula directed Mergan and Randolph.

"Yes ma'am!" they shouted in unison. "And may I say, it's about time!" Mergan said with a smile. Grabbing his staff, the wizard began twirling it in circles over his head and grew taller as the air around him began to twinkle like Fourth of July sparklers. A long, flowing deep blue robe with stars and a tall hat with matching colors replaced his rumpled suit.

He stopped when Cathy gasped, "What on earth?" and almost toppled backwards off her perch. Jerome caught his wife and helped her get repositioned mumbling, "Sorry, Mergan. Ursula warned us. Please continue!"

"Certainly! I apologize for surprising you. Pretend you're watching Fantasia and enjoy the show! It should prove quite entertaining!" With a devilish grin, he pointed his staff toward Randolph and swept it in a circle, pulling leaves off nearby trees and shooting acorns harmlessly at the earth wizard's ankles. Drawing tighter circles with his staff, Mergan forced the leaves to swirl, moving closer and closer to the poor man until Randolph began swatting at them to keep from being hit.

He heard Susan gasp then saw all three looking at each other, trying hard not to laugh. "That does it! I'm tired of your shenanigans!" he yelled, finding it hard to control his own laughter.

Putting on his bowler hat, the earth wizard began sweeping his own staff in the opposite direction. The two wizards were equally powerful, so the leaves and acorns stopped moving and hovered menacingly over both wizards' heads. "On the count of three!" Mergan shouted. "One-Two-Three!" Both wizards swept their staffs into the air, sending their treasures shooting out over Lake Superior like a missile.

"That was amazing!" Susan cheered, watching nature's rocket fly away.

"I thought it best to start with the least threatening revelation," Ursula admitted. "What's the verdict? Did they change in appearance?"

Their answers came in a rush, "Taller! The robes! Their commanding voices! The magic!"

"Excuse me, but I must clarify something," Mergan said, jumping up and putting his hand in the air. "Randolph and I are wizards. It may appear to be magic, but wizardry goes far beyond the ordinary tricks of pulling a rabbit out of one's hat."

"Sorry, but whatever it is, I'm quite certain your, er, skills extend far beyond tossing leaves and acorns around," Jerome admitted.

Appearing satisfied, Mergan grinned saying, "You're forgiven, my dear earthlings!" and sat back to watch the rest of the show.

Calling for attention once again, Traveller said, "Okay, gentlemen. I think you've revealed yourselves quite sufficiently!"

Both had risen in stature to tower over everyone, but in a split second, they'd returned to their previous height, and Mergan's beautiful blue coat disappeared. Sitting side by side, both wizards reached out to lean their staffs against two nearby saplings, then sat back to pull hankies out of their pockets and wipe their sweaty brows.

"I hadn't noticed how identical your mannerisms were until now!" Jerome observed.

"Sad but true. This guy strives to be just like me!" Mergan said, pointing his thumb toward Randolph.

"You wish, old man!" Randolph joked. "However, enough of us; don't you think it's time to show them who Traveller is, Ursula?"

"You both had us fooled," Susan interrupted, speaking for all three of them. "Randolph, how on earth did you hide such powers for so long? You pulled off the simple store owner and rockhounder so well!"

"That's a fact!" Cathy agreed. "You might've already told us, but as you can imagine much has happened, and I fear important information has fallen through the cracks. How on earth could you have hidden the fact that you're a wizard for so long? You've owned your shop forever, and this revelation would shock all of your friends!"

"Our dear earth wizard has only known he had such extraordinary talents since early summer, shortly after Whitney and Edward discovered theirs." Grinning at the memory, Ursula added, "Someday, Mergan and I will tell the story of our first meeting with Randolph. It's a doozie! Let me just say, we were all shocked with the outcome!"

"True, this is all new to me," Randolph admitted. "With the help of these two Yagdians, I dove into my role rather quickly. However, I think it's time, dear friend," he added, looking pointedly at Ursula.

Chapter Eighteen

MORE SURPRISES

"As you're all aware, our dream jumper has risen to the challenges of wizardry remarkably well. He's reached Whitney and Edward for us, and I dare say his talents will continue to be challenged as we progress." Ursula said.

"However, it's past time I showed myself to these wonderful people!" Turning toward Susan, Jerome, and Cathy she admitted, "Remember, we're on the same side!" Suddenly she realized Aiden was no longer beside Ellie. When she looked at the cat questioningly, all she got was a yawn and shrug of her sleek black shoulders. "Where could that dragon have gone. His debut will happen very soon," she muttered.

Just as she prepared to transform, Aiden ran into their clearing, panting with his long tongue hanging out one side of his mouth. "Care to explain?" she mouthed but he just shook head and grinned. "There's a secret here!" she muttered again.

"Okay, Ursula, show your Yagdian self," Randolph encouraged.

"Fair warning," Ursula said, "This may be a bit bright, so I won't take offense if you have to look away. If you have sunglasses, I suggest you put them on!"

All three dug in their pockets and quickly put on their shades and looked expectantly at the leader of the alliance.

"We're ready!" Susan said excitedly. "I can't imagine anything will top what we just witnessed!"

"Famous last words!" Mergan mumbled, as Randolph grinned in anticipation, remembering how shocked he was to see Ursula turn into Traveller.

"May I preface this by saying Whitney saw me for the first time very close to this very spot! She was understandably shocked and even turned her ankle trying to run away." Ursula smiled and added, "I remember she was terrified for herself, but hesitant to leave without Ellie."

"I remember my daughter hobbling around for a day or two! But she wanted to save Ellie, eh? That sounds like Whitney!"

"Whitney set Edward up shortly after that," Ursula said with a chuckle. "Your poor grandson wasn't prepared for my trans-formation but recovered quite nicely indeed! Let's hope none of you turn an ankle in a mad dash to escape from me. Although things have been lighthearted, this will still come as a shock! Prepare to meet an extremely large polar bear on the beach of Lake Superior!"

In a whirling mass of wind, sand and bright explosions of light, the elderly woman transformed into her true Yagdian self. An impressive seven-foot-tall polar bear stood regally before them.

"How! What happened!" the three yelled, tripping over them-selves to stand up. "Behind me!" Jerome bellowed, bravely facing the bear as he pulled the women behind his back.

"Stand back, caveman!" Susan snapped, moving to stand beside him. Taking another cautious step forward, she asked, "Ursula, is that really you?" Her normally strong voice quiv-ered as she bravely tried to control her rising panic. They'd been warned but still weren't prepared for such a dramatic change!

"Yes Susan, it's me," the bear said comfortingly. "But on Yagdi I'm known as Traveller and what I am revealing to you now is my true appearance."

Hearing a loud thump behind her, Susan whirled around to

find Jerome had fallen to the ground with Cathy hovering over him. "Jerome, it's okay! At least I think it is," she said, glancing nervously at the huge bear. "But I'd feel better facing this beast standing up, so please get up!" she pleaded.

Reaching out to help, Susan and Cathy pulled Jerome up and placed the stunned man between them.

"I'll stay right here. Promise!" Traveller said softly. "Only approach me if and when you're ready. Remember, we're all on 'Team Whitney and Edward!'" she added, hoping to remind them she was also Ursula.

The dappled sunlight filtering through the leaves of the mighty tree transformed the bear's white fur into shimmering shades of iridescent colors that were so mesmerizing, Susan couldn't keep herself from leaning closer so she could touch her amazing coat. "I had no idea! You're stunning, Ursula, or should I say Traveller!" she murmured.

"If I didn't trust you were a friend, I'd be running for my life right now! You must certainly be a force to be reckoned with!" Jerome admitted with an embarrassed laugh as the three moved closer and circled the bear.

"You most definitely want Traveller on your side in any battle!" Mergan agreed.

"Are you as powerful as you look?" Cathy asked shyly.

"I can chase enemies running at fifty miles per hour and subdue beasts twice my size. Does that answer your question?" she asked with a big smile that made her intelligent eyes twinkle with delight.

As Cathy nodded, Traveller warned, "Now stand back! Here goes the light show again!" and suddenly Ursula, the elderly woman they were growing quite fond of, was standing in front of them once again.

"I'm glad you're back!" Susan said, giving her a huge hug.

"However, I can see where Traveller would be quite an asset in battle!"

"That's nothing!" Mergan beamed proudly. "My dear friend of many decades has the most strategic mind on Yagdi and is the general of our armed forces!"

"You don't say! That's quite an honor!" Jerome noted, looking at Ursula with renewed respect.

"However, as they say, 'you ain't seen nothing yet!'" Mergan laughed as he turned toward Aiden and Ellie. "Who's next?" he asked with a mischievous grin.

"I'll go first," Ellie said.

"Ellie, did you just talk?" Susan gasped, scooting closer to Cathy as the petite house cat transformed into a majestic black panther six feet long and four feet high.

In stunned silence, they grasped for hands and eyed the large cat warily. The panther seemed to take up far too much space in the clearing that suddenly felt small and confining.

"Please don't be afraid, it's really just me," Ellie purred loudly, standing to once again pad slowly toward them. Stalked by a large panther who looked every bit like the predator she was, the three stood and turned to run.

To ease their obvious distress, Ellie sat down and purred quietly, "I won't come any closer, but let me introduce myself. I'm Ellie, the leader of the Yagdian Panther Clan. I must admit it feels good to show my true colors!"

"Ellie, is that really you in there?" Susan asked, looking for an escape route. Suddenly, Looa came out of nowhere and raced toward the giant cat.

"Looa!" Susan cried, moving to grab her. But the small bird wouldn't stop. Flapping her wings excitedly, she raced to the panther and jumped up and down until Ellie acknowledged her presence. "How are you, little snow goose?" the panther purred, and lay down to let Looa jump on her back.

"Don't tell me!" Susan gasped, turning toward Ursula. "She can't be!"

Ursula started to respond but stopped when Susan threw her hands in the air in exasperation. "What next? A flying baboon?"

Choosing to ignore Susan's sarcasm, Ursula explained, "Looa and Ellie are both from Yagdi and know each other very well."

"Of course they do!" Susan exclaimed with rising exasperation.

"Looa is yet another gift I sent to help you, Susan," Ursula continued calmly.

"Whatever do you mean?" Susan asked, gaping as Looa circled twice and settled into Ellie's soft fur.

"Looa is a very special creature, and part of Yagdi's community. While many of us gain our reputations through battle, Yagdian geese are quite the opposite. They're skilled in soothing fears and discontent. I suspected Whitney and Edward might have to leave you temporarily and sent Looa to ease your worry during their absence."

Dropping onto the ground, Susan pulled Looa off the giant cat and into her lap. "You really do know how to plan ahead, don't you, Ursula? I'm here to tell you, this little bird was everything you thought she'd be. I'm going to miss you when this is all over, little girl," she said quietly, rubbing her face in the bird's soft feathers.

"You know, Susan. I'm willing to bet our Looa has grown to love you and Whitney as much as I. Don't be surprised if she decides to stay as well."

Looking hopefully at the little bird in her lap, Susan said, "You don't have to answer right away, but accept this as an open invitation to stay here on Earth, Looa. But only if that's what you wish!"

"I can't think of a better future than spending the rest of my life here with you and your lovely daughter!" Looa admitted shyly.

"That's so wonderful!" Susan said, grabbing her close.

"That went a long way to distract you, Susan. I hope the rest of you had enough time to adjust as well," Ellie purred, looking from one human to the next. "I was sent by Traveller to protect you and Whitney, and I've felt lucky to be a part of your life every day since!"

When Ellie stood, Susan scrambled to get up. Her thick, black coat sparkled with iridescent colors and her soft voice beckoned the three humans closer. Unable to resist, they moved as one and gathered around Ellie and discovered her fur was as soft as it was beautiful.

"Our little rescue cat is truly magnificent!" Susan whispered in awe of Ms. Ellie's beauty.

"You're every bit as soft as you look!" Cathy added, petting her elegant head.

Susan surprised everyone by getting down on her knees to face the very large cat. "You're incredible! I'm so sorry you had to hide this magnificence for so long!" she whispered.

"It was never a problem," the panther admitted. "At first, I came here simply because Traveller asked me to watch over both of you. However, I truly enjoy living with you and Whitney, so I've asked for a permanent leave from my clan. If you don't mind, I'd like to remain here with you, in the form of a cat, that is!" she promised. "But you'll always be under my protection, so if danger approaches either of you, your enemy will face a very angry panther!"

"Mind? Are you kidding me?" Susan wrapped her arms around the cat's large neck. "I agree, appearing as a cat seems wise, but it's good to know Whitney and I will always have back-up!" Grinning into her deep brown eyes, Susan said softly, "You've just brought me so much happiness! Does Whitney know?"

"She does indeed!" Ellie purred contentedly.

"Look out!" Jerome screamed, yanking his shocked wife behind the closest pine tree. "Run, Susan!" he yelled, frantically motioning for her to join them.

"Pick a bigger tree if you're trying to hide!" Susan teased, totally misreading her friend's crazed behavior.

"It's okay! There's no need to panic!" Ursula, Mergan, and Randolph all shouted. But the pounding of feet and rustling of trees destroyed their attempts to calm the poor man.

Finally, Susan heard the commotion, whirled around and felt her legs give out. She hit the ground hard and winced as red-hot pain shot from her ankle to her hip. Determined to escape, Susan began crawling toward her friends, and was grateful when Jerome ignored his own peril and raced out to pull her to safety.

"It looks like a dragon!" Cathy screamed, putting her hand over her mouth.

"That's impossible!" Susan blurted.

"There's no need to be afraid!" Ursula called out to them again. "Finally!" she muttered when their frantic gazes turned toward her. Walking slowly toward the group huddled behind the tree that was far too small to protect them, she announced proudly, "I'd like to introduce Aiden, the new king of Yagdi! He's one of the good guys and a powerful member of 'Team Whitney and Edward!'"

"Told you there was more!" Mergan said to no one in particular, looking quite pleased with himself.

"Aiden...How..." Susan began, but stopped and gasped when Looa squawked and flapped her wings excitedly then raced toward the dragon. "Looa!" Susan cried.

"Looa, aren't you supposed to be soothing Susan?" The magnificent dragon asked, winking at the bird barely tall enough to reach his ankles.

Reminded she'd shirked her duties, the small bird raced back and jumped into Susan's outstretched arms. Aiden's goofy grin didn't detract from his magnificence. Exuding immense power, he was taller than most of the pines, and towered over the group! Realizing this beast from fairytales could topple their flimsy shield, the three humans slowly emerged from behind their ridiculously small tree.

Susan stared at Aiden's clawed feet, and worked her way up, absorbing every detail of his magnificence. He was three times her height, so she had to crane her neck to see his long nose and the sharp, pointed spine running from his head to the tip of his tail. "It's so hard to picture you as the big goofy dog who drools under our kitchen table, begging for tiny scraps of food!" she said, ignoring her screaming ankle to hobble toward him.

"This doesn't work, does it?" Aiden growled when Susan winced and rubbed the back of her neck. "I can fix this," he said softly, spreading his wings and lowering himself to the ground.

This transformation was the most difficult for the three to wrap their heads around, but they were trying. "I was so wrong to think nothing more could surprise me. Aiden, how could you have contained your true self for so long?" Susan whispered. Smiling fondly at the dragon, she cautiously reached out and touched his shimmering scales.

"I was very young when we first met, Susan. A lot has happened since and not all for the better!" he said, bowing his head.

Suddenly the dragon stood on his back legs, spread his wings wide and gracefully soared into the air. They all blinked in stunned amazement, but Aiden was above the treetops before anyone could say a word.

"He's magnificent. But this is a sight I never planned to see over Lake Superior, or anywhere else on Earth for that matter!" Cathy gasped, watching Aiden circle high overhead.

Aiden was most comfortable in the sky. Diving back and forth with ease and skill, the young dragon gave them an aerial show they'd never forget! He dove head-first toward the water but veered off inches from the surface to shoot back into the sky. Flying straight up at breathtaking speeds, the dragon disappeared.

"There he is!" Jerome shouted, pointing at the tiny speck in the sky.

Happy to be flying, Aiden was hesitant to return, but knew they had much to discuss, so he turned and headed back. The dragon could see much further than any of the others, and located the small group huddled on the beach way before they saw him.

"He's coming down!" Jerome exclaimed, pointing skyward again. They tracked their dragon's descent until he was just below the treetops. Hovering above his friends, Aiden found a spot large enough to land, then gently lowered his massive body onto the ground.

"Just like the kids and Randolph, I only recently learned what I was capable of," Aiden admitted. "Whitney and Edward were my friends, and bravely accepted the daunting task of protecting me while I was still too young to defend myself. They spent this entire summer encouraging me to discover my abilities."

He looked at Susan for a long time before turning toward Jerome and Cathy. "Whitney and Edward were perfect role models for me! Because of their patient guidance, I developed the skills and confidence needed to follow my father as ruler of our world."

Aiden looked up and down the beach to make sure no one was near, then stood up and roared menacingly.

It happened so fast, and was so unexpected, Susan and Edward's grandparents screamed and covered their ears as they watched fire erupt out of the gentle dragon's mouth and nose. His oval dragon eyes shone with fierce determination as he growled, "I will do whatever it takes to bring my friends back to their families, but I will have help. Not only here, but from afar!"

Turning toward Ursula, he continued, "If you agree, I'd like to ask Torryn and Araa to join us in our quest to bring Whitney and Edward home!"

"Agree? I think it's genius! Please do so immediately.

Meanwhile, let's walk back to Susan's house. We have planning to do, and Cathy and Jerome are awaiting a call from their granddaughter." Looking at Aiden and Ellie, she suggested, "I think you should transform before we come upon some unsuspecting soul walking the beach."

"Hold on, this is probably Mallory now!" Cathy said, stopping to pull out her phone. "Yes, dear. I understand. That's wonderful! Great job, Mallory! We'll see you mid-afternoon tomorrow. Call us when you arrive, and we'll give you directions to Whitney's house." After a slight pause, she said, "Oh well, all right then. We'll look for you tomorrow."

Putting the phone in her pocket, she looked around the group, saying, "Due to a last-minute cancellation, Mallory booked herself on a flight leaving in two hours. She's frantic at having to pack so quickly, but I can tell how excited she is to get closer to her brother! She says she doesn't need help with her directions. She knows your address from previous communications with Whitney and will just use her phone's GPS."

"That's wonderful!" Susan said, grimacing as she hobbled toward her friend.

"Are you okay, Susan?" Cathy asked, stepping closer.

"My ankle's sore, but nothing a little time and ice won't cure. I'm just sad because the thought of meeting my daughter's pen pal for the first time without Whitney seems so wrong! However, let's not waste any more time! We should get home and start making plans! And while we're at it, I need to come up with some reasonable excuse to call off Officer O'Neil's search for my daughter."

Chapter Nineteen

TRICKING THE TRICKSTER

$\int$ itting across from each other under "Edward's dome of secrecy," Whitney said softly, "We need to find out if your dome truly blocks our conversations from the trickster. Got any bright ideas how we can accomplish that?"

"I've been thinking about it a lot," Edward admitted, keeping his voice low. "What if we set him up? We can bait him with something and see if he bites."

"Good idea! Maybe something that has to do with my staff. If Mergan's right, he wants to get his hands on that really bad!"

"Good one!" Edward agreed. "How about this? In a loud voice, you tell me your staff has lost its magic down here, and you're tired of dragging it around everywhere. We can see how he reacts. If he brings it up, we'll know he can hear us."

"Perfect!" Whitney said. Fearing the cagy wizard might be lurking nearby, she frowned and looked around suspiciously then murmured, "Before we get started, there's something else we should talk about."

"We need to figure out a way to con Patrick into showing us what his feather can do, and we need to do it fast before he has a chance to get suspicious. I saw that little wizard twirl it between his fingers, and I have to believe it's the same weapon Mergan told us to beware of. We don't know what it can do, but Mergan seemed to think it had powers. Maybe Patrick's abilities will weaken if we get that feather away from him. At the very least, it's a great bargaining chip, don't you think? We might be able to use that to coerce him into helping us get out of here!"

Edward frowned and looked out over the water. "I hate the idea for a lot of reasons. We'd become as devious as him, and that's nothing to be proud of! Second, we're in a world of hurt if it doesn't work!"

After a few agonizing minutes, he finally said, "I still don't like it, but I agree we have to do something, so let's try and trick the trickster! He won't be expecting it, so we'll have the advantage of surprise. We could feed his ego and say Mergan told us about his amazing feather, and we thought it sounded pretty cool! If we pretend to be skeptical of its powers, he might bring it out and do something to prove how special it is."

"I like that!" Whitney said enthusiastically. "We can play 'good cop, bad cop' when he joins us. You be the bad guy and I'll pretend to take Patrick's side, at least part of the time. He might see me as a weak target," she smiled confidently. "He'll find out soon enough I can hold my own!"

"Great idea! I have no problem disin' the guy!" Edward said, grinning mischievously. "You draw his attention to the staff and tell him you're thinking about leaving it behind because its magic doesn't work down here. We'll see how he reacts. The key will be getting him to pull out his feather. If it really does hold magic the trickster will be too distracted showing off to notice I'm moving in."

Shaking his head, he added, "There are a couple of sticky assumptions we're making here. I'll need to overpower him, and he's pretty slick. Then, when you get his feather, you'll have to keep it away. It's risky! Think it's worth a try?"

"It's the only way to find out if the dome works down here and we'll have an advantage if we can take away some of his powers. Let's do this and hope we can pull it off!"

"Let's go for it then," Edward said, getting up quickly. Walking far enough away that Whitney would have to speak up, he nodded for her to begin.

"Hey Edward, what do you think about leaving my wizard staff here when we move on? The magic doesn't seem to work down here and it's too heavy to lug around."

"I get it, but that was a gift from Mergan to you, so I'll leave that decision up to you, Whit," Edward answered, then waved his arm to remove his dome.

Drawing water into his jug, Edward returned to Whitney and sat down. They didn't have to wait long before their friend appeared. His body looked transparent at first, but quickly formed into the one and only grinning trickster. "Good afternoon!" he said happily, sitting across from the kids. "I'm so glad to have someone to talk to."

"Welcome, Patrick. How's it going?" Edward asked, trying to sound pleasant.

"I feel GREAT!" the trickster said with a sly grin. "I heard you talking to your friends earlier. Nice move reaching out to them! It sure didn't last long, but I'm happy for you. How'd you do it?"

Stealing a glance toward Edward, Whitney noticed her friend's slight smile and knew he'd also picked up on Patrick's unintentional, but very welcome clue. The trickster hadn't heard anything while they were inside his dome!

"It's great, but we haven't perfected the connection yet. It was short. About a minute or two, right Edward?" Whitney said.

Before Edward could answer, Patrick chimed in. "I heard your mom's voice, Whitney. Your grandparents were there too, Edward. How nice for both of you! I don't know this Randolph character, but he sounds like a crafty wizard. I heard the nasty things Mergan had to say about me, but that's no surprise!" he added with a pout. "Then I heard someone named Ursula ask if you were able to use your powers, and then I didn't hear anymore.

I'm sorry you were cut off! Better luck next time," he added with a grin.

"Yeah, now that you bring it up, our powers seem to have pretty much disappeared down here," Whitney said sadly.

Standing up, she went over to her staff and picked it up. "And this thing's worthless now. What good is a staff that no longer holds magic?"

Trying to look nonchalant, Patrick walked slowly toward Whitney. "That's a pity your staff doesn't work down here. There are many strange happenings in the depths of the portal. In fact, there are many stories I can share about the wizard clan down here if you're interested. Let's sit down. I love telling stories."

"Hey, I'd like to hear more about that feather you were twirling between your fingers!" Whitney said eagerly.

"That old thing? You told me about that, but so what? It's just a feather, right?" Edward asked, turning toward Patrick.

"Oh, it's very special indeed!" Patrick gloated. "Maybe I'll show you what it can do one day!"

"Mergan tells us it has some powers, but nothing that sounded all that impressive!" Edward said grumpily.

"Mergan doesn't know what he's talking about!" Patrick protested, jumping up. Pulling the feather out of his sleeve, he twirled it between his fingers then pointed it toward the wall behind them. *KABOOM!* The feather blew a deep hole into the wall, shooting rocks in all directions.

"That's so cool!" Whitney gushed, winking at Edward. "It blows things up! What else can it do?"

"Whatever I ask!" Patrick said proudly.

"Can I touch it?" she asked pleadingly.

"Maybe, if I decide to let you."

"How about we trade for a little while? Your feather for my useless staff?" she goaded.

Although his eyes sparked with interest, Patrick instinctively

looked for signs of deceit. Detecting nothing but wide-eyed inno-
cence in Whitney's bright green eyes, he grinned and walked
toward her. "That might be fun, at least for a short while!"

Whitney got up and sauntered toward Patrick, swinging her
staff temptingly in front of her. Edward waited until Patrick was
totally focused on the wizard staff, then jumped up and leaped
into action!

Catching the trickster by surprise, Edward grabbed both his
arms, yanked them behind his back, and held on for dear life. He
was a small wizard, but wiry and very strong, and Edward had to
work hard to keep Patrick restrained as he yanked back and forth,
turning his head at an impossible angle, trying to bite him.

"Now or never, Whit!" Edward yelled, and Whitney jumped
into the fray,

"Ah ha!" she cried triumphantly, snatching the feather out
of Patrick's hand. Backing away quickly, she grabbed her staff,
then nodded for Edward to release him. Certain the wizard would
attack, Edward raced to Whitney, then dropped his dome around
them.

Angry red spots appeared on Patrick's shocked face. He
clenched his hands so tightly blood dripped from his palms, and
with a low, animalistic snarl, he raced toward them. Edward's
shield held, and he smacked into it face first. Screaming in agony,
he held his bleeding nose in one hand, and raised a fist at Edward
with the other yelling, "How dare you trick me! You planned this,
didn't you? I can't take your staff and you're holding my feather.
So, what's next?" he demanded, sinking to the ground.

Leaving Patrick's feather and Whitney's staff safely inside
the dome, they exited their protective shield and moved cautiously toward the trickster. Leaving plenty of space between
them they sat down and tried to explain. "Patrick, we didn't do
this to be cruel. We're just trying to protect ourselves. You're so

unpredictable, we can't trust you. You need to prove that we can," Whitney said firmly.

"How can I do that?" he wailed. "I never do anything right, so even if I wanted to, I probably wouldn't be successful!"

"How about you do something for us as a starter? Can you show us how to get out of here?" Edward suggested hopefully.

Looking at them as if they'd lost their minds, Patrick said cautiously, "We'd need to go right through the wizard clan's camp! Even if we're cautious, Edna knows everything, so we'd never get away with it!"

"I'll bet you could come up with a plan with the right motivation," Whitney said calmly. "We'll hang onto your feather until you do. Let's just call it insurance."

"I can't go far without that feather," Patrick whined. "But it looks like I have no choice. You drive a hard bargain, kids!" he said, staring at both with a hint of respect.

"Until later," he said, then turned and disappeared into the darkness muttering in a low voice only he could hear, "I have some big decisions to make!"

Once he was out of sight Whitney sighed, "He's so dejected. I hope our plan works!"

"Me too!" Edward agreed. "But let's look on the bright side. It's working so far!"

Tucked safely inside Edward's dome once again, Whitney said, "I guess we just proved what Traveller said. We used our heads and tricked a trickster. Your genius sanctuary kept Patrick's big ears out of our conversation, and now we have his feather. But what's next?"

"I know. I'm shocked it was so easy. But we played him perfectly. I just hope we didn't play into some wild scheme of his." Gazing beyond the boundaries of the dome he shrugged his shoulders and continued, "I guess we'll just have to see what happens next."

"I didn't think of that possibility," Whitney admitted. "I better keep you around a little longer," she added with a sideways grin. "Trusting Patrick to get us out of here's going to be tricky because, well, it means trusting Patrick, and we know he's the ultimate joker. We need to devise a plan that works in our favor."

"Glad I come in handy sometimes," Edward joked, but his smile didn't linger. "Whit, we need to stay alert. I have an awful feeling this whole thing might be a trap." Snapping his fingers Edward grinned. "Let's try contacting Mergan. He seems to know this guy pretty well."

"How do we do that?" Whitney asked, intrigued by his idea.

"It seems like Randolph's the key communicator, and that makes sense because he's a dream jumper with all kinds of powers. But your wizard staff holds magic too. Why don't you try using it to contact them? Maybe some of our powers will return while we're under the dome," he said hopefully. "I'd help, but I tried to take that thing from you once and it gave me a jolt I'll never forget, so I won't be trying that again!"

"Yeah, I remember that and the shocked look on your face," Whitney laughed. Wrapping her hands around the staff, she said, "Okay, wish me luck! What do you think I should say?"

"Try abracadabra."

"Very funny. I tried that when I first got it, and it didn't work. But you just reminded me of something really important! I played with this staff for hours and finally figured out 'abracadabra' was the right word but I needed to mix up the letters a little bit!" Holding her staff at arm's length, she commanded, "Ababacra!"

"Wow, it actually worked!" Whitney gasped as it began to glow and wiggle so much that she had to tighten her grip. "Please find Randolph!" she commanded.

When nothing happened, she looked at Edward and groaned, "Now what?"

Randolph's mystified voice cut her off. "Whitney is that you?"

"Yes, yes. It's us Randolph!" Whitney shouted.

"Way to go, Whitney!" Randolph yelled back excitedly. "How on earth did you do that?"

"We took Ursula's suggestion to heart and started using our heads! It was Edward's idea to use my wizard staff while we're under his dome," Whitney admitted. "I told him I'd keep him around a while longer for that! Is Mergan there? And if he is, can you play liaison again?"

"You two certainly make a good team!" he chuckled. "Mergan's right here, but are you sure you want to feed his ego like that?"

"Yeah, we're pretty sure!" Edward confessed with a smile.

"Mergan, phone for you!" Randolph yelled. Turning serious, he added, "Whitney and Edward discovered her wizard staff works while they're safely under the boy's dome. They have news. Are you ready to listen?"

"Absolutely!" Mergan announced as he rushed into the room. "Ask them what we can do to help."

Whitney talked so fast Randolph struggled to relay her information. "We've confirmed Patrick can't hear us, and tell Mergan we just grabbed the imp's feather, and we plan to use it as a bargaining tool. We promised to give it back once he gets us out of here! But we need Mergan's help. He knows more about Patrick than anyone else. We might be playing into some genius plan of his and we're trying to figure out how to proceed."

"They did what?" Mergan shouted when Randolph paused to catch his breath. "Get every bit of information you can from the kids, my dear earth wizard!"

"Patrick seems to know his way around, and we need his help to get out of here before the wizard clan finds us. We all know he's not trustworthy, so we took his weapon and that might have given us the upper hand, at least for the time being." Whitney explained. "We know he could trick us and mess things up worse than they are now. Patrick's all about himself, so if there's something in it for him, we have no doubt he'd turn us in, then it's game over!"

"Very wise," Mergan said slowly, digesting everything he'd just heard. "Reassure the kids they've pegged the little rat perfectly! What can I do to help?"

"Randolph, Mergan seems to know the joker very well," Edward answered. "We thought he might be able to suggest how to proceed."

"Tell them I don't like it," Mergan shared. "I don't like them anywhere near this so-called wizard clan. In fact, Patrick may have made them up as a convenient distraction while he carries out something more devious. Either way, you must stress to the kids they're in grave danger and must use extreme caution. If there really is a clan down there, they've operated under the radar for over a century, so I have no doubt they're powerful!"

After he relayed Mergan's concern, Randolph added, "Hold off for a few hours, kids. I think you're onto something, but I agree with Mergan. It'll be dangerous. Give me time to look through the boxes in my basement. There may be some ancestral clues to help us proceed."

"That makes sense," Whitney agreed. "But we don't want to wait too long. It gives Patrick more time to scheme! Never a dull moment down here!"

"Mergan will help me go through my family's boxes piled high in the basement of the rock shop," Randolph volunteered, and grinned when the wizard's eyebrows shot up in surprise. "We need to find out if there's a connection between my ancestors and this wizard clan, then figure out why they wanted to drag our alliance into the portal. If there's a chance that Patrick's telling the truth, it seems like a worthy endeavor."

"Meanwhile, I agree with Mergan. You two need to be careful. Since we talked, Mergan has done nothing but think of the young wizard and very bad memories are returning. He shared that Patrick was never a good student and developed a real attitude. Mergan admitted he had some skills but got discouraged easily and could be nasty and vengeful. I think you've pegged him, kids. The scoundrel sounds like a petulant child, but one who's extremely dangerous!"

"Tell them to pretend to agree with him as much as they can!" Mergan advised, quite troubled by what the kids may have gotten themselves into.

"We'll begin digging into those boxes immediately. Promise me you won't do anything until we get back to you?" Randolph said.

Whitney and Edward nodded at each other, then Edward answered, "Okay, but try to hurry!"

Just then, Susan came running in with Jerome and Cathy right behind her. "Are you talking with the kids?"

"We are indeed!" Randolph said. "We've been comparing notes about Patrick, the young wizard they've run into. Whitney and Edward, your mom and grandparents are here. Can I relay anything to them? Susan, are you okay doing it this way?"

"Of course!" she answered quickly. "Tell them we're all fine and fully aware of the true identities of each member of their alliance."

Whitney and Edward looked at each other in relief when Randolph described the day's revelations. "Is everyone truly okay now?" Whitney asked hesitantly.

Trying to reassure her daughter, Susan said quietly, "Please tell the kids we just want to get them home as quickly as possible. We now realize how powerful their alliance is, and just hope their friends can come up with a plan!"

"My turn!" Cathy chimed in. "Can you relay the news about Edward's parents not coming, and why, but tell him Mallory will be joining us tomorrow."

"What?" Edward erupted. "Randolph, did you just say Mal's

coming to Michigan? It's probably best that mom and dad are off having fun because I don't think dad would react well at all! Hopefully we'll be home before they even know what happened. But Mal shouldn't come alone!"

"Cathy says it's too late to try and change your sister's mind. It sounds like Mallory caught a plane immediately and with the time difference and twenty-two-hour flight, we expect her tomorrow afternoon," the wizard answered.

"Amazing," Edward said, dumbfounded by his sister's actions. "Doesn't surprise me Mallory got what she wanted! Full disclosure, my sister might be a problem. Let's just say she means well but can be a bit overwhelming!"

Saying good-bye to her daughter felt particularly troubling this time, so Susan reached out for Cathy and Jerome. The three friends sat in quiet agony until Susan finally broke the silence and voiced what they all feared, "Let's hope that's not the last time we speak with our children!"

Chapter Twenty

MALLORY BLOWS IN!

Susan didn't sleep well that night and heard a phone ring sometime before dawn. It was only 4:30, but she'd lost all hope for sleep several hours ago. Tossing the covers aside, she threw on her robe, and found her slippers half hidden under the bed. Shuffling quietly toward the kitchen to put on a pot of coffee, she found Jerome and Cathy already dressed and talking quietly by the fireplace. "Did I miss something? Why are you both awake and dressed at this hour?"

"Did our phone call wake you? It was Mallory with an update," Jerome explained. "She wanted us to know that everything's on schedule, and she plans to be here early this afternoon. We've made several attempts to explain the time difference, but apparently, she doesn't care. At any rate, we couldn't go back to sleep, so here we are."

"Believe me, I get that! Your phone didn't wake me up. Unfortunately, I didn't get very much sleep last night. I don't know about you two, but I'm growing more worried as the minutes pass, especially since we still don't have a plan to bring the kids home." Turning toward the kitchen, she added, "If you plan to stay up and watch the sunrise with me, the coffee will be ready in a few minutes."

Pouring herself a cup, Susan walked onto the deck and collapsed onto the closest Adirondack chair. She needed to stay busy to keep from going crazy with worry! Problem was, there was nothing to do at the moment. "I'm drinking too much of this, but if I can't sleep, I may as well," then sighed as the soothing warmth coated her dry throat.

Grinning as loud snores reached her from the family room, she pulled Whitney's favorite blanket over her and leaned her head back. "Glad somebody's able to get some sleep around here."

Susan woke up and groaned when she noticed the spilled coffee all over Whitney's blanket. Shocked she'd fallen asleep, she bent over to search for her coffee cup, and was happy to find it was still in one piece. She stood up and put it on the table then walked to the edge of the deck. Leaning on the deck rail, she looked out over the turbulent lake and let her eyes wander. The alliance was up early and involved in an impromptu strategy session on the beach. "I hope they come up with something soon," she said to herself, watching Mergan draw lines in the sand with his staff.

"Guess that plan didn't work," she thought, as the wizard frowned and shook his head then wiped the sand clean with his staff.

"This quiet morning might be the definition of 'calm before the storm,'" she thought, remembering Edward's description of his sister. Thanks to her reassurances that no one ever walked this far from town, Ursula, Aiden, and Ellie remained in their Yagdian forms. She watched them work on plans for a while, but the Adirondack chair looked so comfortable, she wandered back over and sat down. She folded Whitney's soiled blanket and put it aside to wash later. Wrapping herself in a clean fleece, she fell asleep listening to the cheerful sound of birds waking up.

• • •

Blinding sunlight woke Whitney's mother out of deep, dreamless sleep. She yawned and opened her eyes slowly, then checked her watch and sat upright. She'd slept the entire morning away! Throwing her daughter's fleece back on the chair, she took her empty cup off the table, grabbed the stained blanket, and went into the kitchen. No one was in the house, so she grabbed another cup of coffee then returned to her perch at the edge of the deck.

Setting her cup down, Susan shook her head to see her daughter's alliance still hard at work down on the beach, so she settled in to wait for Mallory. "Could that be her?" she muttered, straightening up and shielding her eyes to watch a lone figure walk toward them. Whoever it was seemed to be on a mission because she was using the hardpacked sand by the water to move more quickly down the beach.

"I should warn the gang!" she thought, noticing they were arguing, and unaware company was approaching.

Waving her arms and yelling, "Hey down there!" didn't work, so she raced down the stairs. Catching Ursula's attention when she reached the beach, Susan urgently pointed toward the figure walking toward them. Immediately understanding, Ursula turned to the group and yelled, "Transform, now!" Her stern urgent voice penetrated their heated discussion.

"What on earth," Mergan began but stopped abruptly when he saw why she'd yelled at them. "Thanks to Susan's warning, we just avoided what could have been a very sticky situation!"

When the beach walker was close enough, Susan recognized her daughter's pen pal from all the pictures she'd sent with her letters. "Mallory!" she yelled.

"Why is everybody just standing around? You should be out looking for my brother and Whitney!" Mallory yelled, putting her hands on her hips.

"Now, this is someone I'd like to meet!" Mergan said to Randolph, then grinned and walked toward their visitor.

First to reach the teen, Susan said, "Hello, Mallory, I'm Susan,

Whitney's mother. Welcome back to Michigan. I'm surprised to see you walking on the beach!"

"It was a long, boring flight and I needed the exercise! We flew most of the way in the dead of night, and they turned the lights off so people could sleep. As you can tell, I didn't! Just look at the bags under my eyes!" she complained, pointing to her face. "Even worse, they don't serve meals on flights anymore! Pretty rude if you ask me! I'm really hungry!" she announced, looking pointedly at Susan.

"Anyway, like I started to say, I needed the exercise, so when the cab came, I gave them your address but told the driver I'd be walking and asked him to deliver my suitcases. He seemed hesitant so I flipped him a twenty. And here I am!"

"This is a very trying and impossible situation, and I'm still trying to make sense of it all myself! But we'll get you caught up after we find you something to eat," Susan said, raising her eyebrows at Ursula.

Giving Mallory another quick hug, she added, "I'm glad you found us, and let's just say we'll do our best to get your brother and my daughter home. I'm so sorry we're meeting under these difficult circumstances, but it's so nice to finally meet you!"

"You, my dear, will inject much-needed energy into our endeavors. I'm Mergan," the wizard said, sticking out his hand.

"Are you in charge?" Mallory asked as she shook his hand.

"Why of course..." he started to answer, liking this girl more and more.

"He'd like to think so," Ursula interrupted with a laugh. Drawing the shocked teenager into a huge bear hug, she said, "Welcome, Mallory! We've heard a great deal about you!"

"Don't listen to a word Edward says," Mallory cautioned. "He's just a boy and doesn't know what he's talking about most of the time."

"Typical brother-sister relationship," Susan muttered to

herself, but just smiled and said gently, "I'm afraid I must disagree. From what I've seen, your brother seems like a really good guy!"

"He is," Mallory agreed. "Most of the time! Aww, aren't you just the sweetest little thing! You must be Ms. Ellie," she cooed, reaching down to gather the cat in her arms. "I'll bet you miss Whitney too!" she whispered, rubbing her cheek against the silky fur.

Ursula knew her old friend didn't have the patience nor the inclination for social politeness. Giving Mergan a look of caution before he spilled everything way too quickly, she directed the teen's attention toward their dream jumper. "Mallory, I'd like for you to meet Randolph."

"Oh, I've heard about you!" Mallory said excitedly. Gently putting Ellie down, she stuck out her hand and smiled. "Hey Rockman. I'm Mallory. You own the rock shop in town, don't you? Whitney thinks you rock, no pun intended! She loves your stories and believe me I've heard them all word-for-word."

Appearing quite pleased with his new nickname, Randolph grinned and took off his bowler hat to shake her hand. "Whitney is a very polite listener! And might I add, I'm willing to share stories with you anytime, young lady!"

"I'd like that," Mallory said, suddenly distracted by the big dog racing toward her. "Come here, Aiden!" she yelled, kneeling in the sand and opening her arms wide. The large, rather clumsy dog couldn't stop fast enough, so all ninety pounds hit Mallory head on and sent her flying.

"You sure know how to win a girl over don't you, big guy?" she laughed. But when Aiden started drooling all over her new shirt, she scolded, "You're a big dog! Next time, slow down!" When Aiden lowered his head and looked like he'd lost his best friend, she mumbled, "So much for discipline," then leaned over to hug him, transforming Aiden's sad face into an ear-to-ear grin full of long sharp teeth.

• • •

Mallory felt a soft breath of air and sensed something extraordinary! She'd never experienced anything like this and had no clue what to think. There was no wind whatsoever and the surface of Lake Superior was so calm it looked like glass. "What just happened?" she mused.

When her toes and fingers began to tingle, the mystified teen took a few tentative steps forward, curious but still not alarmed. "There's something strange out there," she murmured. Suddenly, about fifteen yards away, the air just above the beach began to shimmer and spark as if filled with electricity. "Whoa! Is anyone else seeing this?" she yelled, watching nervously as waves of air began rolling toward them.

In a sudden brilliant burst of light, Araa and Torryn shimmered into view, and their appearance was astounding! Mallory screamed and turned to run, with Susan right behind her. Their granddaughter's scream brought Cathy and Jerome out of the house and onto the deck. "Mallory!" they shouted and raced for the stairs. Taking them two at a time, they ran fearlessly toward danger.

Although shocked to see her friends travel the stairs so fast, Susan was too concerned about the arrival of two monstrous dragons. On top of that, Mallory's face had turned pasty white, and she'd begun gasping for breath. Susan was a trained veterinarian and knew both were signs the poor girl was going into shock.

"Bet I don't look much better!" Susan thought, racing to help Mallory. She and Ursula reached the frightened teenager at the same time and wrapped their arms around her. Cathy and Jerome arrived seconds later and joined the comforting circle. Brushing Mallory's hair back, Ursula said in a quiet, low voice, "You have nothing to fear whatsoever. You're among friends, but I understand what you see before you must be difficult to grasp." Her magical voice sounded so soothing and her words so reassuring the shocked teen and equally shocked adults soon relaxed.

Before too long, Mallory was breathing normally, and her rosy complexion had returned. Seeing similar positive signs in Susan and Mallory's grandparents, Ursula said softly, "Unfortunately, there's no time to ease into this gently because we have many important decisions to make. Therefore, it's my distinct honor to introduce you to Araa and Torryn, two very powerful and revered leaders from Yagdi."

Watching the scene with rapt attention, Randolph shook his head and muttered, "Ursula did it again! Her skills just deflated what could have been a disastrous situation for everyone."

Even more intriguing, he'd noticed Mallory's humorous expression turn quizzical just before the dragons appeared. The timing couldn't have been coincidental, and it sure looked like she'd been expecting something to happen. Wondering if the wizard had seen Mallory's odd behavior too, Randolph turned toward Mergan, but stopped and grinned.

The cagy old wizard was smiling at him and leaned in to keep their conversation private. "I saw it too, Earth Wizard. Mallory could have simply sensed the two dragons' immense power, or we may have the makings of another extraordinary human on our hands. Either way, it's a very special human who can sense the presence of dragons," Mergan said excitedly, keeping a close eye on Mallory's miraculous recovery.

"Are they really dragons?" she asked, eyeing the huge beasts who kindly stayed far enough away she could relax just a little.

"They are indeed," a deep voice said.

"What was that?" Mallory yelled, whirling around so quickly she almost tripped over her own feet.

"I'm the big dog who just bowled you over!" Aiden said with a sheepish grin. "And the large dragons before you are my parents."

Susan, Cathy, and Jerome sighed with relief and smiled at Aiden. "He did promise they'd be arriving," Susan said calmly.

Sounding quite put off, Jerome grumbled, "Yeah, but I thought there'd be some kind of warning ahead of time!"

"Dragons? No way!" Mallory yelled, staring first at the large dragon masquerading as Aiden then at the two even larger dragons that were supposedly his parents. "I see the resemblance, but dragons don't have families, do they?"

"This is too much!" she shouted angrily. "You can't possibly be the big dog who bowled me over and slobbered all over my new shirt!" she demanded, once again putting her hands on her hips.

When Aiden started toward her, she stuck her hand out and yelled, "Wait just one crazy minute!" Pausing to wipe the sweat off her brow, she rubbed her eyes and muttered, "I must be hallucinating from that long plane ride!"

She finally threw her hands up in defeat and glared accusingly at everyone. "A little heads up would've been appreciated! I want to know what's going on around here, and I expect answers! But before we continue, let me know now if there are any more surprises!"

The young teenager's blunt demand and accurate assumption stunned everyone. Mergan was the first to recover and shocked everyone when he smiled broadly then started laughing so hard his shoulders shook and tears streamed down his face. With lips twitching, they watched their normally serious friend's unrestrained amusement, and soon everyone but Mallory had joined in.

"What's so funny!" Mallory demanded, which only prompted more laughter.

Although she looked terribly offended, it didn't take long for Mallory's sour expression to soften.

"You, my dear, are quite invigorating!" Mergan said, wiping his tears away. Looking around the diverse group, he admitted, "All of you bring unique gifts to our mission, and I feel honored to work with each of you."

The wizard's rare gesture of appreciation left everyone speechless. Finally, Mergan broke the silence to explain, "You're right young lady, I believe there might be a few more interesting surprises to uncover. However, that's enough chit-chat! Let's get down to the business at hand."

"What on Earth?" he growled, realizing Torryn and Araa had suddenly disappeared. "Ah, Ha!" he muttered, noticing a couple strolling along the beach. They were still closer to town than they were to Susan's house, and too far to have witnessed the strange creatures, but they were wandering closer and would be walking past them shortly. "Wise decision!" he muttered.

Grabbing Susan's arm, Ursula whispered, "Fair warning, Torryn and Araa will return and that's very welcome indeed! They will be invaluable assets on the Yagdian front as we begin our search for young Whitney and Edward.

As they walked toward the house, she added, "I must say I now see why Whitney and Mallory have become such good friends! They both have spunk, and neither are afraid to speak their minds!"

Smiling warmly, Susan tucked her friend's arm under hers. "I believe you know my daughter very well, dear friend. I hadn't made the connection because I was too busy thinking how Edward had been very generous when he described his sister as persistent and stubborn."

Turning to Mallory, Susan said, "To answer your earlier

question, there is more to reveal, but let's get some food in you first.

"Sounds good to me!" Mallory said excitedly, picking up her pace.

Watching the girl tromp through the deep sand, Susan leaned toward Ursula and whispered, "Do you think she heard my hint of more to come?"

"We'll soon find out!"

Mergan overheard Edward's sister and turned toward Randolph. "Mallory's quite lively, isn't she! That energy may prove beneficial, but she must give her poor parents plenty to worry about! However, I must agree lunch sounds wonderful, particularly a double enchilada with plenty of cheese! Hey Mallory, do you like Mexican food?" he called to her hopefully, following her up the stairs.

"Come here, granddaughter!" Jerome said warmly when they reached the deck. "We were too distracted to say a proper hello!"

Mallory loved her grandparents and missed them terribly, so she ran into their open arms and enjoyed a much overdue group hug. "We used to do this all the time!" she said, smiling at the memories. "I've really missed you guys!"

However, when they started gushing over her, Mallory raised her eyebrows pleadingly at Mergan as Cathy pushed her to arm's length and said, "You've become such a beautiful young lady."

Groaning inside, Mallory smiled politely then wriggled away. "Susan, can I help with lunch?"

"We've got it!" Susan laughed. "Enjoy spending time with your grandparents!"

"It's bittersweet seeing them so happy, isn't it," Ursula said quietly, following Susan into the kitchen.

"It certainly is, and I'm happy for them! It just makes me more impatient to hug my daughter!" Opening the refrigerator, she peered at the bowls of leftovers and sighed. "How about hot dogs on the grill? I have homemade potato salad and beans to go with."

"Sounds perfect! Quick and easy!" Ursula said. "I'll ask Jerome or Cathy to start the grill," she offered, leaving Susan alone.

Leaning against the counter, Susan sighed and looked out the window. Mallory and her grandparents were huddled around the grill laughing and chatting while Ursula and the two wizards sat down at the table. As always, Ellie and Aiden had placed themselves strategically under their feet.

"I can't believe I'm looking at a polar bear, two wizards, a panther and a dragon!" she thought, shaking her head. "There's Looa too," she muttered, watching her little bird hop under the table. "It's still mind-boggling to me! I can only imagine what Mallory's reaction will be!"

The peaceful scene prompted a flashback to her daughter's birthday dinner on the deck. "It seems so long ago! So much has happened in just a couple of weeks!"

"Thinking of Whitney, Susan?" Cathy asked quietly.

Startled, Susan gasped, "I must've been daydreaming! I just saw you at the grill!"

"I know how hard this is for you but remember you're not alone! I think about Edward every minute and wish we had a plan in place. I hate waiting!" Cathy admitted.

"I know!" Susan frowned. "We need to really push for that, starting right now! Can you help me take dishes and food outside? It feels like we've waited long enough!"

Once everyone had started eating Susan stood to make an announcement. "I get that we all needed to eat, but how's this for a plan? Eat fast, then let's go to Ellie's Point. It would be a good place to get Mallory up to date. Maybe Aiden's parents would be more comfortable joining us where it's more private," she suggested, looking pointedly at Ursula. "We need to take our cue from our kids and formulate a plan of action!"

"Here, here!" Mergan agreed, lifting his glass of fresh-squeezed lemonade.

Susan nibbled a little, but mostly pushed her food around, impatient to walk the beach.

Cathy stood up and gathered plates then nudged Susan as she walked past. "Let's get these washed!"

Eagerly grabbing the bowls of food, Susan followed her friend into the kitchen. "Thanks!" she said, as they put the leftovers in the fridge. "It's just, our kids are everything to us, right? We work so hard to keep them safe! I've never felt so completely helpless and if I don't keep busy and stay focused on getting them home, I'll go mad!"

"I get you, Susan. And so does Jerome. You never have to pretend around us. We're in this together, and we must share our grief as well as our hope. It's the only way to move forward!"

"You know, I feel closest to Whitney here in our home. It almost feels like a bridge between here and our kids!"

"You might be onto something," Ursula agreed, walking into the kitchen. "Sorry, I didn't mean to eavesdrop, but I heard what you just said. The idea of a bridge between worlds has been the subject of many discussions when strange occurrences happen. So, the idea that your home could be a bridge between Whitney and this place she holds so dear may not be that far-fetched. Now let me help so we can take a walk," she said with a wink.

Chapter Twenty-One

RIDING DRAGONS

Mallory skipped out on cleanup and raced down to the beach. Entering the frigid water very slowly, the teen carefully picked her way through the nasty rocks along the shore, pulling up her shorts as she moved out further. Mallory was standing knee-deep on a sandbar, gazing out over the lake when she sensed Torryn and Araa and whirled around so fast she almost plunged face-first into the freezing water.

"You again?" she shouted in irritation as the pair shimmered into view. Mallory looked toward the house hoping to see reinforcements headed their way but sighed and looked back at the dragons. No one was there, but she had to do something! Her legs were numb from the cold, and she was shivering and getting colder by the second.

"Get over it, Mal!" she grumbled and headed back. Wading to shore was even trickier than coming out because she had to keep her eyes on the huge beasts but still try to avoid those obnoxious rocks. She tripped several times but made it back without taking a dive.

As Mallory drew closer to the beach, she recognized how truly striking they were. With her toes still under water, the girl paused then squared her shoulders and bravely marched up to confront the two dragons.

Torryn and Araa waited patiently, hoping Whitney's friend

would adjust to their presence if they allowed her to make the first move. Sure enough, Mallory appeared to relax the closer she came. They both grinned down at the small person glaring up at them, trying to act so courageous. "Hello again, Mallory," Araa said gently.

"Woah, give me a minute!" the girl said, taking a step back.

Torryn winked and said, "Your courage reminds me of young Whitney."

Feeling her face heat up, Mallory stammered, "Whitney warned me about you! She said you're a big flirt!" Looking at Araa, then back down to the indignant young woman, Torryn grinned.

"I take that as a compliment! Would you like to sit and talk a bit while we wait for the others?" Araa asked, stretching the length of her long body into the sand.

Mallory watched as the larger dragon who called himself Torryn settled next to his wife and suddenly felt her defenses fall away. Sitting across from their two rather large heads, Mallory prompted, "Can you describe your first encounter with Whitney?"

• • •

They were still talking about life on Yagdi as the others joined them. "I'd like to get to Yagdi someday!" Mallory announced. "It sounds beautiful!"

"That can certainly be arranged, my dear girl!" Ursula chuckled. "How about we get Whitney and Edward back, then we can discuss a reunion on Yagdi. How does that sound?"

"Perfect!" Mallory said, jumping up. "How far is it to where we're going?"

"Just down this peninsula, about a mile," Randolph answered.

"I have an idea!" Torryn began. "May I suggest Araa, Aiden and I carry the four humans on our backs? It'll save us time!"

"I'd love that!" Mallory shouted, then added shyly. "Can I ride on you, Torryn?"

"That can also be arranged," he winked and grinned to see the flush of red move from her neck to her hairline.

"My friends, what a wonderful idea!" Ursula agreed. "The rest of us can meet you there."

"That'll take hours!" Mallory complained, eyeing the three elderly people.

Susan walked up to Aiden's parents and Araa smiled. "How very special it is to formally meet Whitney's mother! Our earlier arrival was disrupted by unexpected company walking the beach, so we had to depart far too quickly. Susan, your daughter is remarkable, and so very heroic. She must make you incredibly proud!"

That's all Susan needed. Returning Araa's smile with one of her own, she said, "From one mother to another, I agree that Whitney is a very special young woman, but so is Aiden. A special young dragon that is. We all hope to instill enough in our children so they can grow into individuals who make us proud, don't we? I believe that you, Torryn, and I have done an exceptional job thus far, based on who our children are becoming."

"I can see where Whitney gets her sense of decency and confidence," Torryn said in a low melodic voice. "She means very much to our family, but our entire small world shares our appreciation for your daughter's and Edward's brave, unselfish actions. Whitney and Edward were critical in our efforts to restore and keep peace on Yagdi." Pausing to look at Araa and Aiden, he continued, "Thank you for sharing them with us."

Jerome and Cathy were more cautious and maintained their distance. However, they were as eager as Susan to start planning, and anxious to get to Ellie's Point, so they nodded at each other and moved in to join the group.

"Now that we've all properly met, can we please get down to

business? There is much to discuss and much planning to be done!" Mergan announced impatiently.

Randolph laughed at his predictable friend. "I think that's wise, given the circumstances. And I for one don't mind walking the short distance."

Nodding in agreement, Torryn said, "Good! We'll meet you three and Ellie at the point. If Mallory's flying on my back, may I suggest Susan ride on Aiden as her daughter has done in the past while Jerome and Cathy jump on Araa."

"I don't know about riding anywhere on the back of a dragon!" Jerome grumbled nervously.

"I for one can't wait!" Susan exclaimed excitedly. "That just gets us there quicker so we can begin making plans. Plus, I'll get to share an experience with my daughter."

"Good point!" Cathy agreed. "I'm in. Come on, grandpa."

Once everyone was settled, the dragons soared into the sky, but stayed just over the waves to avoid detection. "Whoa there!" Jerome shouted, surprised when Araa shot into the sky. "I never enjoyed carnival rides! Too hard on the stomach!" he admitted.

"You sound just like Edward!" Aiden roared.

"Loons!" Cathy said, pointing to the large black and white bird who'd just surfaced with a fish in her long beak. Three chicks popped up immediately after, proudly displaying their small minnows. The hungry loons quickly gulped down their meals, then ducked their heads under, searching for more.

Sensing a disturbance, the mother loon looked up and discovered they had company. She lifted her body out of the water flapping her wings in warning, then they all dove under and disappeared. As if in farewell, Torryn changed direction. Tipping his huge wings, the dragon led the group off the water and over the peninsula to Ellie's Point.

"Look!" Mallory shouted, pointing to the strange animals racing out of the trees just below them. In her excitement, the teen lost her balance and began slipping precariously to one side. "No!" she screamed, frantically trying to stabilize herself by digging her fingers between the overlapping scales on Torryn's broad back.

Torryn wouldn't have allowed his passenger to fall, but to reassure his inexperienced rider, the dragon shifted his massive body. When Mallory slid back to the center and settled in, he turned his head and winked.

Choosing to ignore his teasing, she yelled, "Torryn! There's a polar bear and a panther down there, and it looks like they're tracking us! And get this! Mergan and Randolph are chasing them! But they're so old! Why would they be doing such a crazy thing?"

Getting no response, she shrugged her shoulders and sat back to enjoy the ride, muttering, "Guess if Torryn's not concerned, I shouldn't be either!"

Soon she felt as if she'd grown up on the backs of dragons. She loosened her grip then let go entirely and spread her arms wide. "So, this is our world from the eyes of a dragon!" she shouted as her knees instinctively tightened to hold her in place.

"Are you laughing at me?" she yelled as Torryn's belly started quivering.

"This intriguing young human seems perfectly suited to voyages atop dragons!" Torryn thought as they approached the end of the peninsula.

The ride was over way too soon. Throwing one leg over Torryn's back, Mallory quickly dismounted then helped her grandparents. "What's going on around here?" she demanded, turning to stare at the approaching bear and panther.

"We warned you there would be more to unveil, Mallory. Meet Traveller and Ellie, two more members of 'Team Whitney and Edward,'" Susan explained.

"Cover your eyes!" Traveller warned. In a brilliant flash of light, she quickly transformed into Ursula while Ellie returned to her small stature and walked in and out of Mallory's legs, purring contentedly. Finally, she sat down and looked up at the girl with big oval eyes, begging to be picked up.

Unable to resist, Mallory bent down and picked her up. "You'll just have to give me time to figure this out!" she whispered into the soft fur around her neck.

"Ah, so you've had a chance to meet two more Yagdians," Mergan said, grinning impishly when she frowned. "For your information, I too hail from that small world. While Randolph is also a wizard with deep Yagdian roots, our dear dream jumper was born and raised on Earth."

Noticing the two old men weren't even breathing hard, the teen stared curiously at the assembled group. "I think I've seen and experienced quite enough strange things for one day! So, if there's more, please save the rest for later!" she cautioned.

"I promised Randolph and Mergan they could have some fun showing off their talents for you," Ursula answered. "However, I think you're right to suggest we continue this later. We need to focus on getting the kids home. As we begin, Cathy and Jerome can answer questions that might arise. Can you live with that for now, young lady?"

"I guess," Mallory mumbled.

As they walked into the clearing surrounding the ancient pine, Torryn pulled the wizards aside. "I believe you might already be aware of this, but that young lady has undiscovered talents! While hesitant at first, she adjusted quickly and rode on my back as if born to do so!"

"Interesting observation indeed!" Mergan said, winking at Randolph. "We have observed some peculiar reactions as well, haven't we my dear earth wizard."

Chapter Twenty-Two

PROCEED WITH CAUTION

Sitting on a stump in the shade of the ancient pine, Mallory was surprised when Susan approached the massive tree, and more surprised when her grandparents followed. She watched curiously as they flattened their hands against the trunk and bowed their heads. It seemed like forever, but they finally turned and joined the rest.

"Grandma, what was that about?"

"The ancient tree we're sitting under hides the portal to Yagdi. Whitney and Edward are trapped somewhere inside," Ursula explained.

"What?" Mallory shouted, jumping up. Running over to the tree, she touched the trunk's rough bark and whispered, "Edward, Mallory, are you in there?"

Mergan was surprised he felt so protective of this young lady. Awkwardly putting his hand on her shoulder, he said softly, "They can't hear you, but we have a way to communicate with them. Would you like to try right now?"

For the first time in her entire life, Mallory couldn't find the words. Looking up at the wizard through tear-filled eyes, she just nodded.

"I'd say that's a yes if I ever saw one!" Taking Mallory's hand in his, he reached his other hand out toward Randolph and Susan. "Shall we?"

They jumped up to join Mergan and Mallory, and immediately wrapped their arms around the tree. Randolph once again placed the stone between his hand and Susan's, then put the skeleton key in the other and reached out for Mallory. Mergan completed the circle, and they began the familiar chant.

"Whitney, Edward, are you there?" Randolph commanded. Surprised by the change in his voice, Mallory looked toward Randolph, but his eyes were closed, and he was frowning in concentration, so she closed her own and just waited.

Suddenly, she heard her brother and shouted, "Edward! Edward is that you?" That shocked the others so much they almost let go but managed to hang onto each other and just let Mallory talk.

"Mal? Is that you?" Edward yelled in response.

Shocked that Mallory could hear her brother, Randolph looked down and gasped. The old skeleton key between their hands was glowing, just as the stone shone between his hand and Susan's.

"Yes! It's me all right! How dare you go on such an adventure without me!" she quipped, trying to keep from crying.

Edward heard the quiver in her voice and understood. His sister had to be just as shocked and sad as he was.

"I sure wish it was under better circumstances, but it's so good to hear your voice, Mal!"

"Likewise, Eddy!" she cried. "Is Whit there with you?"

"I'm here, Mal!" Whitney said tentatively. "I didn't want to interrupt you two."

"Are you kidding me? You're my hero, Whitney! I'm so glad you two have each other! I'm here with your gang of five plus Aiden's parents. They've made Susan, grandma, and grandpa honorary members of the alliance. Everybody misses you terribly! But with Mergan and Ursula cracking the whip, I have no doubt we'll come up with a plan to break you out soon!"

"I like that, Mal! A break-out! So, you've met everyone,

eh?" Edward encouraged. "Spill it. Did you survive all the introductions?"

"Of course!" his sister said, sounding more confident than she felt. "But I have to admit, today was full of surprises, and I'm still trying to wrap my head around everything!"

"Sounds about right, girlfriend!" Whitney agreed. "I feel your pain, and if Edward manned up, he'd agree!" she added, grinning at her friend.

"Hey, just give it time! They're all the good guys you definitely need on your side! Just sit back and enjoy the ride!" Edward suggested.

"How can I enjoy anything when you and Whitney are lost somewhere in this tree?"

"You've just met the best minds and strongest allies in two worlds!" Whitney said emphatically. "While your brother and I are planning a way out of here, you guys will be scheming a way in, so we should be home in no time!"

Susan tried to be patient, knowing Mallory needed some time with her brother, but she couldn't wait any longer. "Whitney, Edward it's me!"

"Mom!" Whitney shouted. "You're here too, that's great! Hey, did Torryn wink at you?" Whitney asked conspiratorially.

"Yes!" Mallory groaned. "Talk about embarrassing!"

"I didn't get the wink," Susan admitted. "But I just took a ride on Aiden's back, so we have an adventure to share when you get home!"

"Wow! That's so cool, Mom! Wait until you take a ride over Yagdi, now that's something else!"

"Your mom was on Aiden while I rode on Torryn," Mallory continued, "And gram and gramps rode double on Araa. Get this, I almost fell off while we were flying to Ellie's Point because I looked down to see a polar bear and a panther racing below us with these two old wizards chasing them. They almost kept up too!"

"Who are you calling old?" the wizards exclaimed together in protest.

"Sounds like you're having your own adventure!" Edward jumped in. "Whitney, remember our crazy ride from the campground to Ellie's Point, with Randolph shooting missiles at those creepy, red-eyed mist creatures?"

"Yeah, unfortunately I do. Seriously Mal, I promise we'll tell you that story, and many more soon! But for now, I'm so proud of all of you! You've taken in a lot in a short period of time! Most would've been running for cover!"

"Edward's grandparents and I considered that a time or two, especially when Aiden revealed himself," Susan admitted. "Mallory adjusted pretty quickly!"

"How can anyone fear kind souls like Aiden and his parents?" Mallory demanded.

"None whose hearts are filled with kindness!" Araa said gently. She'd approached quietly and stood right behind Mallory.

"That's true," Mallory admitted. "But I don't hold kindness in my heart for anyone who wishes to harm my brother or Whitney! In fact, I pity anyone who tries to tell me differently!"

Mergan smiled. "I continue to admire your spunk, young lady!"

"My dear girl, there isn't one among us who feels any differently," Ursula said with calm confidence. "We all have good hearts but will defend the innocent and those we love with terrifying swiftness our enemies have learned to fear."

Torryn roared ferociously, sending fire bolts into the sky over Lake Superior.

"I'm glad you're on our team, flame thrower!" Mallory yelled, then relayed what had just happened.

"Mallory, can you ask your brother if they've tried using our small tokens?" Araa whispered.

Tamping down her curiosity, Mallory shared her message.

"Tell Araa and Torryn everything's working now, including their tokens, but only if we're under my dome," Edward answered. "That's a start!"

Torryn came up behind Mergan and hissed urgently, "Araa and I must leave immediately. Something has come up that needs our attention. If it proves to be important, we'll let you know."

Mergan frowned as he watched the dragons disappear. "I hope their emergency has nothing to do with the safety of our young chosen ones."

"Funny creature, that Patrick!" Whitney said, changing the subject. "He's suspicious of the dome now. He can't see it, so he walks toward us with his arms out, feeling for it."

"Anyway," Edward added, "We're really glad Ursula suggested the dome. We feel much safer, and we're grateful for the privacy!"

"One other interesting piece of news!" Whitney interrupted. "Sorry I keep breaking in, Edward!"

"We're all used to it, Whit! Carry on!"

Susan noticed Ursula, Aiden, Ellie, and Edward's grandparents had moved in closer, as if it might allow them to hear better. "I think I speak for all of us, kids. We're just grateful we can communicate! It's reassuring to hear your voices. Let's make sure it happens often, so we don't sit around worrying!"

"Sounds like a very wise plan!" Whitney answered. "I do have good news to share. I haven't felt the stones on my necklace heat up since we fell through the portal. So, we suspect something down here is interfering with our ability to communicate. But here's the really important news. We were sitting under our shield, and my stones became super warm just before Patrick showed up! It's amazing they work again while we're under the dome! But maybe more importantly, don't you think it's pretty telling they heated just as the trickster showed up?"

"That's very interesting indeed," Randolph agreed, sharing her report with the others.

Ursula jumped in excitedly, "Tell the kids that was a worthwhile experiment, and I'm glad they still work. But they need warnings like that all the time! How about experimenting a little? Suggest to Edward it might be beneficial to see if he could create a portable, traveling dome, just for when they move about. That might make all of us feel better about their risky excursions."

"Wow! That's a great idea!" Whitney said excitedly when Randolph relayed the message.

Casting a worried glance toward Mergan and Randolph, Ursula cautioned, "Randolph, please remind Whitney and Edward to be very wary of Patrick.

"We thought the same thing, Ursula," Edward answered. "Could one very capable liaison please tell everyone not to worry? We promise to use our heads before jumping in!"

Ursula wasn't quite finished. "Randolph, tell them that as careful as we try to be, anyone, myself included, can still miss important things! I caution them to be aware of that and double and triple check all of their decisions as much as they can!"

"Got it!" Whitney said to Randolph. "Tell Ursula she's very wise and her strategic mind is just what we need right now."

"If time permits, Whitney and I will run every plan we make by you first. How does that sound?" Edward promised.

"Whitney, listen to Ursula and listen to your mother," Susan said sternly. "You must both be very, very careful!"

"Got it, Mom!"

"If there's nothing more for now, we need to strategize to get you home, then Mergan and I have business to attend to in my cellar," Randolph said.

Looking truly mystified about everything she'd heard, Mallory volunteered, "I'll fill gram and gramps in on all the news."

Satisfied their alliance was hard at work to rescue them, Whitney and Edward reluctantly said their goodbyes.

Chapter Twenty-Three

CLUES IN THE CELLAR

Using his skeleton key, Randolph opened the door to his rock shop and guided Mergan to the cellar door. "I'm still curious about the key's reaction to Mallory at the portal," he mused. "I'm convinced that girl has gifts!"

"I'm quite certain as well. Maybe they'll grow stronger and become more apparent to Mallory as we continue," Mergan suggested.

"Be careful! The stairs are treacherous!" Randolph warned as he flipped the light on. "Mom had this door sealed up when I was just a child, and it stayed shut until the power company claimed they needed access to the primary electric box down here."

Mergan looked at his friend quizzically. There had to be a story behind Randolph's cryptic explanation, and he couldn't wait to hear it. But for now, he just grumbled and followed Randolph down the stairs.

Hitting a low beam with his head, he yelled, "This is a crime, man! Why have you never bothered to bring your shop into the twenty-first century!" And rubbed his head all the way to the basement.

"I don't come down here very often. Why spend hard-earned money renovating a dingy basement I never see?" Randolph answered, distracted with navigating the stairs.

After dragging twenty old boxes across the cracked concrete

floor to the center of the room, they sat down on the two folding chairs they'd set up under the only light bulb.

Wiping the dust off the box marked "Heirlooms," Mergan sneezed three times. Pulling out a hanky to blow his nose, he grumbled, "I can't believe all the dust and cobwebs down here! You really need to clean this place up, Earth Wizard."

"Maybe someday," Randolph sighed patiently as he dragged a box labeled "Family" between his knees. The light was rather dim but provided enough to see the contents of each of their open boxes.

"This cellar holds frightening memories for me," Randolph murmured, sifting through old pipes and empty decorative treasure boxes. "So, I haven't been down here for a very long time. But thanks to you and Ursula, I discovered I was a wizard and needed to learn more about my family. That's the only reason I'm here now!"

Studying his friend carefully, Mergan said, "Okay, I get it. But can you tell me what happened to you? It had to be traumatic for you to remember an event that happened so long ago."

"Mom caught me looking through these very boxes and got extremely upset! She grabbed my ear, dragged me up the stairs, and slammed the door shut. Pointing her finger in my face, she yelled, 'Never venture into the cellar again! Do you understand, young man?'"

"You haven't been a kid for a very long time, Mergan," he grinned teasingly. "Neither have I for that matter. However, I assume you remember how curious kids can be, and I was no exception. I *had* to return to this cellar because mom forbade it."

"I snuck down here a few days later. I thought I'd been smart and covered my tracks, but parents seem to have an inner alarm when their kids disobey. Sure enough, she caught me nose-deep in one of these boxes and screamed, 'You disobeyed me!' She grabbed my ear once again, and back up the stairs we went.

Shortly after that, dad bricked up the doorway. I didn't think this cellar held anything of significance, so I simply ignored it, that is until my recent discovery."

"That's quite a regrettable story, my friend!" Mergan said sympathetically. "Was this yours by chance?" he asked, pulling out a baby rattle. "If so, you were a powerful chewer! Look at all the bite marks on this thing! Does your family history include golden retrievers?" he asked chuckling.

"Yeah, yeah, enough with the jokes. Let's stay on task," Randolph said good-humoredly. "This looks interesting!" he murmured, pulling out a rolled-up sheet of architect paper. Getting down on his knees he rolled it out on the floor and leaned in for a closer look. It was their family tree, and his dad had hastily written his name across the lower right corner in cursive.

"Look at this, Mergan," he said excitedly, pointing to the paper. "That's my dad's signature at the bottom." Scanning the dates and names, he gasped and pointed. "Mergan, did you by chance know an Edna and Charles Southgate?"

"Well, I'll be!" Mergan gasped and got up to pace. "I remember Edna clearly! Are you saying she's a distant relative of yours?"

"She's right here on top of my family tree!" Randolph said, getting up to face Mergan. "My great grandfather's grandfather and grandmother founded this city in 1843. Before moving into town, my family lived out in the country not far from here. In fact, if I remember correctly, they settled near Susan and Whitney's place, out on the peninsula by our damaged portal!"

"Mergan, could there be a connection between that old Michigan White Pine Tree and my family? It can't just be a coincidence they homesteaded so close to the point!" Growing more excited, the earth wizard looked anxiously at his friend. "Were my great grandfather's great grandmother, Edna, and great grandfather, Charles, banished from Yagdi?"

It was obvious his friend needed time to contemplate this

intriguing development, but Randolph was too eager to wait for answers. "Spill it, old man! What do you know about my ancestors?"

"Sit down and we'll figure this out," Mergan suggested, trying to collect his thoughts. "Edna was a major player in our long-ago battle between wizard clans. Her clan was all about themselves and gaining riches and power, but our group defeated them."

Mergan had another sneezing fit that prompted the wizard to pull out his hanky once again and blow his nose. "Now where was I?" he asked, folding it and putting it back in his pocket. "After their defeat, Edna and her clan were given two options, and chose to leave Yagdi forever, rather than live in the desert on the far side of our world. We never heard from any of them again, and we all assumed they'd perished."

"I wish I could provide more information," he added apologetically. "There were a few crazy Yagdians who reported seeing Edna's clan near our southern mountain range just after they were banished. But we deemed that impossible because our elders had positioned trusted spies near the departure site. They were tasked to make sure the clan left then report the welcome news immediately after. All went as expected."

"You know, now that I think about it," Mergan continued, "those crazy sightings weren't far from Sylern's nest!" Suddenly intrigued, the wizard stared at Randolph and said, "You don't suppose Edna and her group could've been hiding somewhere nearby all along, do you?"

Rolling up his family tree, Randolph stood and turned to Mergan, "What are the chances Torryn and Araa could send scouts to Sylern's abandoned stronghold to check the area for activity?"

"They'd have to be chosen carefully for stealth and their ability to keep information they uncover from leaking into the wrong hands," Mergan answered as he stood up excitedly. "May I suggest you stay here and look for anything you can find on your relatives, particularly Edna and Charles. While you're doing that, I'll contact Torryn and Araa."

Heading for the stairs, he muttered, "Hold on!" and turned back to Randolph. "Aiden's father pulled me aside earlier today. He was going to follow up on something that he admitted 'could be important!' Wouldn't that be interesting if there was something mysterious going on near Sylern's old hangout? I need to go, Randolph, but let's keep in touch and meet back at Susan's for dinner and compare notes." With that, he raced up the stairs mumbling, "Ursula's going to be quite interested in this piece of news!"

"That wizard can move quickly and without grumbling when he needs to!" Randolph chuckled, watching Mergan fly up the stairs. "Maybe Mallory's exuberance is wearing off on our dear friend!" he thought, hearing the grumpy man whistle as he walked through the store, and out the door.

Hoping for more revelations, Randolph returned to his task and eagerly sifted through the contents of more than a dozen boxes. He was sorely disappointed to uncover nothing of significance. Setting the last box on the floor in front of his chair, Randolph sighed and sat down. Taking his time, he looked at it carefully and noticed the flaps were torn, as if they'd been opened and shut many times. "Do I dare hope there's something in here besides baby rattles and deeds to places that no longer exist?" he murmured.

Opening the frayed cardboard gingerly, he discovered a rectangular package wrapped in threadbare muslin cloth. "Someone must have considered this item important because they took the time to wrap it. And it's surprisingly heavy," Randolph observed as he lifted it out of the box and set it in his lap. His fingers shook with anticipation, so he took great care unwrapping what remained of the frayed material. "This looks very old," he murmured, gazing curiously at the cover. It was a photo album, worn and tattered with age. But the gold lettering near the top was still legible, even under layers of dust.

"Southgate Family! I wonder if this could be what we need!" he gasped opening the cover. Old black and white images of two people glared up at him, as if annoyed by the unexpected and unwelcome intrusion. "Edna Southgate, Leader, and Charles Southgate, deceased," he read, running his fingers over each picture.

"Charles died," he muttered sadly, lowering his head to mourn the passing of an ancient relative he'd never known. After a few moments, he solemnly touched Charles' face then wrapped the album in old Christmas wrapping paper that happened to be lying nearby. "This holds important information! I must get back to the others!" he yelled and raced up the stairs.

• • •

"Christmas present?" Mergan grinned, looking pointedly at Randolph's package wrapped in green tissue paper decorated with Christmas trees.

"Everybody, gather around! We must contact Whitney and Edward immediately!" Randolph shouted as he ran into the dining room, ignoring Mergan's jab. Gently placing his package on the table, he removed the wrapping paper, then grinned triumphantly and stood back.

"An old photo album!" Ursula exclaimed, walking between the two wizards. "Your family? And doesn't that say 'Southgate' on the cover?" she asked, getting excited.

"It is my family, and it does indeed appear my distant relatives were part of an ancient wizard clan!" Randolph said, opening the cover. "Meet Edna and Charles Southgate, my great grandfather's great grandmother and great grandfather."

Nodding toward Mergan, he pointed to the two portraits

staring up at them and announced, "These are the faces behind the family tree the wizard and I discovered earlier today."

"That's her all right!" Mergan marveled, turning to Ursula. "My dear friend, this is the leader of one of the banished ancient wizard clans!"

"Oh my!" Ursula gasped, sitting down to stare at the album. She gazed into their faces for a long time then looked up at Randolph. "This must bring both joy and unease to your heart, my friend."

"No matter what disquiet this brings," Mergan said encouragingly, "you have uncovered a treasure trove of information we must delve into right away, my dear wizard. But first things first. My stomach's telling me it's almost dinner time, how about we celebrate with Mexican food tonight?"

"Cathy and Jerome are in town getting dinner as we speak," Susan announced, walking into the dining room. "I'll call in your requests!" But she noticed their intense expressions and frowned. "You look concerned and excited at the same time," she said, walking over to the album. "Who are Edna and Charles Southgate?"

"Those just happen to be my distant relatives!" Randolph answered with a gleam in his eyes. "If Mergan is correct, they were members of a wizard clan banished from Yagdi over a hundred years ago. This could provide clues for our young chosen ones. If by some miracle Edna is the leader Patrick claims to have met, then we must tell them she's a distant relative of mine."

He turned to Mergan and Ursula with a questioning look. "I just wish there was some way to share these photos with them. Any ideas?"

"That's a challenge worthy of consideration!" Mergan said, frowning and pulling on his lip. "There has to be a way. We just need to uncover it. In the meantime, my brain could use nourishment! Since you're taking requests, a 'Hungry Man's Platter' for me! And make sure it includes tamales, tacos and enchiladas!" he added, rubbing his stomach enthusiastically as he sat down.

"Are you certain one platter will be enough?" Ursula joked as Randolph and Susan rolled their eyes.

But Mergan was already engrossed in Randolph's photos and didn't respond. "There's Hector! I remember that nasty wizard!" he growled, turning to another page.

"One 'Hungry Man's Combo Platter' with tamales, tacos and enchiladas coming up," Susan said as she placed the call. While waiting for Cathy to pick up, she tapped Mergan's shoulder. "Do you have a second choice, just in case?" she hissed.

"No second choices!" he barked without looking up. "I'll buy the ingredients and deliver them to the chef myself if need be!"

"Cathy?" Susan said, holding up her hand to shush everyone.

"I'm here Susan but...STOP! TURN AROUND!" she yelled.

"All right! All right!" Susan could hear the crunch of gravel as Jerome turned the car around.

"Cathy, what's going on?" Susan asked nervously, putting her cell on speaker so everyone could hear. *"Cathy, what's going on and where are you?"*

"There it is!" Cathy shrieked. They heard tires squealing then Jerome shouted, "That's him all right!"

"Cathy, talk to me!" Susan demanded.

"Susan, we just saw that horrible old man who threatened all of us in your driveway a few weeks ago! Do you remember? The man who didn't look quite right in human clothes?"

After a moment of stunned silence, the room erupted. "Don't approach him!" Randolph yelled. "He's extremely dangerous! Just get out of there!"

"But he's right here, only a mile or so from your house!" Cathy warned. "We caught him skulking in the bushes!"

"Aiden, don't do it!" Ursula screamed trying to intercept the dog before he got out of the house. Unfortunately, she was too slow, and arrived on the deck just as Aiden transitioned into a dragon. She watched in dismay as he flew straight up from the beach then shot toward town. He was moving so fast and so high the young dragon was a blur even to Ursula's keen eyes.

Walking back into the room, Ursula cried, "Aiden just went after Sylern!" and dropped into a chair.

"Ursula, please explain what just happened," Susan asked nervously, sitting down next to her.

"I shouted for Aiden to stop, but he kept going!" she cried. "That horrible creature is the very one who kidnapped your daughter, Susan. He escaped the wrath of our young king on Yagdi, and I think he has regretted that ever since."

Pulling her chair around to face Susan, Ursula continued, "Aiden looked so grim! I fear he'll do everything in his power to capture that creature, and the confrontation has me very concerned!"

"I get that you're worried, Ursula, but I want that thing punished for what it did to Whitney!" Susan responded angrily.

"Rest assured, if our young dragon is successful, that's exactly what will happen!" the elderly woman promised, squeezing Susan's hand reassuringly.

Realizing they had to act quickly, Ursula stood up and took charge. "Mergan, you said you just spoke with Torryn and Araa. Can you reach them again? We must tell them Sylern's here!"

"On it! I'll meet them on the beach and explain the situation!" Mergan shouted as he pushed the door open and raced out. The small group jumped nervously when it slammed shut then settled around the table to wait for news.

"Let's go find Jerome and Cathy," Susan urged, picking up her keys. They were almost to the front door when it flew open and Edward's grandparents piled in, both talking at once.

"Hold it!" Jerome shouted, turning to Cathy. "How about I explain, and you share any details I've left out?"

When Cathy nodded, he turned to the group. "You're never going to believe what happened after we hung up! That creature leaped into the air and took off like a missile. But our dragon appeared out of nowhere and pulled him out of the sky! It was an unbelievable battle. Aiden gave as much as he got, but Sylern hung in there until the bitter end! I never saw such long claws in my life! I admit Cathy and I looked away several times because we were so worried for Aiden and couldn't do anything to help. Both beasts dug into each other with fangs, biting into shoulders, backs, anything they could reach!"

"Thank goodness, Aiden was the victor! He's dragging the other beast over all the gravel he can find, much to that thing's dismay," Cathy finished.

"We heard the creature crying out in pain as we turned the car around," Jerome added, taking the food from Cathy. "We'd already gotten dinner and were headed back when we saw 'em! I'm thinking we may have to put that on hold. Aiden and our uninvited guest should be here any minute!"

"Just put it in the fridge!" Susan agreed grimly. "I suspect you're right. We won't be eating anytime soon!"

Chapter Twenty-Four
INTERROGATING A MONSTER

They needed to inform Whitney and Edward immediately, so for the sake of time, Susan and Randolph joined hands without including Mergan, and hoped they'd still connect.

"Let's hope that beast didn't hear anything of importance, but who knows how long Sylern's been skulking around us? If he heard where the kids are, it could spell doom!" Mergan moaned, pacing back and forth in front of the fireplace.

"Indeed, if they don't respond right away, I'll be very concerned!" Ursula admitted.

They kept their eyes glued on Randolph and Susan, but there was too much nervous energy in the room for anyone to sit down.

"Whitney, Edward, we need to talk!" Randolph repeated urgently.

"That's the fifth time," Susan muttered, looking nervously at the earth wizard.

"Randolph, we're here. You sound upset. What's going on?" Edward finally answered, detecting his serious tone. "Sorry for the delay. We were down by the waterfall and didn't hear."

"So glad to hear your voice. I'm assuming Whitney's right there too?"

"Yeah, I'm here!" she answered right away, then waited.

"Right to the point, both of you. That's what's needed at this moment! Let me explain!" Randolph continued.

"First, we're all safe and glad you're both okay too!" Susan said with relief.

"Glad to hear that, but something's going on. Fill us in!" Whitney said anxiously.

"Edward, your grandparents just saw Sylern!" Susan said, looking at Cathy and Jerome. "We wanted you to know that monster is here! Aiden captured him and he's dragging him to the house as we speak."

"Hope he's finding every jagged rock along the way!" Whitney said. Remembering the evil creature's demonic smile was enough to send shivers through her entire body!

"That's exactly what he's doing!" Randolph answered hurriedly. "However, our fear is he may have been lurking around here the past couple of days and heard your location. If he's connected to the wizard clan Patrick speaks of, he may have already relayed that information.

"Randolph, tell them I've contacted Aiden's parents, and they insist on helping us interrogate our prisoner. In fact, they sound eager to do so! They've rounded up a few trusted scouts and sent them to the beast's deserted stronghold to do a little reconnaissance. They might come up with something useful," Mergan said, then continued pacing nervously around the small room.

"Aiden's here!" Jerome yelled and looked to Ursula, figuring the head of the alliance could take it from there.

"Please be careful, kids!" Susan pleaded.

"We need to cut this short and take care of business. We'll contact you shortly!" Randolph promised, racing out of the room with the rest of them.

Spurred into action by Sylern's anguished cries the group raced frantically down the stairs and reached the beach just as Torryn and Araa shimmered into view.

"What on earth is that?" Mallory cried out as she got her first look at the beast.

"That, my dear, is the creature who captured Whitney!" Torryn said striding toward his son. Towering over the prisoner, he commanded, "Stand up at once!"

"I think I'm fine just where I am!" their old enemy one mumbled insolently.

Aiden growled and tightened his chokehold around their captive's neck and smiled with satisfaction when the beast started gagging and clawing at his hands. Batting Sylern's fists away the young dragon watched his parents lumber toward them menacingly. Their eyes gleamed with the promise of revenge and Aiden knew they intended to inflict great harm on their enemy.

"Let's interrogate first, then we can finish him off!" the young dragon suggested, his ear-to-ear grin looking every bit as vengeful as his parents.

Spreading his huge, muscular wings, the ancient tried to bluff his captors. "No one has ever held me prisoner for long! I will avenge your outrageous behavior and believe me I know of many creative ways to do so!" he growled threateningly.

Eager to accept Sylern's challenge, the dragons moved in. His bluff also backfired with the one holding him around his neck because he felt Aiden's grip tighten even more, making him extremely uncomfortable and unable to move.

The ancient one squirmed and tried to step back but was surrounded before he could do so! Although Sylern stood an impressive ten feet tall, the dragons were much larger and towered over him!

"Didn't get away this time, did you?" Torryn taunted, ignoring Sylern's attempts at intimidation.

Throwing her hands up, Mallory cried, "Doesn't anything look normal around here? Is there something in this Lake Superior water that turns ordinary creatures into freaks of nature?"

"Many of us look quite different indeed, young one. However, our heritage is the cause, rather than Lake Superior," Ursula answered with a patient smile.

"Mallory, please let them continue!" Susan interrupted impatiently. "I for one want to see justice for my daughter. This beast must pay for causing Whitney such grief!"

"All right, I'm sorry!" Mallory murmured, keeping her eyes on Aiden's captive while she moved between her grandparents.

"Are you ready to give us answers?" Torryn demanded with a contemptuous sneer.

"Or what?" Sylern goaded, taking a chance they were all too kind to hurt him.

Proving their intent was deadly serious, father and son lifted their heads and roared, then stepped in far too close for the beast's comfort. With a surprised gasp, Sylern once again tried to back up, but Aiden snapped his jaws menacingly and squeezed his neck tighter. "We have reliable sources and do not need your information. Even if you offered, we would seriously doubt your sincerity!" the young king answered. "However, if you surrender, we may consider alternatives to your future that aren't quite so bleak."

"Either way," Torryn added, "Our new king has captured you with no hope for escape, and I suggest you keep that in mind as you decide your next move!"

"We have a few questions before you finish him!" Mergan growled. "These are my friends, Sylern," he began. "You know the power I have, and I surround myself with those of similar strength. As Aiden suggested, there may be more palatable alternatives for your future if you answer truthfully. What do you say?"

"Depends on what you demand. I can't promise anything!" Sylern snarled.

"We have only three questions. Do you work for the wizard clan, specifically Edna Southgate? When did you return to skulk around us *and* what have you heard?"

"Ah! You've heard of Edna? That surprises me! That clan leader's been quite careful to keep herself and her clan's activities hidden in the tunnels for decades," Sylern admitted, giving away much more than he should have.

Ignoring the valuable information, Susan shouted, "You captured my daughter once and I won't let you harm one hair on her head ever again!"

Grinning deviously, Sylern took the opportunity to play with the woman. "Your daughter and her friend will be in big trouble when I return and share their location with Edna! Don't expect to ever see Whitney again!"

Susan gasped then lunged at the beast in a rage before anyone could stop her. Grabbing the tip of the closest wing, she squeezed and wrenched with all her strength until she felt bones break between her fingers.

"How dare you!" he roared as deadly fangs sprang from his mouth. But his pain was so distracting he wasn't fast enough to use them before Ursula swooped Whitney's mother away.

Sensing defeat, Sylern decided to take a different course and sat down in the sand. He stared at each of his enemies with keenly intelligent, hawk-like eyes, then rested his head on two clawed fists, as if he'd given up.

But his act fooled no one, and they were ready for his attack. "Look out!" Torryn yelled, pushing Araa out of the way just as the beast whipped its tail around. Striking with deadly accuracy, the sharp, triangular barb sitting at the end of his tail sliced a deep gouge in the sand where Araa had been standing.

Sylern turned to Susan with a cold, calculating smile, revealing row after row of long, dagger-sharp teeth. Susan was so distracted, she wasn't prepared when his tongue shot out of his mouth like a serpent. Before the poisoned tip struck her cheek, Aiden grabbed it and pulled. Sylern's eyes widened, and he began gagging and squirming. "Give it up, Sylern! I won't allow you to hurt any of my friends! However, I might let you live long enough to drag any measly information you may have into the open. And we can do so with or without pain. It's entirely up to you!" the enraged young dragon roared. He only let go when Sylern went limp and cried, "I surrender!"

Confident their dragons were capable of countering any of Sylern's moves, the rest moved to safety to let them focus on the task at hand without the distraction of worrying about them. They watched Torryn take a silken cloth from around his ankle, blow on it then wrap it around their prisoner's wrists.

"These hurt!" Sylern complained, pulling, and twisting at his constraints. But the cloth bands had powerful dragon magic and sprung back into position like a rubber band after each anxious contortion.

"What now?" the monster mumbled. While he appeared to have given up, his eyes were filled with hate, so no one lowered their guard.

Suddenly, Ursula transformed into an equally powerful beast, and the huge polar bear menacingly approached her enemy. "You will do everything we say without question and without delay!" she growled menacingly.

Looking toward the dragons, she prompted, "Torryn and Araa, can you share what you've put into action, and update us on their progress? It may very well persuade our prisoner it's in his best interest to cooperate."

"Splendid idea!" Mergan yelled. "Looks like our friend has received encouraging news!" he added, noting Torryn's victorious grin.

"I did indeed, minutes ago!" Torryn began, looking threateningly at Sylern. "We sent spies to the mountains in the southern desert hours ago on a very special mission. They just reported there's evidence of activity near your abandoned nest. The grasses and bushes in the immediate area were trampled in patterns that seemed to indicate numerous well-used paths."

Turning toward Susan, he explained, "We were investigating the possibility Sylern hadn't been working alone when he waged war on Yagdi and snatched your daughter!"

Returning his gaze to the prisoner, Torryn dropped his bombshell. "We appeared just as the war was ending and witnessed Randolph's impressive battle with you, Sylern. That exchange made the dragon army realize you weren't nearly smart enough to make such detailed battle plans. Therefore, we suspected someone was commanding your movements. We just didn't know who. So, we revisited events leading up to the final battle and over time and much research we learned enough to suspect a wizard clan had been involved and was probably controlling your actions."

"How dare you!" Sylern roared, but Aiden pushed him back down before he could jump up.

"After Randolph's discovery, we're now quite certain you've been working for Edna Southgate!" Torryn roared.

Sylern was shocked, but quickly masked his reaction with arrogant indifference. "I have nothing more to say!"

"I don't think that's an acceptable response!" Randolph shouted.

"Ah, we meet again, Earth Wizard!" the beast sneered, grinning wickedly. "You think an ancient who's eons old would stoop to obey one of your ancestors? That's so ludicrous it's almost laughable!" he cackled. Suddenly, the beast went slack, and his eyes closed. They heard murmuring then he looked at them with a big grin and jumped up excitedly.

"Enemies approach, and you can thank Randolph for this timely offensive! Turn around!" Sylern roared defiantly.

• • •

"Susan, take Mallory and her grandparents with you and race to the deck. Don't ask questions, just go!" Traveller implored.

Once they'd reached safety, the Yagdian general whirled on her alliance and shouted, "Form a line of defense!"

The two wizards grabbed their staffs and flanked Traveller while the dragons lined up to the left of the giant bear and Ellie prowled restlessly on her right. The terrified humans felt like they'd fallen into a late-night horror show as they watched the chaotic scene before them.

Hordes of small animals suddenly appeared from every direction, and all seemed to be headed toward a spot on the beach about fifty yards away. They scurried through the grasses, climbed from trees, and popped out of the sand. "There have to be hundreds!" Mallory gasped.

Suddenly, as if commanded to do so, every one of them turned to race over the nearest dune and headed straight toward the alliance. Traveller roared, "Surround them before they reach the house!" and raced across the beach, leaving deep footprints, and sending sand flying. Obeying her command, the alliance worked together efficiently and effectively. Spreading out, they raced alongside their ferocious general, all matching her lightning-fast offensive.

"I *knew* there was something going on!" Susan moaned.

"Whatever do you mean?" Cathy cried.

"I've been treating an overabundance of small critters for a few days. Many were fine physically but seemed to be suffering from severe emotional trauma. I was suspicious about the sudden numbers and preparing a summary for the Board of American Vets when Whitney disappeared. As you can well imagine, that became top priority." She looked with horror at the rodents racing toward the alliance. "This wouldn't be happening if I'd told Ursula!"

"Now, you can't know that!" Cathy said, trying to comfort her distraught friend.

"Those silly rodents don't stand a chance," Mallory muttered and almost looked away, not wanting to see the demise of such poor little creatures. But suddenly they began morphing into horrifying creatures of all shapes and sizes. "No way! It's gotta be the water!" she gasped. "Oh, no you don't!"

She glared at Susan and her grandparents. "We need to help, or at least be ready to fight if we have to," and with that she ran to grab a big, metal shovel. Shocked at Mallory's boldness, the others quickly found weapons and raced back to the rail.

They watched in horrified fascination as every small creature suddenly became a fearsome abomination! Some grew fangs and long nails and lumbered awkwardly through the sand, as if they were unaccustomed to standing upright.

"Oh, that's just wrong!" Mallory muttered, watching some of their bodies elongate into snake-like creatures, losing their arms and legs, and slithering through the tall dune grasses.

Another group sprouted enormous wings that carried them high into the air. Much larger than eagles, their barbed tails swished back and forth threateningly as their long, deadly talons reached out, ready to grab a victim.

The terrifying creatures moved toward the deck with evil intent, but the alliance bravely raced to cut them off before they were able to reach their friends.

Suddenly, Mallory heard Randolph's deep voice above the chaos and gaped in wonder. She watched the wizard face the deadly onslaught and raise his arms, his long suit coat flapping in the wind as if inviting danger. "My Rockman looks just like one of the powerful wizards from fairy tales!" she cried.

"Stop and hear me!" Randolph commanded, but they ignored him and kept coming.

Remaining calm and resolute in his purpose, Randolph

raised his staff high above his head. Suddenly growing mightier in both stature and boldness, he bellowed, "Sylern is no longer your leader. You obeyed me once and must do so again! Heed my warning! If you do not stop this disgraceful offensive, you will suffer our wrath!"

The deep, authoritative command stopped the creatures in their tracks as effectively as a brick wall. Just as they'd done on Yagdi, each one deferred to the earth wizard's unmistakable power and obeyed. Within seconds, they'd all returned to their true selves.

Inspired by her Rockman's courage and amazed at his incredible transformation, Mallory cheered, "Go Randolph!" as the monstrous beasts morphed back into small rodents.

Unfortunately, everyone was so distracted by their earth wizard's stunning authority over the creatures, no one paid attention to Sylern. They missed the creature's jubilant sneer; unaware he'd slowly but surely removed his bindings.

Pleased with his effective distraction, the ancient one spread his wings and launched into the air. Realizing their mistake too late, Aiden was preparing to race after their enemy when Torryn stopped him.

"Why?" Aiden demanded.

Torryn's frustration matched that of his son, but the dragon sincerely felt his plan was best for this moment. Realizing his son suffered from the impatience of youth, he hurried to explain.

"Go now, but stay out of sight and don't capture him, whatever you do! I'm quite certain he's headed to Edna. If we give him a little rope, he'll hang not only himself, but Edna and her clan as well. He'll lead us right to them! Once we've confirmed their entrance, we can launch an attack before they grab Whitney and Edward!"

Admiring his father's foresight, Aiden nodded in

understanding. Then with a menacing roar he streaked into the sky and was soon out of sight.

"We must inform the kids!" Mergan shouted. "They may not have much time and must be prepared to defend themselves!"

He raced up the stairs to the humans. "Susan! As soon as our earth wizard joins us, let's contact Whitney and Edward. While they prepare for an attack, they need to know we'll be blowing the doors off Edna's stronghold very soon!"

Chapter Twenty-Five

REVEALING AN ANCIENT

"**I**s anyone there?" Whitney shouted. "Still nothing!" she said, turning to frown at Edward. "What do you think happened? They sounded so frantic!"

"I don't know, but I'm sure we'll find out soon enough. In the meantime, just keep trying if it makes you feel better."

"Hey, portal to earth, is anyone there?" Whitney yelled.

"Where'd you come up with that?" Edward quipped, rolling his eyes.

"Same place I got 'biker boy!'" she snapped, but her irritation vanished when she heard her mom's voice penetrate the ominous quiet of the cavern.

"We're here, kids!" Susan assured them, sinking into an Adirondack chair. Suddenly realizing she was talking to her daughter without a connection to Randolph, she watched the dream jumper collapse into the chair next to her. He was grinning at her and pointing to his stone.

"It's glowing!" she gasped.

"Yes, it is indeed! I think I can accurately assume we've created enough of a bond that you can communicate with the kids anytime we're near each other."

Susan grinned back, then focused on her daughter. "We have much to share with both of you. Sylern escaped, and we assume he is headed back to Yagdi. Aiden is following, and we hope the beast will lead us to its boss. If that's Edna and the wizard clan, we should soon discover their location. The Yagdians know far more history than I, so I'll defer this conversation back to them for now."

"Let the kids know we'll contact them as soon as we hear from Aiden. If our plans go as hoped, we'll be knocking on their door very soon!" Mergan proclaimed boldly.

Randolph did so, then added excitedly, "I have more intriguing news! I found a very old family album, and guess who was on the inside cover?" Unable to wait, the earth wizard forged ahead. "Edna Southgate, my ancient relative. We're quite certain she's the very same woman Patrick speaks of meeting!"

"Get out of here!" Whitney gasped. "I wish we could see her picture so we could know whether that trickster is telling the truth when he describes her!"

"Randolph, see if they're certain all of their tools are available to them. If they are, please tell them we know a way to do just that!" Ursula exclaimed.

"They are!" Whitney answered Randolph excitedly. "Everything works, but only when we're sheltered under the dome. I think we already mentioned that to Torryn. Didn't he tell you?"

Susan could hear the confusion in her daughter's voice and pictured her deep frown. Suddenly overcome by loneliness and dread, she sighed and grew pensive.

"No, but in Torryn's defense, we were all focused on Sylern at the time," Randolph explained.

"I've been giving this some thought," Mergan spoke up. "Randolph, please tell the kids I believe that with an encouraging nudge, the magic in those tokens will project an image from my mind onto the wall of Edward's dome. If you can relay the image from my mind, it should work," he said excitedly.

"Shall we give it a try?" Randolph asked after he'd relayed Mergan's idea.

"We're under the dome right now," Edward answered, pulling the small token out of his pocket. "Let's do this!"

"There she is!" Whitney screamed. "Good old black and white! Too bad her photo was taken before color had been invented!"

"Describe what you see!" Randolph demanded eagerly, holding the photo of Edna at arm's length. "I want to confirm this is really working."

"Her eyes are very dark, and she looks intelligent," Whitney began.

"She has a long face with dark lips and a prominent nose," Edward added, studying the photo carefully.

"She's wearing a dark dress with a huge, pointed collar and she wears a hat that sits high above her head, like Mergan's!" Whitney said then added quickly, "This may be all off, but your relative looks torn between anger and sadness, Randolph."

"That's her!" Randolph exclaimed, putting the photo back on the table. "The kids have described this photo perfectly!"

"That's good news!" Mergan shouted and danced an awkward but enthusiastic jig around the room. "That may very well be the turning point in rescuing our young chosen ones!"

"Exactly right!" Ursula agreed. "Randolph, please tell the kids they now have an important advantage. They know what Edna looks like and can use that knowledge to determine whether Patrick continues to lie or is telling the truth by simply asking him to describe her."

"Hold on!" Whitney objected. "We're not great with black and white images, so what if he says she's got blonde hair? How do we know that's not true?"

"Great question!" Randolph jumped in. "You can assume anything dark will appear black, while lighter colors take on lighter shades. So blonde hair would be white in the photo, and so on."

"Got it!" Whitney said, sounding a little more confident. "Now, tell us more!"

"Randolph, tell the kids first and foremost, they must find out if Edna is in fact the leader," Ursula instructed. "Our young wizard could be tricky and describe Edna while leaving out the important detail that someone else leads the clan. I suggest they pepper him with questions they know the answers to and see how he responds. Demand he describe Edna and see if the image painted by the trickster matches the woman we've seen."

Also, remind the kids to stay mum about seeing Edna's picture. Let the young wizard assume they don't have a clue what she looks like and give him full reign to act accordingly. Finally, tell Whitney and Edward it's imperative they report back to us *after* talking to him but please do so *before* following him anywhere," she urged.

"Tell Ursula that makes perfect sense, and we'll do just as she suggested!" Edward promised. "By the way, you can mention I've been practicing her 'travel dome' idea and have pretty much figured it out. It's big enough to protect Whitney and me, and if Patrick agrees to help us get out of here, I'm certain we can squeeze him in too. It could be a huge advantage!"

"That's excellent, honey! But please be careful!" Susan pleaded, breaking off abruptly so the kids wouldn't hear her quiet sobs.

Whitney heard her mom's anguish and struggled to keep from tearing up. "Aw mom, I promise to be careful! We can't wait to get home, and each time we talk with all of you, our confidence grows that we'll see you all soon!"

Just like at the portal, Mallory heard the entire conversation. Unable to stay quiet any longer, she said softly, "Hang in there, Eddy. And Whitney, that goes for you too! It takes a lot to impress me, and you and your alliance have successfully amazed me!"

"We have much to do on both ends, so keep in touch!" Randolph said as he stood up to end the discussion.

"Love you!" Susan shouted.

"Love you more!" Whitney answered.

After they'd signed off, Mallory announced, "Before we all part ways, there's something I need to say. I know I can be a pain, and I'm too demanding sometimes, but I wasn't kidding when I said I was impressed with your alliance. You're all so powerful, but I believe that power is inspired by your love and admiration for one another," she said, looking shyly around the group. "Whitney and Eddy are lucky to have found you!"

"When this is all over, I'd like to run a few tests on you, young lady. That is if you agree," Mergan grinned.

"I'll bet you say that to all the girls!" she teased. "But yeah, I'm in!"

Susan silently watched their banter with very mixed feelings. While she had grown fond of her new Yagdian friends and shared Mallory's respect for them, as long as Whitney was still in danger, she couldn't help wishing they'd never entered her daughter's life!

• • •

"Here goes," Whitney said nervously. "Time to trick the trickster and see if he came to play for real!"

"We have a good plan, thanks to our allies, and I'll make sure that joker knows he can forget ever getting his feather back unless he earns our trust. That means telling us the truth and helping us get out of here, preferably unharmed. But that will also mean going against Edna, and I really think he's afraid of her!" Edward noted with concern.

"Yeah, that's true. But he's all about himself, so we have to prove it's in his best interest to side with us against Edna and her clan. I know that won't be easy!" Whitney admitted with a sigh.

"We'll find out soon!" Edward said, nodding toward Patrick.

"Are you still in that silly prison?" the trickster taunted, sauntering up to them.

"Not today but stay at arm's length for now!" Whitney warned.

Patrick winced as he realized they still didn't trust him, and he was struck by a sudden stab of loneliness.

"Maybe he really wishes we liked him," Whitney thought, surprised by his reaction.

"I think I can get you past Edna," Patrick offered.

"Would you really? You'd do that for us, Patrick?" Whitney asked, remembering Mergan's advice to play along.

Grinning at her naive acceptance, he said excitedly, "Of course! But I can't do that without my feather!"

"I already told you the feather won't be returned until you prove you can be trusted, and that means two things," Edward announced, putting up one finger. "Number one, you get us past Edna without her knowing. Do I make myself clear?"

Patrick put his head down and nodded, so he raised another finger. "Second, you must find a way to get us out of here. *Both* need to happen, or it's game over and you'll never get your precious feather back!" Edward finished, crossing his arms.

Glancing at each other while they waited, Edward winked and mouthed, "This'll work!"

Patrick responded just as he'd hoped. "Okay! I promise, but let me scout it out first, then we can go together."

Edward shook his head and held his ground. "Not gonna happen. We go together or not at all. If we catch wind of you going on a solo operation, the deal's off."

"All right, already!" the trickster grumbled. "I'm ready if you are!"

"Good to hear!" Edward said. "But before we go, Whit and I need to know what we're getting into. Okay if we ask you a few questions?"

Considering that quite harmless Patrick agreed immediately, confident he could deflect anything he didn't want them to know.

"We want to know about Edna," Whitney requested. "Anything you can tell us will help. What does she look like, what kind of wizard is she and does her clan follow her commands?"

"Edna's easy to pick out!" Patrick said, eager to describe the woman, but not wanting to give too much away. "She has bright blond hair and wears pants all the time. She commands the clan with a tight fist, and everyone listens to her."

Noting the partial truth, Whitney pushed the trickster, hoping he'd correct some of his intentional misinformation. "That's interesting! I thought you said she had black hair and brown eyes earlier. Am I wrong?"

"If you can't believe me, I won't work with you!" Patrick yelled and disappeared in a flash of light.

They looked at each other in dismay, then Edward quipped, "I thought that went quite well, don't you?"

Whitney was so surprised her friend was joking about something that *didn't* go as planned, she burst into laughter.

"I think we need to talk with Mergan!" she suggested. "Dome of silence please!"

Under the privacy of Edward's dome, she picked up her staff and felt it warm up and begin twitching in her hand, as if eager to do something. "Randolph, we need to talk!"

The dream jumper responded immediately. "We're here! Did you talk with Patrick, and if so, how did it go?"

"About as well as a fish out of water!" Whitney said sadly. "I know Mergan suggested we go along with Patrick as much as possible, but when I questioned his description of Edna, he got all upset and said he couldn't work with us then disappeared! Did I blow it?"

Mergan nodded as Randolph shared Whitney's concern, then answered, "Tell them not to worry. I don't think they 'blew it' at all. Explain to them that I'm quite confident the little imp will be back. However, the kids may have alerted Patrick they know more about Edna than he'd thought, and that might prove worrisome."

"Maybe the mighty Mergan has a plan for when Patrick returns?" Edward asked hopefully.

"Let's see if he's more willing to share what he knows about Edna before turning to Plan B," Mergan suggested.

"And what's 'Plan B?'" Whitney asked as Randolph continued relaying messages.

"To be determined," Mergan answered honestly. "Tell them to keep us posted but to expect the varmint to return, and I don't think they'll have to wait long."

They waited impatiently for several minutes and were getting up to grab more water when Whitney grabbed Edward's arm and hissed. "Mergan was right, here he comes!"

"Didn't think we'd see you again today," Edward said, trying to sound nonchalant.

"I decided you two are my best bet to get what I need," Patrick shot back. "I know you tried to trick me, but I've experienced deceit many times and understand your hesitancy to trust me."

"Welcome back, honest Patrick!" Whitney said warmly. "You do know we can tell which Patrick is with us, don't you?"

"I'm beginning to realize that you both have hidden talents," he admitted.

"Just what do you need, Patrick?" Edward asked.

"First and foremost, I want freedom from worrying that witch of a clan leader will change her mind and come looking for me."

"And?" Edward prompted. At Patrick's quizzical look, he explained, "You said, 'first and foremost.' That usually indicates there's more."

"Ahh! Caught that, did you?" Patrick grinned.

"Oh no! Stay with us!" Whitney cautioned. "We need an honest conversation."

Patrick's sad smile surprised both of them. "Sorry, fooling people comes more naturally than working with them. I too have a problem with trust!"

"There you have it! Bravo, a breakthrough in honesty! You know what? I like that!" Whitney said with a huge smile.

Patrick's heart melted! Whitney's genuine smile was directed at him, and that rarely happened! So, he smiled back and continued cautiously. "As long as we're working on honesty and trust, I should disclose that what I *really* want is justice from Mergan's horrid treatment. I promised Edna that I'd find you and bring you back, along with the rest of the clan, not that I wanted to see harm come to any of you, but I wanted to laugh at Mergan when he was slapped behind bars."

Putting his head down, Patrick admitted, "I see now that wouldn't have been enough, and I would have always wanted more!"

"I get that we're having a breakthrough and you're finally being honest, maybe for the first time. But what you're telling us is pretty serious!" Edward admitted, eyeing Whitney. "That's a huge worry for us, so why should we believe that you won't be taking us straight to Edna?"

"Because I want my feather back! It's as important to me as your staff is to you, Whitney. If it helps, I really don't want to run into her either. So, if I help you get out of here, it's a win-win for me too!"

"Okay, that makes sense!" Edward said but added sternly, "You need to know we won't agree to anything if it means you get Mergan behind bars. He's our friend and there's no chance in this world or any other we'd help you do that!"

"What did he do to you that was so awful?" Whitney probed, truly mystified. "I know he can be gruff, but he's got a really kind heart!"

"HA!" Patrick laughed. "You think so, eh? Did you know

he called me 'Scheming Trickster' just because I liked to play pranks on others, including him? I was already suffering from low self-esteem, so that really stuck and I hate him to this day. I blame my miserable childhood and terrible experiences in wizard school on his heartless treatment of me."

They shared an empathetic glance, then Edward turned from Whitney and cleared his throat. "Did he treat you differently than all the other young wizards he tutored?"

Remaining true to his word to speak the truth, Patrick scrunched his nose and considered Edward's question for quite some time. "Yes, I truly think he did. However, I own some of that blame myself. I tested his patience frequently, and he blew up frequently, so we got along as well as oil and water."

"So, you think you were part of the problem, Patrick." Whitney said gently.

"Maybe," he admitted slowly, then stood up and stretched. "Shall we move on to a more pleasant topic?" he asked hopefully.

"Just one more question," Whitney said, walking to the young wizard. When they were eye-to-eye, she asked, "Can you promise to keep an open mind if I can get the two of you together to talk this out?"

"I don't know!" he moaned. "I've spent my entire life scheming up ways to get him back, so that's a big ask!" Putting his hand to his chin, Patrick considered her offer, then asked suspiciously, "You'd really do that for me? What do you get out of the deal?"

Expecting his reaction, Whitney explained, "Apparently this is new territory for you, but I don't always make deals just to help myself. I'm asking for you to make a deal to help both you and Mergan."

Trying to gain his trust, she added, "I want a dear friend and one who may turn out to be someone I enjoy hanging around with, meaning you Patrick, to see if you can work things out. That's what I'd get out of it."

"That's not much!" Patrick said suspiciously.

"It's everything!" Whitney yelled, throwing her arms up impatiently. "I like helping others, and I'd like to help you and Mergan patch things up."

"Well, I'll be!" the trickster muttered. "This is a first and something I must consider carefully. Can I answer that later, young chosen one?"

"How'd you know we were chosen ones?" Edward demanded.

Looking a bit put off, Patrick sighed and said, "Edna knows who you both are and that's what she said your alliance likes to call you."

"Whitney, Edward, are you there?" Randolph interrupted.

"We're here, with Patrick," Edward replied, warning the wizard they had company.

"Aiden followed Sylern and just reported back! He found the entrance and told us that Edna herself came out to welcome her pet lizard back. He fears she'll soon know everything, and that means you're both in big trouble!" he reported urgently.

"You must find someplace to hide, and quickly! Torryn and Araa are joining their son right now, so it won't be long before the dragon army arrives. Until then, you must stay out of sight!"

"Will do, thanks Randolph!" Whitney turned wide-eyed to Edward. "Let's hide!"

Chapter Twenty-Six
A FRAGILE TRUCE

"I feel so helpless!" Whitney screamed, pulling Edward in close. Taken aback by their raw emotion, Patrick didn't know what to do. Sylern's return changed everything! Edna would soon discover their location, that is if she hadn't already done so. "We need to act fast!" the young wizard muttered, looking nervously around the cavern then back at Whitney and Edward.

He'd promised not to approach the clan without them but decided he had to take that risk. "There's something I must do," he declared, looking apologetically at the teens, and then disappeared in a flash of brilliant light.

"How like that phony to leave us right now!" Edward growled, pulling Whitney to sit down beside him.

"I thought I'd gotten through to him! Guess I was mistaken once again. After all we've been through, how can I still be so naive, Edward?" Whitney cried.

"That's a part of you, Whit!" he said, reaching for her hand. "You want to see the good in everyone, even those who don't deserve your sweetness!"

"Thanks for trying," she said with a sad smile. "But I wish I was a better judge of character. Why can't I recognize deception, and why do I struggle to admit there are some who won't ever change? Believe it or not, I'm still hoping Patrick won't deceive us, and that he had a good reason to leave. I'm hopeless!" she cried.

"Shhh. It'll be okay, Whit," Edward said, awkwardly patting her shoulder.

They tried contacting the others several times but all they got was silence. "This is driving me insane!" Whitney cried, standing up to pace.

"Whit, stop! He's back!" Edward hissed, raising his arm to cover them with his dome.

Whitney put her hand out to stop Edward, then whirled around to face Patrick. "Friend or foe? We need that answer right now, trickster!" she yelled angrily.

"Friend! You must trust that right now, or we won't make it out of here alive!" Patrick's eyes were wide with panic, but he was staring at them with fierce determination.

Afraid she couldn't judge the trickster's true intentions, Whitney looked toward Edward for direction. He nodded, then they turned as one to confront the young wizard.

"Tell us why we must trust you and be quick about it!" Edward snarled, his fists clenching in frustrated anger.

"You surprised me earlier Whitney," Patrick admitted softly. "I've never had anyone offer to do anything whatsoever for me, and simply didn't know whether I could believe you. I came back because I want to!"

Pausing for a deep breath, he announced "I want all of us to get out of here safely, so I went to spy on the clan! And I did so for a reason," he continued, raising his hand to keep the teenagers from interrupting. "I knew full well you'd try to keep me from going, but I had to find out more."

"Well? What did you discover?" Edward prompted, moving closer.

"Listen to me before you judge my actions!" he cried, throwing his hands in the air. "I learned so much! I'm not certain how, but they've discovered your location. They know I'm here with you, and Edna assumes I reneged on my promise to bring the two of you to her and she's furious! She's mobilizing her minions to attack this very spot. If they find us, they'll drag all three of us to that witch of a leader and I promise you the outcome won't be pleasant!"

"What do you suggest we do now?" Whitney asked cautiously.

"You must follow my lead, no questions asked, and you must do so immediately!" Patrick demanded.

"You're insane!" Edward scoffed incredulously. "How could you think we'd do such a crazy thing?"

"Because Edna and her clan will be here any moment and you're out of options! I'm leaving, and your next move is up to you, but I strongly suggest you follow me!" With that, the wizard ran toward the water.

Reaching the rocky shelf by the edge, Patrick turned toward them one last time. "It's go time! Whitney, you've seen me underwater a few times. Trust me when I say this pond holds magic and it's our only hope for escape!" Then he turned and dove in.

Racing to the water, they peered down to search for the trickster. They could see a long way down, but Patrick was gone! Tortured with uncertainty, Whitney and Edward turned toward each other, aware their survival depended on what they did next.

"Let's do this!" Edward said, holding out his hand. Whitney linked her fingers with his, and they nodded solemnly to each other. Then, in a giant leap of faith, they turned and dove together into the shimmering pool.

• • •

Grateful they were both strong swimmers, Whitney and Edward used powerful strokes and descended quickly, looking for Patrick as they dove deeper. Relieved when the wizard shimmered into view, they changed direction and reached him in no time. He grinned and gave them a thumbs up then swam toward the edge of the pool.

They followed Patrick's lead, but suddenly felt a strong resistance. They paddled harder but moved forward more slowly and began to worry they weren't going to make it! Just as they approached the rocky edge, they noticed a small river flowing into the pool and realized they'd been swimming against its current that whole time!

They saw Patrick swim through a five-foot high crevasse of solid rock, apparently carved by the river, and followed. Whitney was nearly out of air and beginning to panic, but there was no way to surface here, and the underwater canal flowed as far as she could see.

They swam through an arch in the rocks and surfaced in an underwater cave. "Thank goodness!" Whitney gasped, gratefully gulping in air. While treading water, she looked around their amazing shelter. "How on earth did you find this, Patrick?"

"For me to know..." he began, then corrected himself. "Sorry, old habit!" he admitted with a sheepish grin.

The young wizard dog-paddled to the rocky ledge. Pulling himself out of the water, he leaped up and shook his head until water stopped flying off his long hair. "Come on, we have things to do!"

Exhausted from their swim, Whitney and Edward lazily allowed the current to pull them to shore, but as soon as they could touch bottom, they dragged themselves out of the water and collapsed next to Patrick.

Allowing them time to catch their breath, Patrick explained, "When I left the clan, I figured one day I'd need an escape route, and made that discovery a priority. I looked everywhere, and eventually searched underwater and found this."

He looked at the kids admiringly. "Good thing I assumed

right. You're both amazing swimmers like me, but if you hadn't been, I don't think you would've made it!"

"Good to know," Edward said, not even pretending to hide his disgust. "That kind of information would've been more helpful *before Whit and I dove in!*"

"I know. You're right," Patrick agreed. "But like I said, you were out of options, so my decision to include you in my escape was the right one at the time!"

Whitney noticed the hint of annoyance in the trickster's demeanor, and quickly jumped in. "Okay boys, take your corners and relax a minute. You can duke it out later, but we have some important decisions to make!"

"Sorry!" Edward said, putting his hand out to the young wizard.

"You're excused!" Patrick said, with a mischievous grin, and shook Edward's hand.

"Okay, if you're done playing gotcha, let's make a plan!" Whitney suggested. "Patrick, we need to get out of here, and I need to know my mom and everyone else is okay!"

"Yeah, those two things are critical, but we need to be smart about it," Edward agreed. "Patrick, can we still get out of here, now that Edna knows where we are, or at least where we were?"

"Not easily," Patrick admitted. "I know my way around the tunnels better than most of her clan members, so there's a good chance we can evade them. But, like you said, we have to be extremely careful! That woman's deviously clever and sometimes it feels like she has eyes in the back of her head; she seems to know everything!"

"So, what's our next move?" Whitney asked. "And, by the way, I *really* want to trust you, so please don't give me any reason not to, okay?"

"You know, trust goes both ways," Patrick whined.

"Look, you need to stop whining and help us make a plan!" Edward snarled.

"You're both right," Whitney quickly intervened. "We're *all* in big trouble and that means we need to rely on each other to get out of this mess!"

Although he sounded hesitant, Patrick shared, "I know another way around the clan's fortress, but we need to move quickly. If we can surprise Edna by moving toward them rather than away, we might have a fifty-fifty chance of getting around her clan's townsite. Then it's clear sailing through a short maze of tunnels that lead us back into Yagdi's foothills."

I could never make it to the maze of tunnels alone. She never trusted me and always sent her minions to watch over my every move! The only time I could sneak away was when I tagged along with mining groups. Edna never came, and that gang of misfits didn't care if I wandered, so that's how I learned my way around. It took time, and I might've gotten caught. But as it turns out, it was well worth the risk, wouldn't you say?"

He didn't like the trickster's emphasis on speed, and *really* didn't like the fifty-fifty odds, or less. However, Edward saw the wisdom in Patrick's words and knew they had no choice but to follow him. "For once I agree with you. Let's move, and quickly!"

"Wait! There's something more pressing that we need to do!" Whitney reminded Edward. "We really must try to contact the alliance! Good thing I held onto my staff for that." Looking toward Patrick, she asked, "Can we do that here, or is there a better spot?"

"Here's as good as any, and better now than closer to Edna," the trickster suggested.

"OK, good!" Edward agreed. "Let's join forces, Whit. Maybe both our voices will cut through this underwater hideout!"

Whitney watched her staff glow and quiver in her hands then she nodded to Edward, and they shouted in unison, "Hey, is anyone out there!" Hearing only silence, Whitney took a deep breath and was prepared to give it another try when she heard Randolph.

"Whitney? Is that you? Hey everyone, it's the kids!"

"Mom! Everybody, we're here!" Whitney shouted. "We're safe for now and needed to know you were all okay!"

Picking up on their 'safe for now,' Randolph glanced at Susan, then Edward's grandparents and asked worriedly. "Where are you? Fill us in first, then we'll tell you what's happening here."

As he listened to the care and concern in their voices, Patrick realized how much he wanted to be a part of something better, with good people he respected and trusted, and grew despondent. He'd wasted so much of his life turning people away because he'd been so full of hate and the need for vengeance.

Whitney's excited voice pulled Patrick from his unpleasant introspection. "That's great news! The dragon army is making final plans to confront the clan!"

"Hang in there just a little longer! The big bad dragons are on their way!" Mallory shouted.

Edward couldn't help but smile. "Thanks sis. I think we've got it covered on this end, but thanks for your support, and by the way, you'd hate it down here in the dark!"

"Okay, just because you're in big trouble doesn't mean you can make fun of my silly phobia about dark tunnels and dark anything! Honestly, Whitney, I don't know how you tolerate that boy!"

"Sometimes I wonder that too, Mal! But we need to get out of here, so is there anything else before we sign off?"

Randolph shared Whitney's abrupt request, which prompted a rare compliment from Mergan. "Tell her she's learning! And that she's right! We must finish this conversation so we can go about the business of ending the very real threat from Edna. If all goes as expected, the dragons will arrive before that woman locates them."

"By the way, Patrick's here too!" Whitney said, and Randolph quickly shared the unexpected news.

"*What?*" Mergan bellowed.

Patrick sighed when Randolph described the old wizard's reaction, then said defiantly, "Yeah, tell the old man it's me!" then he leaned back against the wall and pouted.

"Oh, oh! Please remember we need you Patrick, and I believe you need us!" Whitney said anxiously, then encouraged Randolph to make sure Mergan played nice for now. "I hope he and Patrick can have a long chat when this is all over, but for now, let's put the claws away!"

"That's my girl!" Susan cried proudly. Reaching out for Cathy's hand, she said softly, "I know you don't want to hear this, but I'm so glad she has Edward there with her!"

"They're both going to be home very soon! I can feel it!" Jerome declared emphatically, putting his hands on Cathy's shoulders.

"I hope with all my heart you're right," Susan whispered.

"Randolph, tell the kids to stay close to each other as they approach Edna and her clan," Mergan advised. "First and foremost, they must remain safely out of sight. Once we have the clan under control, we'll rescue them."

"And tell that young trickster to listen carefully to these words!" he continued in a loud, authoritative voice. "If one hair on the head of either Whitney or Edward is out of place when I see them, he'll have none left on his, and worse! Make sure he hears that!"

Patrick almost stood at attention when he heard Randolph's commanding voice but stopped before making a fool of himself. He just rolled his eyes and said, "Just tell the old man not to worry! His ancient brain might fry from the stress!"

Smiling at Whitney, he added in a much more subdued voice,

"I promise to guard these two with my life. Whitney was the first to say she'd like to know me better, and that was powerful. I treasure her willingness to see beyond my rather abrasive exterior."

When Randolph shared Patrick's heartfelt sentiment, Mergan looked at Susan with a puzzled expression. "Whitney has befriended one I never would've expected could be a friend to anyone. Your daughter is remarkable!"

"Honey, Mergan just said you're remarkable!" Susan said proudly.

"Mom, you always told me when people work hard to push you away, they really need for you to come closer!"

Susan gasped. "That's so true, and who would've ever thought that lesson would mean so much to us!"

That memory brought another thought to her anxious mind. "Patrick, can you hear me?"

"Yes ma'am!" Patrick replied, confused she was actually talking directly to him.

"Please bring my daughter and Edward home!" she cried, then cut off before they heard the apprehension in her voice.

Patrick heard her despair and promised in a voice ringing with sincerity, "Whitney's mother, you have my word, and I don't ever make promises I can't keep!" then smiled warmly at the kids.

Randolph relayed Patrick's vow and the old wizard was once again shocked by his sincerity. Mergan coughed then said in a subdued voice, "Randolph, tell those three I think we're all on the same page, and tell Patrick his heartfelt vow has lightened my heart. We'll let them know as we hear more news."

Whitney and Edward exchanged surprised glances as they watched the young wizard speak with Susan. Leaning in close to Whitney, Edward quietly admitted, "He's a trickster, and a good one at that! But I'm starting to believe his heart is in the right place now!"

Chapter Twenty-Seven

CAPTURED!

"There's Aiden!" Ursula shouted, leading the rest onto the deck and down the stairs.

"I need to return to Yagdi but wanted to touch base with the alliance," he announced as they joined him.

"It's so good to see you, Aiden," Ursula said. "I've never felt so helpless! Here we are stuck on Earth, unable to get to the kids, and that's terribly frustrating! I'm actually tempted to dig up my old wurfing machine that's still buried deep in the sand not too far from here. However, events are happening so fast, I fear it would be too late by the time I pulled it out and made it functional. There must be a way to use our vast experiences to help our young chosen ones!"

Trying his best to mask his own concerns Randolph reminded everyone, "Whitney and Edward have become quite masterful at getting themselves out of trouble. We must assume they'll do so this time too."

"You're right Randolph. Aiden, you and your parents can plan the first offensive. In the meantime, the wizards, Ellie and I will go to the portal and see if we can't find a way to open it."

She turned to Mergan. "This house seems to have unique qualities, almost as if it's a bridge between us and the kids. I think we need to make sure someone is always here to cover that avenue of communication."

"It's decided then. We'll part ways, but everyone must stay in touch, and that means communicating frequently, even if just to check in," Mergan said.

Struck with another idea, the wizard looked at Aiden questioningly. "As a last resort, could we try riding to Yagdi on the backs of dragons?"

"Only if all else fails!" the young king cautioned. "That's not been entirely successful in the past."

"I don't care!" Mallory implored. "I'd ride on any of your backs to save Whitney and my brother! Not only that, but I have complete confidence that any one of you would do whatever it took to keep me safe!"

Deeply moved, Aiden took a step toward the outspoken teen and bowed low. "You honor the dragons with your trust, Mallory. And your bravery matches that of Whitney and Edward!"

"I, too, am willing to try anything!" Randolph added. "Let's move forward and adjust plans as more information comes to light."

"I really must return," Aiden said, and moved a few yards from the group so his takeoff wouldn't throw sand in their faces. They watched the young dragon spread his iridescent wings then effortlessly sail into the sky.

"Let's get busy," Mergan said in his usual abrupt manner. Although he feared what would come next, the wizard was determined to conquer all obstacles in the way of bringing the kids home and knew with absolute certainty everyone on this beach felt the same fierce dedication.

Feeling left out, Susan, Cathy and Jerome huddled together and conversed in low voices for several minutes. Finally, Susan nodded and turned toward the rest. "The three of us have listened to your discussion and various plans, but none include us. We all want, no we all *need* to do something to help!"

"There has to be something we can do!" Jerome declared earnestly. "They're our kids!"

"I for one wouldn't mind holding down the fort here," Susan offered, brushing away a stray tear. "Ursula, you said this house was important. Is there something we can do here?"

"There is indeed! This will be the first place our dragon allies will come, and you can let us know when they do."

"But we have no way of communicating, so how do we stay in touch?" Susan asked.

"Aiden's mother and I had the same concern, Susan. So, knowing that we would have to split up, Aara provided a solution. Everyone, put your hands out," Ursula said with a sly grin.

Looking at their friend quizzically, they all did as she asked.

Ursula placed a small token in each of their hands, then stood back and crossed her arms. "You are the proud owners of a very unique method of communication. No matter where we are, you can reach anyone in this group with a simple command, and that includes Aiden and his parents, even while on Yagdi. You might even be able to reach the kids, that is if they're under Edward's protective dome."

"But this is just a cute little dragon," Cathy said, holding up her token.

"The dragon army uses that 'cute little dragon' to transmit information among their troops. It's quite handy and keeps fragmented groups up to date on activities elsewhere. Much the same way, they'll allow us to speak with each other when we're not together. Just hold the token tightly and talk. We'll all hear you."

Noticing their confusion, Ursula continued, "How about we do some practicing? Half of us can stay up here and the other half go to the beach. What do you think?"

"I can text with the best of them! You can count on me for help," Mallory shouted, racing out the door.

Hoping the tiny tokens would work as Ursula described, the

two families followed Mallory to the beach, eager to practice until they felt confident with this strange new way of communicating. But strange or not, they knew it might make the difference in getting their kids home!

. . .

Bringing out another precious granola bar, Edward broke it and gave half to Whitney, who immediately offered a piece to Patrick. Although the young wizard looked at it hungrily, he refused and stood up then walked to the small pool. Kneeling at the edge, he cupped his hands, and took quick sips of water.

The teens did the same, then refilled their Yetis and tossed them into their packs.

"Okay, let's do this!" Edward said, standing up to stretch.

"Follow me," Patrick said, diving into the water. Whitney grabbed her staff and nodded at Edward. This time, they knew what to expect as they confidently dove in.

"That was invigorating!" Whitney shouted, breaching the surface last.

"Oh no!" she cried when she saw Edward and Patrick. Both were standing close to shore with several ornery looking thugs holding their hands behind their backs!

Whitney noticed her friend's silent plea to swim away while she still could, and shouted defiantly, "Not gonna happen, Edward!" But she did take her time swimming to shore while trying to come up with something to get them out of this mess.

She still carried her staff but was quite certain they wouldn't let her keep it. Nothing worked unless they were under the dome anyway! "We just have to be ready and hope an opportunity falls into our lap," she thought grimly.

"There she is! Glad you could join us, young chosen one," Whitney heard as she pulled herself up and onto the rocky ledge.

As she stood up, a woman she assumed was Edna stalked out of the shadows like a predator.

"Grab her staff and be quick about it!" she yelled, pointing to Whitney.

A rather old wizard with a face full of deep wrinkles approached and grabbed the staff. "Whoa!" he yelled, dropping it to the ground.

"Oh, don't be such an infant!" Edna snarled sarcastically. "If you can't handle it, just pick it up with your little pinky and toss it in the pool. This young lady won't be needing it any longer."

Edna's gopher grimaced with pain when he picked up her staff, but he gritted his teeth and held on long enough to give it a good toss into the water. Whitney was so busy watching the current carry her staff away, she didn't notice Patrick was also carefully following its path. When it was pulled under the waterfall and taken out of sight, they both looked away.

"Edna, I'm so glad we finally met!" Whitney said sarcastically, returning her attention to the clan leader. "Looks like you're afraid of little old me and my big bad staff!"

The ancient leader laughed. "I like your style, young lady! Under different circumstances, I might actually enjoy spending time with you."

Turning to Edward, she added, "I've heard about you too, young man. I know you both have talents, and I also know they are strongest when the two of you are together, so we'll try to keep that from happening!"

Finally, she glared at Patrick. "Welcome back, traitor! I guarantee you won't enjoy the punishment I have in mind for you!"

"Edna, don't you see? This was all part of my plan!" he protested. When she turned and started to walk away, he threw Edna some bait he didn't think she could resist. "The least you could do is to hear me out!"

Whirling around, Edna moved so fast they couldn't keep track of her until she was in front of Patrick and pointing her finger in his face. "You have run out of all nine lives, young trickster! There is nothing more I care to hear from you!"

"Not even if I told you I could bring the rest of the alliance to your doorstep?" Patrick asked with a devious grin, intentionally turning his back so he wouldn't have to look at the kids' horrified stares. They must believe he'd betrayed them for his plan to work.

"Patrick, you told me..." Whitney began. The young wizard cut her off with a cold, calculating laugh that made her shiver. Without looking at her, he sneered. "This wise leader knows my reputation is well deserved. She also knows I wouldn't dare risk her vengeance by deceiving her!" Patrick said arrogantly. He finally looked into Whitney's tormented eyes and struggled not to wince.

Edna didn't detect trickery in the young wizard, and even more telling, the shocked expressions in both chosen ones convinced her the trickster was speaking the truth. "He probably promised them the moon," she thought, feeling a grudging respect toward the young wizard for pulling off such a traitorous act.

There were more important things to be done, so she conceded, at least for the time being. "You might still come in handy, *if, and only if* you can deliver the rest of the alliance to me!" She flicked his nose with a fingernail and turned to lead everyone to their stronghold.

Whitney tried hard to communicate with Edward, but as she'd expected they kept them separated and even positioned them so they couldn't see each other. "We must really scare them!" she thought. "Could Edward make a dome if given the opportunity," she wondered, feeling a tiny ray of hope. "And could I create a distraction?"

As they were shoved in front of Edna, Whitney seized on the opportunity. Turning toward Edward, she raised her eyebrows and looked pointedly toward his arms, and hoped his subtle nod meant he'd understood.

"Let me formally introduce myself," the woman declared haughtily, bringing Whitney's attention back to their captor. "I'm Edna, leader of this ancient wizard clan that once ruled Yagdi."

Eying the teenagers up and down as she walked slowly around them, the horrid woman suddenly stopped in front of Edward. Whitney noticed his grimace and watched his jaw clench, but he didn't say a word. "What are you doing to my friend?" she yelled, seething with frustration and anger.

"Not much, just a little probe into his thoughts. That kind of information can come in handy. For example, I just discovered you were encouraging this young man to find an opportunity to cover you both with his protective dome."

"You surprised me," Edward shouted. "You will *not* enter my mind again!"

"You're both quite remarkable, in spirit and bravery. However, you sorely underestimate my vast capabilities," Edna sneered, then turned to her minions.

"I must attend to an urgent matter, so take the young ones to separate cells, and make sure they can't see each other," she commanded. "Patrick, you stay right here!"

Whether it was intentional or a lucky slip, Whitney and Edward were dragged right past Patrick. Edward made eye contact and mouthed, "This isn't over!" Ignoring the threat, the trickster dramatically rolled his eyes toward the teen's pants' pocket and was rewarded when Edward's eyebrows shot up and he gave a subtle nod of understanding.

When Whitney was led past him, she leaned in and hissed, "You've proven how poorly I misjudged your character! I hope never to see your dishonest face again!"

He just grinned and feigned indifference as she was taken away. It really hurt, but Patrick had perfected his ability to deceive so well, he'd managed once again to fool the clever clan leader. Edna had indeed noticed the trickster's lack of concern for the two teenagers and smiled with satisfaction.

Once the kids were out of sight, Edna walked purposefully toward him. "Well, young trickster, I suppose you may have one more life in you, but I want to hear exactly how you plan to bring the alliance into the portal."

"First and foremost, I'll need your assistance in the matter," Patrick began.

Taken aback, Edna cocked her head and eyed the young wizard carefully. "Why do you need me, Patrick?"

"The portal has been damaged, but I know you have a way to bring it back into working order."

"Good assumption, young man!" she said. "However, only my most trusted assistants know where I keep that information, and you're not currently among that esteemed group."

"If you don't bring me on board, you won't get the alliance. Simple as that!" Patrick said sternly, even though his insides were turning and twisting nervously.

Edna poked his mind, just a quick in and out to assess whether Patrick's intentions matched his words.

He'd expected such behavior and was well-practiced in blocking his mind. He just had to picture a huge metal door slamming shut. It wasn't detectable but worked every time, and this was no exception. He smoothly blocked her entrance, and his barricade held up so perfectly, she didn't detect his underhanded move and stepped away with a satisfied nod.

"The blueprints lay beside my seer, and you've already discovered where that's hidden. However, I now have guards at my door, so don't expect to enter without my knowledge ever again, young wizard."

"I must get back to the kids, but don't go far, for I will need your services very soon. Jackson will ensure you don't snoop around before that." With that, Edna twirled around and marched out of the room.

Patrick could finally relax. There was no one around, so he grinned. "Jackson, eh? He's stepped up in the world. However, I imagine for the right price he'd still feed me information as he has before."

Whistling at this stroke of luck, the young wizard headed toward his informant guarding Edna's private suite, doing his best to appear casual and unhurried.

Chapter Twenty-Eight

METAMORPHOSIS!

Sparing no expense, Patrick generously paid off Edna's guard. However, gaining entrance into her suite was only half the battle. He had to work fast! Grateful to find the seer just where it had been and thinking that was a ridiculous oversight for such an intelligent woman, Patrick located the blueprints for repairing the portal.

"Too bad I don't have my feather to help me locate the information!" Patrick thought. "However, its magic is now where it's most needed. It may very well save their lives! So, I'll just have to be satisfied with committing everything to memory."

Accomplishing his task much faster than even he believed possible, the young wizard rolled the blueprints up with a satisfied grin and put them exactly where he'd found them. Then, he walked out whistling and gave the greedy guard a wink and a thumbs up.

"Lucky for me, the mechanism to unlock the portal isn't far from here," he muttered. Turning the corner, and finding no one in sight, he made a beeline to the control room.

Cracking the door open just a sliver, he peeked in to make sure the room was empty. "Thank goodness!" His eyes darted quickly around the room until he found the small device he was looking for, then he snuck down the long, narrow room to the end of the very last table. It looked innocent enough, but when he tried to open it, the case remained latched tight.

"Good thing I remember this step!" he thought, sitting down in front of the small black box. "The Road Travels Both Ways," he said with a smile and unlatched the box.

"Now to open the portal!" But just as Patrick put his finger on the key, he heard the latch on the door click into place and looked frantically for a place to hide. The thick curtain running the entire length of the wall was close, so he ducked behind it and held his breath. It was full of dust, and he felt his nose beginning to twitch. He couldn't afford to sneeze right now so he slowly raised his hand and clamped his fingers around his nose, then he froze, hoping the curtain hadn't moved and given away his hiding spot.

Seconds later, four sets of boots clomped down the aisle right toward him.

"Edna said to look everywhere! There's nothing in here that trickster would be interested in, so let's make this quick and move on!" one of them grumbled.

Other than crossing his toes and pinching his nose shut, Patrick didn't move. He stayed perfectly still, hoping they didn't look *everywhere*, but fearing they'd pull the curtain back any minute! Patrick chanced taking a breath only when he heard the door shut behind them, and their steps retreat down the hall.

Slipping the curtain back slowly, he peeked then sighed with relief. The room was indeed empty once again. "Sounds like Edna discovered my absence, so this may be my last opportunity!" he hissed and returned to the black box. With a quick command, he opened it and wasted no time hitting the red button he'd seen in the blueprint. Surprised but pleased when he saw *"PORTAL NOW FUNCTIONING"* flashing across the top in deep red, he grinned at completing his first task, shut and relatched the box, then raced to the door.

"From now on, operate using the sneakiest tools in your

toolbox, trickster," he encouraged himself, opening the door just enough to peek out.

"Thank my lucky stars!" he sighed, finding the hall empty. Everyone was busy looking elsewhere for him, so it shouldn't be terribly difficult to sneak out of the stronghold and into the sunlight. Closing the door softly behind him, he crept to the first intersection and ran into a group of young wizards. Hoping they weren't privy to Edna's frantic search for him, Patrick put on his best smile and said, "Beautiful day! Anyone care to join me for a few minutes in the Yagdian sunshine?"

Relief washed over him when they didn't seem to know him, nor did they act concerned about some escaped thief in their stronghold. Grateful no one accepted his invitation, Patrick waved a friendly good-bye and hurried to the large concrete doors at the entrance.

"Project for her eminence," he called to the guard, and once again felt relief when the doors opened slowly, stopping when there was enough room for him to run through. "Keep 'em open! I'll just be a few minutes! Orders from the queen!"

Patrick scurried through the tunnels and reached the entrance in no time. He'd been living in the dark so long, the light was blinding! Blinking rapidly and shielding his eyes, he crawled over a nearby ledge, and dropped into a small clearing.

"That sunlight feels amazing! Hope I get back out here soon!" he said, then pulled out the small token he'd stolen from Whitney's pocket. "Good thing I'm a skilled pickpocket too!"

He wasn't sure how it worked, so Patrick rubbed the small dragon and hissed, "Mergan, talk to me old man!"

He waited impatiently, but after several minutes of silence, he tried again. "This is Patrick. We need to talk now!"

"Patrick, what on earth!"

"Shhh!" he said quickly. "Keep it down! I'm outside and this conversation must be lighting fast! Edna's got Whitney and

Edward. I tricked her into thinking I intentionally brought the kids to her, then baited her by promising to bring the entire alliance here to the stronghold! She bought it, but I fear she's onto me now, so we don't have much time!"

Peeking nervously over the ledge to make certain no one was near, he dropped back down and continued. "I've opened the portal, Mergan! We're in the mountains right next to Sylern's den. Hurry! I don't know how long the kids have. I'm going back in to find Whitney's staff and I'll try to get it to her. I believe Edward remembers he has my magical feather, but that's still unproven. If so, it might come in handy."

"Patrick!" Mergan exclaimed. "I owe you! You've done something unexpected, and wonderful indeed, young wizard! Expect our new king and his parents to arrive before us, and we'll follow shortly after!"

"Got it!" Patrick replied and climbed back over the ledge and raced inside.

"Step two completed!" Patrick thought, giving the guard a thumbs up as he flew through the door. "One more to go!"

Speeding through the tunnels to the cavern, he heard Edna screeching, "I want that trickster's head!" Thankfully, it sounded far away, but he still kicked his speed up a gear and raced down the tunnels with even more urgency.

To the best of his knowledge the speedy route he'd discovered remained a secret. Even so, he stayed alert but thankfully didn't encounter anymore clan members. He raced into the cavern and didn't slow down until he got to the pool. Looking toward the spot he'd seen Whitney's staff disappear, Patrick smiled with relief when it reappeared under the waterfall and a sudden fast current brought it right to his feet. Knowing this would hurt, Patrick took a deep breath and reached down to bring Whitney's lifeline out of the water.

The electrical shock from the staff was so severe Patrick

dropped it and shook his arm until the painful tingling stopped. "You can do this because you must!" he growled. Taking another deep breath, he grabbed the staff once again.

The bolts of electricity zapping his arm were so excruciatingly hot the young wizard kept looking to see if he was on fire. Patrick managed to hang on and ran back to Whitney and Edward, hoping it wasn't too late.

Skidding to a stop outside the entrance to the main hall, he heard Whitney cry, "Stop it!" Dropping her staff, he peeked around the corner and gasped. Edna was standing over Edward, and he instantly recognized both her intent and Edward's extreme agony. "Wait for the right moment, Patrick!" he hissed to himself.

But it was so hard! Whitney was crying and urgently pleading with Edna to stop while Edward was sitting cross-legged on the floor, holding his head in his hands. The poor kid was rocking back and forth, and his agonized moans sounded low and way too quiet. "At least his hands are free," the young wizard thought hopefully. "Come on, Edward, grab that feather!"

Just then, Edna snarled, "Edward, this will all stop at once if you cooperate!" which made him wonder how long the poor guy had been suffering from her horrible mind probe.

"Tell me the location of both the alliance and the trickster and I'll make the pain go away," she promised.

Pushing himself slowly off the floor and onto his knees, Edward glared at the maniacal woman and groaned, "Not going to happen, witch!"

Patrick smiled proudly at the defiance blazing in his new friend's eyes. But growled when Edward fell back down with a pitiful cry and rolled back and forth, trying to remove the pain that had reentered his head.

"Stop, Edna! Can't you see your mind torture isn't working!" Whitney shouted.

"Go, Whitney!" Patrick thought, when he noticed the red

spots dotting the brave girl's wrists. The teenager was so furious at Edna, she'd worked at the bonds around her wrists until the ropes had become frayed. They looked ready to pop with just a slight tug.

Grabbing her staff off the floor, Patrick ignored the sudden pain as he jumped out of his hiding spot. "Come on, one last pull, Whitney! You can do it!"

Clenching her jaw, Whitney gave her wrists one last mighty tug, and the rope broke free.

"Catch!" he yelled, tossing her staff through the air. As if drawn to the girl, it sped right into her freed hands.

With frayed rope dangling from her wrists, Whitney reached up and grabbed her staff. She stood tall and proud, looking every bit the powerful, protector warrior she was meant to be. The furious heroine had finally broken through her earthly bindings to seek vengeance on the evil woman causing her friend so much pain.

"Paybacks can be brutal, Edna! Begone!" Whitney bellowed, punching her staff toward the shocked woman.

"No!" Edna yelled, her arms and legs flailing helplessly as she flew backwards and smacked against the rock wall, sending large boulders tumbling to the floor. Moaning in pain, Edna covered her head as dislodged stones rained down on her from above. With a low, menacing growl, she shook her head and tried to get up.

Filled with rage, Whitney stalked to Edna and glared at the woman who'd grinned so cruelly while her best friend writhed on the floor in unimaginable pain. Suddenly, her staff and hand began glowing in oranges, yellows and purples. "The colors of Yagdian sunsets!" she gasped.

When the colors exploded and rays of light filled the room, Edna shrieked, "No! It can't be true!"

Whitney felt the change in every fiber of her body. Determined to make sure Edna never tortured Edward, or anyone else ever again, she ruthlessly punched her staff toward their enemy and bellowed, "Begone!"

This time, Whitney gave it a little twist at the end that sent Edna flying the entire length of the huge meeting hall. She slammed against the far wall with a loud smack and crumpled to the ground. The powerful ancient sat there, mumbling non-sensical words as if she couldn't believe some mere child had the audacity to attack her and had the ability to cause so much pain.

Whitney frowned and stalked purposefully toward the old woman cowering on the floor. As she glared down at their enemy, Edna looked up and pleaded, "No! Please! I hurt all over! Just let me be!"

"Why should I? You call Patrick a trickster, but you're that and worse! You live to hurt people. Give me one good reason why I should show you mercy when you ignored Edward's agony and his pleas to stop?" Whitney growled, growing more incensed by the second.

"You'll pay for what you've done to my friend!" she yelled, raising her staff above her head. "Edna, Begone!" she shrieked, and with an upward sweep of her staff, the woman rose until she hovered just off the ground. While Edna kicked and screamed, Whitney bellowed, "This.One's.For.Edward!" and swung her staff from side to side like an enraged conductor, sending the enemy flying back and forth in dizzying circles.

"Now you look like the witch you truly are, only without your broom!" Whitney shouted. She enjoyed seeing the same anguish on the evil woman's face she'd hated seeing on poor Edward's minutes ago and raised her staff high into the air. "Now, this one's for you!" she yelled, throwing Edna so forcefully she hit the ceiling and fell to the floor in a heap.

Not giving their enemy time to recuperate, Whitney punched

her staff toward Edna with such force, the woman went through the wall behind her!

No longer the brunt of Edna's mind jabs, Edward had almost completely recovered and desperately wanted to help Whitney. But when he tried to stand up, his legs were so weak he wobbled precariously. Patrick raced over and put his arm around the teen's waist to keep him from falling over. Smiling grimly, the young wizard pulled his feather out of Edward's pocket and held it up. "I'll let you do the honors. Simply twirl it between your fingers, and the feather will do whatever you command," he explained, handing it to his new friend.

They watched Whitney stalk over to Edna, appearing eager to deliver more punishment. Pointing to her, Patrick winked at Edward. "I think, given everything you and Whitney have endured together, it's fitting that you end this together!"

"Whitney," Edward gasped, staring in wonder at the girl standing before him. When she turned toward him, Edward was so awed by the power radiating off his friend and the fiery determination glinting in her eyes, all he could say was, "You're amazing!"

"Edward! You're okay!" she cried out happily. At his nod of reassurance, and noting Patrick was there to help, Whitney turned back to Edna and began a slow, methodical stroll toward the woman who dared torture her best friend.

Surprising all of them, Edna emerged from around a corner and raised her arms at Whitney. "Don't mess with me, little girl!"

Shocked the woman had bounced back so quickly and not certain Edward had fully recovered, Whitney bravely raised her staff to defend all three of them. Edna's furious black eyes sparked with an evil gleam. Maybe it was weakness or overconfidence, but the wizard made an uncharacteristically grave error. She underestimated the resilience and determination of the three standing before her; something she would regret forever.

The irate woman was so focused on Whitney she paid no attention to Edward or Patrick and marched purposefully toward the young upstart. Patrick knew what was coming when she raised her arms and heard Whitney scream then drop to the floor in agony. "She's in Whitney's mind, Edward. It's now or never!"

"Edna! I'd like to join the party!" Edward taunted, hoping to distract her long enough to give Whitney time to regroup. When the powerful woman turned his way, he proudly watched his amazing friend quietly rise and creep toward their opponent.

Unaware Whitney was approaching, Edna snarled at Patrick, "Well, if isn't the traitor himself! And young Edward, how nice of you to recover so quickly. That just means double the fun when I make you grovel in pain once again!" she growled, sounding much like a wild animal.

All three felt the stab of pain, but Whitney was so furious, she ignored it and leaped at Edna from behind. Catching her adversary by surprise, they grappled in the air then fell to the ground. They hit so hard, Whitney's grip loosened, and Edna took full advantage of the moment. Tumbling away from the girl, the wizard jumped up and directed a powerful bolt of energy toward her young attacker. Whitney used her staff to block the deadly onslaught then twisted it to send the flow of energy sailing back toward her enemy. As Edna batted away her own force of nature, Whitney leaped up and raised her staff to face her nemesis.

"Well, aren't you just full of surprises!" Edna hissed, and put her arm up, ready to attack. This time Whitney was faster. As if understanding each other's intentions, Whitney brought her staff into the air, and yelled, "Begone!" as Edward threw out his hand and twisted the feather as Patrick advised, and commanded, "Pain, leave us and enter Edna threefold!"

Shrieking in agony, Edna whirled toward Whitney. Raising her arms, the ancient moved her hands in a dizzying circle, up and down and back and forth. Whitney felt a breeze against her cheek then gaped in disbelief as a tornado formed, took aim, and headed straight toward her.

Using her staff, the teen imitated Edna's earlier movements, and just as she'd hoped, the approaching twister stopped then began circling in the opposite direction. It made a wide, sweeping turn, then raced toward Edna.

Edna hadn't expected such skilled defense, but she had plenty of tricks in her arsenal and never ran from her enemies. Trying to decide which upstart to attack first, she whirled to glare menacingly at Whitney, then turned to Edward and finally Patrick. While Edward held the feather up threateningly, she watched the two young men move together then wait for Whitney to join them.

When Whitney raised her staff and poked her shoulder mockingly, Edna shrieked, "Playtime is over!" then leaped into the air, twirled three times to gain momentum, and kicked a leg right at Whitney's head. Patrick had expected this maneuver because he'd used it quite often himself. The young wizard flew into the air and deflected Edna's kick just before she struck the girl.

Knocked off balance, the woman crumpled to the floor. Her opponents wasted no time rushing in and hovered over her menacingly. Whitney was holding her staff at the ready, while Edward twirled Patrick's feather mockingly, keeping it frustratingly out of reach.

"Edna, make my day and do something stupid. I'd love to mess with your mind as you did mine, and I believe Patrick's feather will help me do just that. What you felt earlier was just the appetizer. Would you like the main course?" Edward asked with a challenging smile.

Edna quickly realized things weren't going her way, at least for the moment. Feigning defeat, she wrapped her arms around her legs and began moaning dramatically, "I give! I give!"

Hearing her cries, frantic clan members rushed in from all

directions but skidded to a stop to stare in amazement. Three youngsters were standing above their leader while Edna lay on the ground, moaning pitifully. Unsure what to do without her direct orders, but knowing they'd be in deep trouble if they did nothing, they stared at each other with wide, anxious eyes.

"Get them!" one clansman yelled, and that was all they needed to hear. Raising their fists, they ran forward to free their leader.

"Look out, Whitney, we've got company!" Edward shouted and nodded toward the mob of angry clan members heading their way.

"Let's do this! Spread out but stay together!" Whitney yelled.

Edward glanced at Whitney and once again marveled at how confident and inspiring she looked, calmly holding her staff in both hands, prepared to end this assault. Winking at his incredible friend, he turned to Patrick. "Like she said, let's do this!"

With grim determination, Whitney raised her staff and faced the charging army. "Begone!" she shouted, punching it toward the sea of wizards.

Eager to join their fierce friend, Patrick and Edward placed the feather between their hands. Raising it high above their heads, they shouted, "Begone!" Patrick's small but powerful device sparked and crackled with energy. As they spun it faster and faster, the sparks grew into flames and finally exploded into hot bolts of fire that struck their enemies with deadly accuracy.

"Again!" Whitney shouted when they kept coming.

All three leaped forward, shouting, "Begone!" and watched the front line of minions turn to ash from the flames or tumble backwards from the waves of energy from Whitney's staff. Staring at the kids with shocked expressions, the rest of Edna's clan turned and ran.

"Yes!" Whitney cheered. "Don't stop! We've got 'em on the run!" Power flowed from all three as they yelled one final "Begone!" then raced after the frightened clan, following them through the entrance and into the tunnels leading out of the cave. In hot pursuit, Whitney, Edward, and Patrick rounded a corner, skidded to a stop, and gaped in disbelief.

The entire clan had run into three very menacing dragons. Aiden, Torryn, and Araa looked quite surprised, but managed to grin at the young warriors. "Looks like you have this completely under control!" Aiden said proudly, taking in the unexpected scene.

"Stop this instant or be incinerated where you stand!" Torryn bellowed to a few he caught trying to sneak off. Although the caverns holding the clan's stronghold were wide and high, they barely allowed the dragons enough room to walk.

"She made us do it!" someone cried, pointing to Edna. "We're decent folks, but fear made us follow her!" Every clan member raised an arm and pointed to their former leader, crying, "It's all Edna's fault!" Hoping they wouldn't be incinerated on the spot, each one fell face down on the floor and stayed there.

The dragons didn't believe nor trust any of them but considered none a threat. So, they turned away and stared at the three young warriors. Recognizing the unbridled fury still simmering just below the surface, especially in young Whitney, Aiden approached cautiously while Torryn and Araa shackled Edna to ensure she was no longer a threat.

Chapter Twenty-Nine

TYING UP LOOSE ENDS

Whitney's legs were so weak, she couldn't stand anymore. Edward reached out and grabbed her, but she felt his arms quivering as he struggled to keep them upright. Patrick noticed and wrapped his arms around both of them. Aiden joined the group, and they clung tightly to each other, their hearts filled with unbelievable joy. Everyone was safe, and this time they were quite certain the battle was truly over!

Whitney squeezed Edward's hand then wriggled free and smiled at Patrick and Aiden. "There's a story behind your appearance, young king, and I can't wait to hear it, but there's something I must do first."

Drawing Patrick in for a huge hug, she whispered, "You're my hero, young wizard! How can I ever thank you for such bravery? We're here and alive because you risked your life to bring my staff to me, and you shared your feather with Edward at just the right moment."

"I'm sure thanking me will take a long time, and I look forward to your ongoing praises!" Patrick grinned. Then, with a heavy sigh, he looked apologetically at both kids. "I'm so sorry I had to deceive you and cause you so much grief!"

Patting the despondent young wizard on the back, Edward handed Patrick his feather. Glancing at Edna he said, "It looks like you cleverly deceived all of us. I predict she'll soon get what she deserves!" he added, pointing his thumb toward the failed leader.

Hearing loud voices coming from the direction of the dark hallway, Whitney glanced nervously at her three friends and mouthed, "Now what?" They were exhausted but if it became necessary, they would fiercely defend each other. Their worried frowns turned to laughter when their alliance and families raced through the door and ran to meet them.

Piling into Susan's arms, Whitney couldn't hug her mother tightly enough, while Edward was smothered by his grandparents and Mallory. "Wow, you're all on Yagdi!" he yelled, coming up for air.

"Talk about traveling long distances to help a friend!" Mallory teased but gave it up immediately to smile brightly at her brother. "You know I'm just kidding!" she said, pulling him in close. "But don't you dare go on another adventure without me!"

Then she turned to gape at Whitney. "You're a superstar, girl! Look at you all brave and conquering bad guys! Who would've thought?"

Mystified and trying to make sense of what she'd just done, Whitney grinned and shrugged. Whoever, or whatever she'd become, even if just for that moment in time, she had to admit she'd been pretty amazing!

Feeling the sleek panther quietly rub against her, Whitney looked down and grinned at Ellie then reached out to stroke her soft fur. "I still hope our wonderfully normal life on the shore of Lake Superior includes a very unique rescue cat named Miss Ellie!"

"I look forward to that immensely!" Ellie answered in her beautiful, melodic voice.

They were interrupted by a sudden scream. "Leave me alone!" Turning toward the entrance once again, they watched Traveller, Mergan, and Randolph shove Sylern into the room with so much force he tripped and fell on his face. "Enough already!" he complained, rising slowly.

"You are so done!" Traveller growled. "Between you, Edna and her clan, we're going to have quite a lengthy trial ahead of us! Personally, I think it's a waste of time. You should all go directly to jail, and they may as well throw away the keys because you won't be getting out in this lifetime!"

Spying Edna, the Yagdian bear turned toward Mergan. "I think we have some unfinished business with this woman, wouldn't you agree?"

"I do indeed! Randolph, can you handle Sylern while Traveller and I have a little chat with this lost ancient?" Mergan asked.

Randolph grabbed Sylern by the ear and dragged him back toward the entrance. "Does this answer your question? I'll get him securely behind bars then join you."

Mergan and Traveller walked purposefully toward the woman who'd caused so much agony and unnecessary grief.

"Get up!" Mergan growled, and the formidable pair watched the evil woman rise, prepared to strike if Edna tried anything. She felt the anger simmering in each, ready to explode, and feared their wrath. But the ancient leader squared her shoulders and managed to pull off an air of righteous indignation.

"How dare you treat me this way, wizard!" she snapped at Mergan. "Don't you know who I am?"

"It's for that reason we struggle with a difficult decision," Traveller admitted with a low, ominous growl.

"Whatever do you mean?" Edna asked petulantly.

"Speaking only for myself, I find it to be an extremely difficult challenge to refrain from punishing you right here, and right now!" the bear warned, her voice calm but dripping with a threatening undertone.

When Edna sneered, Traveller roared, "I see your intentions, ancient one. You'd like nothing more than to appear terribly wronged."

Looking fondly at the group of friends and allies surrounding them, she continued. "I'm afraid that ship has sailed, Edna. There isn't one among us who isn't aware of your atrocious deeds, if not to them personally than to a loved one. And none would ever be foolish enough to consider you wronged in any way whatsoever! As a matter of fact, I'm quite certain none among us would hesitate to demand swift justice for your cruel, selfish deeds."

"How dare you!" Edna began, but Mergan's thunderous yell stopped her cold.

"How dare *we*, you say?" Mergan asked, leaning in so close they almost touched noses. "Old one, do you not see the irreparable damage you've done? The lives lost, the unspeakable acts against Yagdi and its citizens, as well as Earthlings?"

Suddenly appearing taller, Edna snarled, "Old man, you're past your prime and I fear you've finally lost your mind!"

Mergan wasn't prepared for her sharp jab to his brain, and bent over in pain. However, Patrick had been expecting such bold behavior. "Cease this minute, Edna!" he cried, stepping forward. Then, a bit more dramatically than was necessary, the young wizard twirled his feather in front of her face, tickling and goading until she exploded.

"You're a poor excuse for a wizard, and not worthy of my time!"

"Gotcha!" he yelled, grinning proudly at Mergan. "Talk about sharp minds becoming weak! I was able to distract you from Mergan far too easily. However, I know for a fact you won't commit any more mind probes, Edna!" Patrick promised, lifting his feather and muttering words only he could hear.

"Put that silly thing away! It's an embarrassment!" Edna screeched and turned to continue her assault.

After a few tense seconds, Mergan grinned and said, "I think it's safe to assume young Patrick just took that power from you, old woman! I feel fine, other than having to put up with your seriously wrinkled face far too close to mine!"

Traveller and Mergan smiled at Patrick then turned toward Whitney and Edward. In another dazzling light show, Traveller transformed into Ursula and gathered the two teens into a fierce bear hug. "I understand you were both magnificent!" she said proudly. When she finally let go, Mergan clapped Edward on the back and hugged Whitney saying, "My pride in you both is surpassed only by how relieved I am to see you once again!"

Walking back to Patrick, Mergan smiled and tipped his hat at the young wizard. In a voice loud enough for everyone to hear, he announced, "Let everyone hear my sincere and utter thanks to this young man for all he did for us, and particularly for our young chosen ones!

"Even incredibly astute wizards can make mistakes. However, I own up to mine. Considering you a trickster with no chance of ever changing was a rare error in judgement on my part. I hope you can forgive me and allow this old wizard the distinct honor to tutor you once again."

Rendered speechless, Patrick just gaped at the tall wizard standing before him. He'd never seen Mergan smile, especially not at him, and this was a shocking development.

"I would be the honored one, sir!" he mumbled, feeling suddenly awkward and shy.

"It's done, then! We'll begin immediately. That is, after our celebration which I certainly hope will include Mexican food, especially enchiladas and tamales."

"Aiden, can you and your parents see that these misfits are all securely locked up, then meet us at Susan and Whitney's house?" Traveller asked.

"Wait!" Mallory yelled, holding up her hand. "Hold on just one Yagdian minute!" Looking pleadingly first at Mergan, then her grandparents, she said, "We just got here! Don't you think it's a bit much to expect me to leave without seeing Yagdi?"

"She has a point," Mergan chuckled. "I suppose we could enjoy our Mexican dinner at 'Traveller's Bar and Grill?'" he added, looking hopefully at his dear friend.

"I must agree it's too intriguing not to take advantage of this unique opportunity. However, only for the afternoon," Susan said firmly. "I'm anxious to get my daughter home!"

"I can live with that!" Mallory said happily.

"Sorry I'm arriving late to the party. It took longer to subdue Sylern than we'd expected," Randolph explained as he rushed toward the group. "However, I did hear the suggestion to remain on Yagdi for a few more hours." Looking pointedly at Edna, he added, "I was going to stay behind a little longer anyway because I must take care of some unfinished business! Shall we meet at the entrance to the portal?"

Mergan and Ursula exchanged worried glances then pulled Randolph aside. "Do you want company, dear friend? We'd be more than happy to stay back and referee!" Mergan said almost gleefully.

"I'm quite certain I can handle an old lady," Randolph said confidently. "Thank you for the offer, but I'd prefer this to be a private conversation."

Ursula smiled and winked. "I have no doubt you can hold your own. You've grown in both power and confidence in a very short time. Remember to use that power and reach out to us if you need help." Poking Mergan in the ribs, she added, "Let's leave Randolph and Edna to their discussion."

Watching his friends walk away, Randolph hoped he'd made the right decision and wasn't being overly confident. Squaring his shoulders, he turned and headed toward the cell holding his distant relative.

. . .

Linking her arms with Whitney and Edward, Mallory practically danced down the mountain, gawking at the huge, colorful parrots and sampling the seeds from Traveller's guadapops. "Hey, save some for our meal!" the bear laughed.

"Look up, Mal!" Whitney encouraged and grinned when her friend gasped. "Something else, right?"

"I can't believe I'm just seeing this, and only because you pointed it out!" Mallory said, craning her neck to look at Yagdi's two suns. "The purple one is so elegant, but the huge yellow one really grabs my attention!"

Hearing Mergan's surprised yelp, she looked at the wizard quizzically than burst into laughter. "What did you call those amazing birds?" she laughed as several took turns dive bombing the outraged wizard.

Whitney chuckled. "Last time this happened, one actually landed on Mergan's shoulder! When he reached up to shoo him away, the bird leaned in and squawked. It almost looked like that bird meant to irritate him. And boy did it ever work!"

When Mergan's feathered friends finally flew away, he squared his shoulders and smoothed his jacket. "Parinches," he said, answering Mallory's question. "They're called p-a-r-i-n-c-h-e-s. Would you like for me to spell that, young lady?"

Ignoring the wizard's sarcasm, Mallory noticed the two towers gleaming in the sun and ran ahead of the group to investigate. Arriving at the settlement before everyone else, she walked to the middle of the bridge and looked into the water. The huge fish swimming back and forth captured her attention, and Mallory felt herself relax for the first time in what seemed like forever.

Traveller smiled as she watched Edward's sister race away. "Does Mallory remind you of Whitney the first time she saw Yagdi?" she asked her old wizard friend walking beside her.

"I was just thinking the same thing!" Mergan said with a grin. "I truly believe we may all finally be at peace, and enjoy a long, wonderful life as friends!"

When they joined her on the bridge, Mallory pointed to the banners flying high above. "What do they stand for?"

Mallory's excitement was contagious, and Whitney was remembering her own joy at seeing Yagdi for the first time. "Let me explain!" Whitney jumped in. "Now, that one with the bright green background and two suns one yellow and the other purple, is the Yagdian flag. The other one, the banner with stripes of green, blue, yellow and red, like the colors in the Parinches we saw, is the flag for this settlement."

Smiling at Traveller, she continued, "See the bold lines through each of the stripes? Those markings translate to 'Welcome, all good creatures.' This is the largest settlement on Yagdi, and the place Traveller and Mergan call home, at least when they're not off fighting bad guys," she added, grinning at both of them.

Unable to remain far from her daughter for too long, Susan walked up and put her arm around Whitney's shoulders. "I for one am anxious to tour this settlement, but my stomach is telling me we need to get to 'Traveller's Bar and Grill' sooner rather than later!"

"Absolutely!" Mergan agreed, rubbing his stomach. "I can almost taste my dear friend's delightful dishes!"

"We'll see what I can come up with," Traveller laughed.

"We must part ways for the time being," Aiden said gruffly. "Three dragons walking the crowded streets of this settlement is a bit much and we're eager to share today's important developments with the other dragons."

Seeing everyone's crestfallen faces, Torryn said, "Traveller will inform us when you head back up to the portal. We'll say our good-byes there."

Whitney sighed as the three dragons disappeared. "I'll never forget the first time I saw those incredible creatures!" Then she turned and said, "Time to explore Yagdi's largest settlement!"

Traveller surprised Mergan by filling her huge kitchen with Mexican food. As she brought out platter after platter of steaming dishes, the bear admitted, "You must return to Earth often to get true Mexican dishes. However, I must admit this is quite satisfactory."

They enjoyed the feast and each other's company until everyone had their fill. After a satisfied burp, Mergan pushed away from the table and announced, "As wonderful as this has been, I'm afraid the time has come to return to Earth." Nodding at Traveller, he added, "And we'll travel every step together this time!"

"I don't think we'll argue this time, do you, Edward?" Whitney asked, turning to her best friend and grabbing his hand.

"No way!" Edward agreed. "Ready to go home?" he asked Mallory.

"I guess, but if I pass Mergan's silly tests, maybe I'll be back!" she said, looking hopefully toward the old wizard.

"I'm afraid that might have to wait for the time being," Cathy said hesitantly. "We were going to wait until we got back to Earth to tell you, but your parents got home sooner than they'd expected. As you can well imagine, Mallory, they saw your cryptic note and called immediately. They were understandably upset, and your father insists you both come home immediately, and I quote, 'be prepared to explain yourselves!'"

Whitney felt like her whole world had just caved in, but for once in her life, she had nothing to say. She stole a glance at Edward and saw his shocked disappointment. He looked at her and grinned sadly then shrugged his shoulders. Squeezing her hand tightly, he cleared his throat then stood up bringing her with him. "That may be his wish, but I can't say it's mine!"

"Obviously, things need to be worked out," Cathy said quickly.

"How about we save this discussion for later and enjoy the rest of our time on Yagdi?"

"Well said," Traveller joined in, then stood up. "Leave the dishes for later. Let's take a quick tour of the settlement, then head to the portal. As before, the wizards and I will be joining you, along with Ellie of course. Aiden has said he'd like to travel with us once again as well. It'll be a crowded portal, but that's a good kind of crowd!"

Chapter Thirty
BITTERSWEET ENDINGS

"Edna!" Randolph shouted sharply as he approached the temporary but quite sufficient cell that housed his ancient relative. "Recently discovering we're kin has intrigued me and prompted many questions. I believe we're long overdue for an enlightening conversation. Although I fear there's much to regret about your past, and possibly that of others in my family, I hope to find something, anything I can feel proud of. I expect you'll have plenty of time in prison to ponder our conversation and any lessons learned as a result."

"I've kept track of you over the years, young Randolph. I'm quite proud of your transformation from store owner to wizard and look forward to this conversation more than you could possibly imagine," Edna answered. The truth of her words shone brightly in the woman's deep brown eyes as she met the earth wizard's intense gaze.

Surprised by her eagerness to talk with him, Randolph felt suddenly awkward and avoided eye contact as he sat down outside her cell. He was sadly aware of his evil relative's devious nature and was prepared for all forms of trickery. Sure enough, as soon as he was sitting, she placed her fingers around the bars and looked at him pleadingly.

Unable to refuse, he reached over and touched her hand and felt the zap of electricity. It was strong enough to jerk his body, but he was able to counter the effect. With a sad smile, he dropped his hand. "Looks like I was wise to assume you'd try to play me!"

"What did you expect? I have very few options at this point, young one!" she snapped.

"I expect common decency!" he roared, shooting out of his seat. "If we can't have a civil conversation, this won't be worth my time or effort. Therefore, you must make a choice right now. If there's a shred of kindness left inside your darkened soul, let it shine through now or we'll never see each other again. I'll leave you to rot in prison, alone and unloved!"

Shocked by his outburst, Edna stared at her relative then smiled grimly. "Randolph, will you please sit down?"

"You must promise me no more tricks of any kind!" he demanded.

"Okay, okay!" she agreed and sighed as he returned to his seat. Peering through her cell, she felt a tear tickle her cheek and swiped angrily at it. "That was embarrassing!" she murmured. "No one has ever seen me cry, just as no one ever saw me cower in defeat until today. You and your alliance must be very proud of your young Whitney! She's become quite formidable. However, losing to a mere child isn't an easy pill to swallow, dear Randolph."

Randolph decided to stay quiet and let her stew. Wriggling uncomfortably, she finally stood up and prowled around her small enclosure like a wild animal. Suddenly, he realized that's just what this ancient woman had become, and asked, "What happened to you, Edna? How did you become so cold, vindictive, and callous?"

"Nothing I couldn't handle!" she shot back defensively. Randolph watched her pout for several long minutes, biting his tongue so he wouldn't say a word. He saw her shoulders sag as another tear dropped down her cheek, but he remained quiet and simply studied her. Suddenly, Edna's mask of haughty indifference disappeared, and she seemed rather vulnerable. Desperately hoping she wasn't tricking him again, he waited for Edna to break the silence.

"I think I was born without a heart!" she whispered in a voice so quiet he had to lean in to hear her.

"Why do you say that?" he encouraged.

"I can't remember doing anything kind to anyone without an ulterior motive," she admitted. "I was always struggling to get ahead, especially because I was a female wizard with lofty dreams. As a young woman, I was determined to settle for nothing less than becoming the leader of a clan. I clawed my way up the ladder to accomplish that and left many family members and potential friends behind in my quest for power and status."

"Do you regret any of that now?" Randolph asked, secretly hoping she would admit she did.

"Not one minute, and I'd do it all over again!" Edna said proudly, regaining some of her arrogance.

"Can you tell me anything about your husband and did you know my mother? I don't remember her very well because she died when I was quite young."

"Charles was an insignificant part of my life, and I rarely think about him," Edna admitted. "He was weak, but that allowed me to mold him as I saw fit. He was a good partner because of that, and my husband got along with everyone and that helped smooth all the ruffled feathers I created."

"As far as your mother, I never met her, but your father and some of my clan members stayed in touch for many years."

Taken aback, Randolph urged, "Whatever did they talk about? They couldn't have had much in common."

"My dear boy, your father's great grandfather was part of our clan! He left in the dead of night with a handful of clan members and journeyed to Earth. They all separated, and your father's great grandfather ended up settling in Ontonagon, Michigan."

Rocked to his boots, Randolph gaped at Edna then shouted

indignantly, "There's no way any of my relatives were among the banished clan!"

"You're too smart not to get this, so take a moment to think about it!" Edna shot back. "You're related to Charles and I and that means you're a part of my clan, even if very distantly!"

Randolph let that sink in for a minute then sighed. "I guess I just didn't want to admit it, but what you say does make sense." Then he frowned worriedly.

"Whatever is the problem?" she prodded.

"Honestly, I don't want to have any of your tainted blood flowing through my veins," Randolph admitted. "Realizing I must carry some of your traits makes me wonder how much evil I store in my own soul."

Edna pushed her hand through the bars of the cell, and this time when he grasped it, the dream jumper was relieved to feel nothing but cool, soft skin. "Out of necessity, I've mastered the art of gauging the character of fellow wizards very well, and I see only goodness and decency in you, dear Randolph. That must come from your mother."

"Like I said, I was just a young child when my mother passed away. Unfortunately, I just remember her boxing my ears anytime I tried to snoop through the old bins of family heirlooms in the cellar."

"That's because she loved you and didn't want you to know you were a wizard," Edna explained. "She was human, but your father fell in love with her and eventually spilled the beans on our family's disgraceful removal. She had to worry you would become a monster."

"Hmmm, I guess I can finally forgive her, then," Randolph said, and felt a heavy burden lift from his shoulders. However, when he looked at Edna, she'd become pensive once again, which intrigued him.

"Edna, one minute you can be cold as ice, but right now you appear to care about me. Do I dare believe that's true?"

"You are the first..." Edna began but stopped abruptly. When she tried to pull her hand away, Randolph held on and pleaded, "I must leave you soon. Please answer me, Edna. Do you care about me?"

"I've spent over a century building barriers. I was worried that if I cared about someone else I'd become weak, and that was something I couldn't afford!" Her black eyes were sparkling with pleasure when she added, "You are the first one to break through those sturdy barriers, Randolph! So yes, I do care about you. And do you know what? It's about time!" she admitted and winked.

Grinning at his relative, Randolph admitted, "I think I may just come back for a visit from time to time, that is if you want my company."

"I'd like that very much!"

"You've made me realize I should reconnect with my father very soon, and I thank you for that, Edna!" Randolph said, standing up. "Now it's time I rejoined my alliance." Tipping his hat, he bowed and left.

• • •

Dazzled by Yagdi, the families marveled over the strange plants and gaped in wonder at the amazing creatures walking past them and playing with their children in the parks. After several hours, Susan reminded everyone, "Remember, I agreed to stay, but only for a short while. I think it's time we head home."

Although it was difficult to leave so soon, everyone was in great spirits as they walked up the mountain path that led to the portal.

Leaning toward Whitney, Edward asked, "Remember how

happy and excited we were last time we followed this very same path? After that huge celebration?"

"Yeah, it's like deja vu all over again! Let's hope it ends better this time!" Whitney said, looking nervously at her friend.

"I know, those memories kinda freak me out right now too!" he admitted.

Bored with their two-way conversation, Mallory teased, "I'll leave you two lovebirds alone for a little while," and raced away.

Embarrassed by Mallory's innocent teasing, Whitney felt her face heat up and lowered her head, hoping her hair would cover the evidence. Neither said anything for several long, awkward minutes and Whitney began to squirm nervously. Struggling over what to say and how to say it, she jumped when Edward grabbed her hand.

"Don't worry, Whit! Mallory's harmless but she can be oblivious to everything!" He gave her hand a squeeze. "I don't know what's going to happen, but we're meant to be together!"

Hearing a promise somewhere in there, Whitney's heart grew lighter, and she picked up the pace. Swinging their hands back and forth, she jabbered about anything and everything, intentionally avoiding the discussion of Edward going so far away. Around the world to be exact!

Mallory joined Mergan and his new student just in time to hear Patrick needling the old wizard. "I'll plan our tutoring sessions, old man. All you must do is show up!"

Mergan's fierce scowl made her laugh. "Oh, come on! You can dish it out but hate it when someone teases you back. Get over it, my wizard friend!" she said, winking at Patrick.

"Sorry young wizard. I was just kidding," Mergan apologized. "I must remember my manners can be rather stern, and my intentions somewhat vague. Those are habits I hope you'll help me correct!"

Mergan looked toward Mallory and grinned at her satisfied

expression. "I'm going to miss your impudence, young lady! I enjoy our bantering immensely and hope our little exam is just the beginning of a long, delightful friendship."

Everyone entered the portal somewhat anxiously, and Whitney felt the familiar butterflies in her stomach as they headed back to Earth. Moving closer to Edward she whispered, "By the way, I agree!"

She'd expected Edward to squeeze her hand reassuringly because he always did, and she loved it! But this time, when his grip tightened, her best friend was shaking. Looking up in alarm, Whitney's breath caught to find him staring down at her. His smile was warm, but why was he looking so serious? Smiling back, she squeezed his hand and asked, "Are you okay?"

"Never better, Whit! As Mergan would say, I think we're on the same page. For now, that has to be good enough," then he quickly changed the subject. "This summer was incredible, but it sure turned our lives upside down! I still can't believe all that's happened to us!"

"Yeah, who knew we'd be fighting bad guys and going through a portal to another world!" Whitney laughed.

"Makes you wonder what comes next!" Edward added, smiling at his best friend.

"You were the best part of my summer! And we're a great team, so I hope we're together to face whatever that may be!" Whitney admitted, feeling her face heat up again.

Edward noticed and nodded with a smile. "Like I said, we're on the same page!"

GLOSSARY

Aiden: Meaning "little fire." Young dragon from Yagdi. Child of Torryn and Araa. Will be ruler one day.

Alliance: A relationship among people that have joined together for mutual benefit. Members of an alliance are called allies.

Aquamarine: From the Latin word meaning "water of the sea," it is Colorado's state gemstone and has a color between blue and green. It's been used as a talisman for wanderers and explorers, who thought it brought them good luck. In very ancient times, it was even believed to counteract the forces of darkness.

Araa: Mother of Aidan. Meaning "rare and beautiful."

Bluff: A small, rounded cliff that usually overlooks a body of water.

Chosen one: One chosen at birth due to their extraordinary capabilities. Their "gifts" exceed normal talents.

Dragons: The mighty protectors of Yagdi.

Eye agate: A rare agate stone that displays one or more circular concentric marks, known as "eyes." Formed over a billion years ago, they are some of the oldest stones on Earth. Folklore says they have magic to share and are known to detect evil and will find a way to warn the person wearing them.

Guadapop: A fruit that grows on vines far up the mountain. Used for pies and salads or eaten fresh off the vine. The seeds are harvested and reserved for special meals and guests.

Ice-cold stones: A sign or warning that danger is imminent. Most importantly, the battles on Yagdi are not going well, putting the lives of the "chosen ones" and the dragon in peril.

Lake Superior: Largest of the Great Lakes of North America, and the world's largest freshwater lake by surface area. It is 350 miles long (east-west) and 160 miles wide (south-north) with 2,980 miles of shoreline. It is the coldest, deepest, and highest in elevation of any of the Great Lakes. The lake's average depth is 489 feet, and at 200 feet, its water remains a constant frigid thirty-nine degrees. Between late spring and late fall, the shore can be shrouded in fog when the land surrounding Lake Superior heats up much more than the water. There have been 350 shipwrecks, with most occurring during fall storms called "northeasters."

Looa: Yagdian loon with abilities to soothe and comfort.

Mage/Magician: A learned person who practices magic.

Magic: The use of special power to make things happen that would usually be impossible. A special exciting quality that something seems different.

Mergan: A mage from Yagdi, and Traveller's teacher.

Merlinite: A stone named after the wizard Merlin. It's usually black and white and combines characteristics of two other stones, agate and opal. Folklore says wearing it will attract powerful magic and good luck in one's life. It can be calming and can identify dark thoughts and strengthen intuition.

Mist creatures: Evil, red-eyed creatures that travel within the mist.

Moonstone: A semitransparent or translucent, opalescent, pearly-blue gem. Folklore claims this stone is formed by moonlight and contains a powerful "good spirit" within it. It is believed to bring you good luck.

Ms. Ellie: Ferocious black panther on Yagdi; Black Bombay cat on Earth who lives with Whitney and her mother. A protector. The Bombay cat is a rare breed with a short jet-black fur coat that's sleek and panther-like. Loyal, attention-seeker, active and curious, round short nose, and head with golden eyes.

Nightmare: A frightening or unpleasant dream.

Parinches: Large, colorful, parrot-like Yagdian birds.

Pen pals: People who regularly write to each other, particularly via postal mail. Usually, strangers whose relationship is based primarily, or even solely, on their exchange of letters.

Peninsula: A piece of land almost surrounded by water or projecting out into a body of water and ending in a point.

Polar bear: A large white bear, *Ursus maritimus*, of the arctic regions. "Nanuk" in Inupiat is symbolic of a strong protector. Several Inuit legends depict polar bears as humans in disguise.

Portal: A door, gate, or entrance. First recorded in 1300, from a medieval Latin word "portalis," meaning "of a gate."

Premonition: A strong feeling that something is about to happen, especially something unpleasant.

Protégé: A person who is guided and supported by an older and more experienced or influential person.

Purmot: A defensive or offensive move by certain "chosen ones" to forcefully push outward with both arms to harness the strength of the wind. This action removes, or pushes away, your enemy. It can also be used to force something to move toward your enemy.

Quartz: One of the most well-known minerals on earth. The crystalline form is hexagonal in shape, looking much like a prism. It's quite transparent and has many colorful shades. Ancient tales say the crystal quartz was formed long ago from the breath of the White Dragon and holds magic. It holds a very positive energy and is seen as a protector.

Randolph: Store owner who learns there's far more to him than meets the eye. Extremely powerful indeed!

Rockhounding: A nonprofessional study and hobby of collecting rocks, minerals, and fossils from the natural environment.

Seer: A devise used for communication by a select few.

Staff: A thin, lightweight rod that is held with one hand. Traditionally made of wood, it is used by magicians for magical purposes.

Sylern: A "great old one" with ancient origins in the distant cosmos. Enemy with hawk-like eyes, clawed talons, and huge muscular wings. Can only be challenged by one more powerful than itself.

Tentacles: A slender, flexible limb or appendage an animal uses for grasping.

Thunderstorm: Form in a type of cloud known as a cumulonimbus, or dark rain cloud. They are most likely to occur in the spring and summer months and during the afternoon and evening hours. It's an electrical, or lightning, storm during which you hear thunder and see lightning. A severe thunderstorm can bring flash flooding, fires from lightning striking Earth, hail up to the size of softballs, and winds up to 120 miles per hour.

Tiger's eye: A powerful stone banded in brown and gold. Provides courage and confidence to those who wear it. Allows only a select few to see into the future.

Torryn: Father of Aidan. Irish for "chief." Mighty ruler and protector of Yagdi.

Transform: The act of making a thorough or dramatic change in form.

Traveller: A protector and giant polar bear in her world.

Triathlon: An endurance multisport race consisting of swimming, cycling, and running.

Upper peninsula of Michigan: Also known as upper Michigan, or the UP. First inhabited by Algonquian-speaking Native American tribes, then explored by French colonists. It's bounded mostly by Lake Superior to the north. Current residents are called "Yoopers," derived from UP-ers. The Straits of Mackinac separate it from the lower peninsula of Michigan, and the Mackinac Bridge spans the five miles between the two land masses. Completed in 1957, it is one of the largest suspension bridges in the world.

Ursa Major constellation: The Great Bear, the most prominent northern constellation containing the seven stars that form the Big Dipper.

Ursa Minor constellation: The Little Bear, or Lesser Bear, the northernmost constellation, containing the stars that form the Little Dipper, the outermost of which, at the end of the handle, is Polaris, the North Star.

Ursula: A female name from a Latin word meaning "bear."

Wafting: A defensive or offensive move by certain "chosen ones" to wave their arms in an arc through the air, with fingers spread while touching a Merlinite stone with the other hand. This action creates a protective barrier, or dome.

Warrior: Someone brave who is engaged in an activity, cause, or conflict.

Wizard staff: A powerful tool that enhances the powers of wizards and others with special gifts, like Whitney.

Wurfing: Form of travel between worlds. A portmanteau, meaning it combines or blends the form and meaning of two or more words. In this case, the two combined words are "world" and "surfing."

Yagdi: Traveller's world: "The Land of Dragons." Combination of Yandi, a Chinese tribal leader, born from a mighty dragon, and Huangdi, a legendary tribal leader. Considered the ancestors of the Chinese people.

Thanks for joining Whitney and her alliance in *The Polar Bear and the Dragon* series: *Dawn of an Alliance, Dream Jumper,* and *Perilous Passage.*

Would you take a minute to review it? Go to Amazon.com/ The Polar Bear and the Dragon and click on Customer Reviews.

Your comments are invaluable to my growth as an author! Thank you!

Debbie

ABOUT THE AUTHOR

Inspired by the interests of her middle-grade students, Debbie Watson now creates tales with compelling characters readers can relate to and admire. Although written for middle grades and young teens, this author has discovered that magical realism and important life lessons appeal to a variety of readers.

Debbie, her husband, and their two dogs live in northern Michigan and when she isn't writing, they enjoy traveling and exploring the great outdoors. The rugged shoreline of Lake Superior is a favorite destination, and the setting for her series, *The Polar Bear and the Dragon*. Her coming-of-age fantasy adventure consists of three books: *Dawn of an Alliance* (first), *Dream Jumper* (second), and her newest addition, *Perilous Passage*.